Jane Lambert studied Modern Languages at Stirling University, taught English in Vienna then travelled the world as cabin crew, before making the life-changing decision to become an actor in her mid-thirties. She has appeared in *Calendar Girls*, *The Curious Incident of the Dog in the Night-time*, *True West*, *Witness for the Prosecution* and *Deathtrap* in London's West End. *The Start of Something Wonderful* was inspired by this rather risky career change.

Her latest novel, *A Scottish Teashop in Napoli*, will be launched in July 2025 by Bedford Square Publishers.

THE START OF SOMETHING WONDERFUL

JANE LAMBERT

H Q

ONE PLACE. MANY STORIES

HQ
An imprint of HarperCollins*Publishers* Ltd
1 London Bridge Street
London SE1 9GF

www.harpercollins.co.uk

HarperCollins*Publishers*
Macken House, 39/40 Mayor Street Upper,
Dublin 1, D01 C9W8, Ireland

This edition published by HQ, an imprint of HarperCollins*Publishers* Ltd 2025

1
First published in Great Britain by
HQ, an imprint of HarperCollins*Publishers* Ltd 2018

ISBN: 9780008764432

Printed and bound in the UK using 100% Renewable
Electricity by CPI Group (UK) Ltd

MIX
Paper | Supporting
responsible forestry
FSC
www.fsc.org
FSC™ C007454

This book contains FSC™ certified paper and other controlled sources
to ensure responsible forest management.

For more information visit: www.harpercollins.co.uk/green

This book is dedicated to my mum, who believed I could write, and to my dad, who told me to get on with it.

PROLOGUE

Reasons for and against giving up the glitzy, glamorous world of flying:

Pros:

No more cleaning up other people's sick.

No more 2 a.m. wake-up calls, jet lag, swollen feet/stomach, or shrivelled-up skin.

No more tedious questions like, 'What's that lake/mountain down there?' and 'Does the mile-high club *really* exist?'

No more serving kippers and poached eggs at 4 a.m. to passengers with dog-breath and smelly socks.

No more risk of dying from deep vein thrombosis, malaria, or yellow fever.

No more battles with passengers who insist that their flat-pack gazebo *will* fit into the overhead locker.

No more wearing a permanent smile and a name badge.

No danger of bumping into ex-boyfriend and his latest 'I'm-Debbie-come-fly-with-me'.

Cons:

No more fake Prada, Louis Vuitton, or Gucci.

No more lazing by the pool in winter.

No more six-hour retail therapy sessions in shopping malls the size of a small island – and getting paid for it.

No more posh hotel freebies (toiletries, slippers, fluffy bathrobes, etc.).

Holidays (if any) now to be taken in Costa del Cheapo, as opposed to Barbados or Bora Bora.

No more horse riding around the Pyramids, imagining I'm a desert queen.

No more picnicking in Central Park with the girls, à la Carrie, Samantha, Charlotte, and Miranda.

Having to swap my riverside apartment for a shoebox, and my Mazda convertible for a bicycle.

'Cabin crew, ten minutes to landing. Ten minutes, please,' comes the captain's olive-oil-smooth voice over the intercom. This is it. No going back. I'm past the point of no return.

The galley curtain swishes open – *it's showtime!*

I switch on my full-beam smile and enter upstage left, pushing my trolley for the very last time . . .

'Anyrubbishdoyouneedalandingcard? Anyrubbishdoyouneedalandingcard?'

Have I taken leave of my senses? The notion of an actress living in a garret, sacrificing everything for the sake of her art, seemed so romantic when I gaily handed in my notice three months ago, but now I'm not so sure . . .

Be positive! Just think, a couple of years from now, you could be sipping coffee on the *BBC Breakfast* sofa . . .

Yes, the rumours are true . . . I have been asked to appear on Strictly Come Dancing. *God only knows how I'll fit it around my filming commitments though.*

Who are you kidding? A couple of years from now, the only place you'll be appearing is the job centre, playing Woman on Universal Credit.

This follow-your-dreams stuff is all very well when you're in your twenties, or thirties even, but I'm a forty-year-old woman with no safety net if it all goes pear-shaped. Just as everyone around me is having a loft extension or a late baby, I'm downsizing my whole lifestyle to enter a profession that boasts a ninety per cent unemployment rate.

Why in God's name, in this wobbly economic climate, am I putting myself through all this angst and upheaval, when I could be pushing my trolley until I'm sixty-something, then retire comfortably on an ample pension and one free flight a year?

Something happened, out of the blue, that catapulted me from my ordered, happy-go-lucky existence and forced me down a different road . . .

'It's not your fault. It's me. I'm confused,' Ben had said.

'I don't understand,' I said, almost choking on my Marmite soldier. 'What's suddenly brought this on? Have you met someone else?'

'No-ho!' he spluttered, averting his gaze, handsome face flushed.

'But you always said we were so perfect together . . .'

'That's exactly why we have to split. It's too bloody perfect.'

'What? Don't talk nonsense . . .'

'I don't expect you to understand, but it's like I've pushed a self-destruct button and there's no going back.'

'Self-destruct button? What do you mean? Darling, I understand life in the cockpit can be stressful, but I do wish you'd open up to me more, talk to me about . . .'

'Look, don't make this harder for me than it already is. It's time for us both to move on. And please don't cry, Em,' he groaned, eyes looking heavenward. 'You know how I hate it when you cry.'

I grovelled, begged him not to go, vowing I'd never again drag him around Primark or talk during *Match of the Day* again – anything as long as he didn't leave me.

Firmly removing my hands from around his neck and

straightening his epaulettes, he glanced at his watch, swigged the dregs of his espresso, and said blankly, 'Good Lord, is that the time? I've got to check-in in an hour. We'll talk more when I get back from LA.'

'NO!' I wailed. 'You know very well that I'll be in Jeddah by then. We've got to talk about this *now*. Ben . . . Ben . . .!'

For three days I sat huddled on the sofa in semi-darkness, clutching the Minnie Mouse he'd bought me on our first trip to Disneyland, as if she were a life raft. I played Lady Gaga's 'I'll Never Love Again' over and over. I wondered if Lady Gaga had ever been dumped without warning, leaving her heartbroken and bewildered, and the pain of it all had inspired her. If only *I* had a talent for songwriting, but I didn't, so I channelled *my* pain into demolishing a family-sized tin of Celebrations chocolates.

Cue Lily, my best friend, my angel on earth. We'd formed an instant friendship on our cabin crew training course. This was cemented when she saved me from drowning during a ditching drill. (I'd stupidly lied on the application form, assuming that it didn't really matter if I couldn't swim, because if I were ever unfortunate enough to crash-land in the sea, surely there would be enough lifejackets to go round?)

'Look, hon, this has got to stop,' she said in an uncharacteristically stern tone, a look of frustration on her porcelain, freckled face. 'Okay, so it's not a crime to scrub the toilet with his tooth-brush, but who knows where that could lead? You've got to stop playing the victim before we have a *Fatal-Attraction* scenario on our hands.'

'Eight years, *eight years* of my life spent waiting for him to pop the question, and now he's moving out to "find himself". I think I'm entitled to be a little upset, Lily.'

Prising Minnie out of my hands and hurling her against the wall, she straightened my shoulders and looked deep into my puffy eyes.

'I promise you that, in time, you will see you're better off 'without that moody, selfish, arrogant . . .'

'I know you never thought he was right for me, but there is another side to him,' I said defensively. 'He can be the most caring and sweet man in the world when he wants to and I can't bear the thought that we won't grow old together,' I sobbed, running my damp sleeve across my stinging cheeks.

'Come on now; take off that bobbly old cardie. I'm running you a candlelit bath, and you're going to wash your hair, put on your uniform and high heels, slap on some make-up and your best crew smile, d'you hear?' she said, pulling back the curtains. 'And while you're in Jeddah, I want you to seriously think about where you go from here.'

'But I want to be home when Ben . . .'

'You always said you didn't want to be pushing a trolley in your forties, and how you wished you'd had a go at acting. Well, maybe this is a sign,' she said, gently tucking a strand of greasy hair behind my ear. 'It's high time you did something for *you*. You've spent far too long fitting in with what Ben wants.'

'It's too late to be chasing dreams,' I sniffed, shielding my eyes from the watery sunlight. 'I just want things to go back to how they were. Where did I go wrong, Lily? I should have made more effort. After all, he's a good-looking guy, and every time he goes to work there are gorgeous women half my age fluttering their eyelashes at him, falling at his feet. He can take his pick – and maybe he did,' I whimpered, another torrent of tears splashing onto my saggy, grey jogging bottoms.

'Get this down you.' Lily sighed, shoving a mug of steaming tea into my hands as she frogmarched me into the bathroom. 'And don't you dare call him!' she yelled through the door.

Perhaps she was right; she usually was. She may be a big kid at heart, but when the chips are down, Lily is the one you'd want on your flight if you were struck by lightning or appendicitis at thirty-two thousand feet.

For the last year or so, hadn't I likened myself to an aeroplane in a holding pattern, waiting until I was clear to land? Waiting for Ben to call, waiting for Ben to come home, waiting for Ben to propose, waiting until Ben finally felt ready to start a family?

Yes, deep down I *knew* she was right, but I was scared of being on my own. Did this make me a love addict? If so, could I be cured?

Chapter 1

Finding My Inner Dog

January – New Beginnings

Where the hell am I? Blinking, I prop myself up on my elbows and slowly take in the swirling, green, psychedelic wallpaper, and the assortment of quirky knick-knacks that clutter every surface.

Four months have passed, and yet sometimes I still wake up expecting to be back in our king-size bed, in our White Company-esque bedroom, and for Ben to be lying beside me.

My throat tightens and hot tears prick my eyes.

Forget *Eat, Pray, Love.* It was Kevin Wilcox who made me do it. Having read his story in one of the Sunday supplements, it was like he was whispering in my ear, telling me to 'Get a move on,' to walk away from my old life and leap into the unknown.

DREAMS REALLY CAN COME TRUE

Former computer programmer, Kevin Wilcox, 40, went for broke when he gave up his 50k-a-year job to become a profes-sional opera singer. 'My advice to anyone contemplating giving up their job to follow their dream is to go for it,' said Kevin, taking a break from rehearsals of La Traviata *at La Scala.*

There was my affirmation; proof that there were other people out there – perfectly sane people, who were not in the first flush of youth either, but were taking a chance.

That's what I'd do. I'd become an actor, and Ben would see my name in lights as he walked along Shaftesbury Avenue, or when he sat down to watch *Casualty*, there I'd be, shooting a doe-eyed look over a green surgical mask.

'What a fool I was,' he'd tell his friends ruefully, 'to have ever let her go.' Hah!

But revenge wasn't my only motive. Faux designer bags and expensive makeovers were no longer important to me. I wanted the things that money can't buy: like self-fulfilment, like the buzz you get on opening night, stepping out on stage in front of a live audience. Appearing through the galley curtains, proclaiming that well-rehearsed line, 'Would you like chicken or beef?' just wouldn't do any more.

I swing my legs out of bed and Beryl's burnt-orange, fluffy rug tickles my toes. How I miss the cool, clean feel of polished wood underfoot.

My blurry gaze lands on *Diana, Forever in Our Hearts*. I can't help but smile as I remember the day I viewed the room when Beryl, my landlady, had proudly shown me her extensive collection of china figurines, which she guards as fiercely as the Crown Jewels.

'This was at a high point in her short life,' she'd told me mournfully, clutching Diana to her ample bosom. 'The moment when she took to the floor with John Travolta during her state visit to the White House.' There followed a moment of respectful silence, then pulling a hankie from her sleeve, she gave Di a little dust and returned her to her spot, next to the limited-edition Smurf family, the matador, resembling a camp Action Man in white tights and cape, baby Jesus in swaddling clothes, and the Eiffel Tower snowglobe with built-in music box.

I tiptoe along the landing to the bathroom and there, lurking in the shadows, like a feline Mrs Danvers, is Shirley, Beryl's sluggish, obese, spoiled-rotten cat. Those speckled, almond-shaped eyes bore through me unflinchingly. Ever since I refused to open the back door for her and forced her through the cat-flap, I've had a chilling suspicion she's been plotting her revenge.

I enter the avocado-green bathroom and tease the mildewy, slimy, plastic shower curtain across the rusty rail. I turn the tap full on, and the shower head – about as much use as a watering can – emits a trickle that would leave your petunia bed gasping. A startled spider tries to make a break for it up the side of the bath, but slithers back down, leaving me to do a kind of naked *Riverdance* as it swirls around my feet.

What I'd give to be languishing now in my sparkling-white, Italian-tiled bathroom, complete with walk-in power shower and scented candles.

Hey, don't be such a wuss! Stay focused. This evening's drama class will reaffirm that all this hardship is going to be worth it. It will. It *will*.

Ever since I'd played the Tin Man in a school production of *The Wizard of Oz* I'd wanted to act. Being tall at an all-girls school meant I never got to play Nancy, Maria, or Dorothy. But I didn't care.

I'd write my own shows, which I'd perform for Mum, Dad, Sammy the dog, and the neighbours. I loved to tell stories; to share, to feel, to emote. I was a shy, gawky kid with a vivid imagination and acting allowed me to disappear into a role.

My bedroom walls were plastered with posters of *Breakfast at Tiffany's*, *Pretty Woman*, *Doctor Zhivago*, and *Dirty Dancing*.

I'd dress up for the Oscars and pose on the red shag pile, tell the interviewer what an honour it was just to be nominated, rise slowly from my seat in disbelief, and accept my award, fighting back the tears as I thanked my parents, my friends, and God for making this possible.

So what got in the way?

'Drama school?' spluttered Miss Crabb, my headmistress. 'Don't be ridiculous. Acting's not a career! What about university?'

'You need to wake up, Em,' Mum said despairingly, rolling her eyes. 'I should never have let you go to *Saturday Showstoppers* when you were ten. It's put silly ideas in your head. Now, what about the Foreign Office? You're good at languages . . .'

Persuaded that teachers and mums know best, I packed my dream away and scraped through university, where I spent more time acting in and producing plays than studying stuffy old Schiller or fusty Flaubert. I wisely left academia behind and joined Amy Air. If I wasn't allowed to be an actress then I would at least pay off my student debt doing something fun and adventurous.

New York was my favourite route. While the rest of the crew would spend our brief stopover snuggled up in the hotel with room service and a movie, I'd dash along to Times Square on West 42nd Street and buy a ticket to a Broadway show. Jet lag miraculously forgotten, I'd be transported to a magical world far from turbulence and sick bags.

When the curtain came down, I'd skip along the shimmering streets of the Great White Way back to the hotel, reliving the performance in my mind, imagining the scene backstage: the post-show euphoria, the drinks, the conversation. And a bit of me regretted that I hadn't believed in myself enough to ignore the naysayers and pursue the one thing I felt truly passionate about. Secretly I never stopped hoping though, that someday, somehow . . .

Then I met Ben and the dream was buried for good. Charming, charismatic, athletic, sophisticated, dashing-in-uniform Ben, a modern-day superman, in control of a Boeing 787 Dreamliner – and of my future happiness.

Now in my thirties, time was running out if I wanted to have children, and though he didn't say as much, I knew Ben and I were destined to be together forever.

Fast-forward eight years, and here I am, forty, heartbroken, childless, with no home to call my own.

But through all the despair, there's a little voice deep down whispering to me, telling me to turn this crisis into an opportunity; to have the courage this time to follow my intuition, to listen to my heart, take responsibility for my own happiness, and not allow others to dictate the course of my life.

Okay, so it's taken nearly a quarter of a century to reach this place, but this time nothing and no one is going to hold me back.

* * *

DRAMATIC AR S CENTRE

I peer through the driving rain at the shabby sign tilting dangerously in the wind, many of its bulbs burnt out.

As I chain my bike to the rack, a rush of feverish excitement and anticipation sweeps over me.

I run up the glistening steps two at a time, my holdall containing new jazz shoes, sports bra, leotard, and leggings swinging from my shoulder.

The heavy wooden door creaks as I push it open.

A group of young beautiful things who look like they belong on the TV series *Glee* are huddled around the noticeboard.

'It says here *Mamma Mia!* recalls should wait outside studio three on the first floor.'

As they scamper upstairs, relief washes over me and I head for the loo.

I tie my soaking-wet hair into a high ponytail and apply a dash of lippy.

'Here we go,' I say, high-fiving my Lycra-clad, slightly lumpy reflection. 'You can do this.'

Pasting on my best flight-attendant smile, I bounce out of the door to the noticeboard.

Portia Howard's method acting class takes place in the basement of this former warehouse. As I enter the room, my springy gait quickly disintegrates into an apologetic tiptoe. Seated on benches at opposite ends of the room are other nervous newbies of all shapes and sizes, some staring at the floor, others checking their phones in absolute silence.

'Hi,' I whisper, squeezing in between a serious-looking chap in trackie bottoms, striped shirt, and tie and a mousey, bespectacled woman with frizzy hair. They both smile weakly, staring into the middle-distance.

Moments pass. 'At my audition I had to imagine I was a plastic bag,' I snort, in an attempt to break the ice. 'In a force-ten gale.'

Not a sound. Not even a cursory titter. Why do I always feel it's MY responsibility to fill awkward silences?

The door flies open and Portia, taller than I remember from the audition, enters centre stage, her black maxi skirt swaying, a red vintage shirt, and fingerless gloves complementing her boho-chic style.

'Welcome, everyone. Whether you're here with a view to becoming an actor, or simply to build your confidence, I hope by the end of the course you'll leave with a better understanding of who you are, what you're capable of, and a self-belief that will drive you forward in your personal life and career. So, let's start by getting to know one another. Have any of you ever been speed dating?'

There's a sharp, collective intake of breath.

'Don't worry,' continues Portia quickly. 'What you do in your spare time is your affair.' The room fills with air once more. 'But this exercise works on the same principle. Let's move the benches closer together with ten of you on either side. When I ring the bell you have two minutes to find out as much as you can about the person opposite you. When the bell rings again, the people

12

on side A stay seated while those on side B slide along a space.'

The bell rings and the nervous, icy atmosphere of earlier melts away as the room is filled with noisy conversation and splutters of laughter, culminating in chaos when, in true Laurel-and-Hardy style, one of the benches tips, depositing two speed daters onto the floor.

Exercise over, Portia waits for everyone to settle down. The only sound is heavy breathing.

'Breath control, projection, and body language – essential tools whether you're addressing an audience of theatregoers or clients,' she purrs in her resonant, velvety Joanna Lumley-esque voice, beckoning everyone to stand up. Placing her palm just below her breastbone, she continues, 'Take a deep intake of breath, fill your lungs with air, like a balloon. Now, pushing the diaphragm in and out, I want you to pant like a dog.'

Pant like a dog? Oookay. Well, if I can successfully portray a plastic bag blowing in the wind, then a panting dog impression should be a breeze (excuse the pun).

'No, no, no!' Portia says, gliding over to my side, her dangly earrings tinkling like wind chimes. 'I don't want to see any movement *here*.' She firmly taps my shoulders. 'It must all come from down *here*,' she continues, as she prods my diaphragm.

'Now try again. Fill those lungs . . . that's it, and let out short, sharp breaths. I want my hand to *feel* that diaphragm bouncing. There, you see, you've got it!'

I'm chuffed I've got it, but all the same, I can't help feeling I sound like a cross between a chat-line hostess and a woman in labour.

'This strengthens the diaphragm, loosens the facial muscles, allows more air into your lungs, helps your voice to develop, and improves your posture,' says Portia, as if reading my mind.

'The next exercise is a good warm-up before an audition or performance. It's called the Wet Dog Shake. Okay, everyone, let's imagine you've just come bounding out of the sea, and now

13

you're going to shake yourselves dry,' she says, as she drops to her knees, her long, tapered fingers splayed out in front of her on the grimy floorboards. 'Let's start from the top with the nose' (she starts wiggling her nose) 'now the head, tongue, the shoulders' (she shimmies her shoulders) 'legs . . . come on . . . bark if you wish . . . go for it . . . release your inner dog!'

James, Mr Respectable-Bank-Manager by day, catches my eye, and we exchange an incredulous look. Sally, the mousey, bespectacled, hitherto rather timid accountant, has hurled herself into the exercise with rather more gay abandon than necessary, tongue hanging out of the corner of her mouth, resembling not so much a shaking dog, as someone having stuck a wet hand in the toaster.

'Come on, you can do better than that!' pants Portia. 'Instead of huddling together like a pair of sniggering school kids – James, Emily – follow Sally's lead. Let yourselves go! What are you afraid of? Making fools of yourselves? If you want to be actors, you have to learn to let go of your inhibitions. I want to *see* those tails wagging. I want to *feel* that sea spray *flying* off your coat. Wag that tail. Shake, shake, shake yourselves nice and dry. Wag, wag, wag. Come on . . .!'

A few nervous titters echo around the room, but then slowly, tentatively, like lemmings, we all follow Portia's lead, and our class becomes less *Glee*, and more *Geriatric Gym*.

'See, that's not so bad, is it? Now roll onto your backs and kick those legs high in the air!' she cries, her pewter bangles clinking like rigging against a sail mast.

As a former BAFTA nominee (I googled her), Portia Howard obviously knows her stuff, but I can't quite picture Dame Helen kicking her legs high in the air and panting like a dog prior to a performance.

'This is ridiculous,' blurts out Poppy, whose every sentence ends with a question mark. 'Basically, I don't hold with all this horseshit.'

Her strained, cut-glass tones echo around the room as we all stare at her bug-eyed, legs suspended in mid-air.

Rising to her feet and smoothing her skinny jeans, she continues, 'Release your inner dog? What has all this pretentious rubbish got to do with being an actor? I don't believe for one moment that Keira Knightley has *ever* had to crawl around a filthy floor on all fours, pretending to be a dog, so I don't see why I should.'

'Good point, Poppy,' says Portia calmly. 'Keira has probably never done the Dog Shake, and you certainly don't have to if you don't wish. But exercises like this teach you to be more fluid in your movement, to release blockages in energy, so that you can express emotion through your body – as well as build up the stamina to cope with eight shows a week, without . . .'

'Yah, but I'm basically not interested in theatre. I plan to go straight into TV and films. I don't know about the rest of you,' she says, scanning the class, perky nose in the air, 'but I want to learn about camera technique, about close-ups and continuity, and . . . giving the director exactly what he wants . . .'

'Whoa, whoa, whoa,' says Portia, holding up her hands. 'My class isn't about showing you a short-cut to fame and fortune – if I knew that, do you think I'd be here now?' she says with a half-laugh.

'Obviously not,' Poppy fires back. 'But *I* have no intention of ending up some middle-aged has-been, teaching drama in a damp and dreary basement for the rest of my life.'

Catching her breath and her composure, Portia replies with a little, enigmatic smile, 'Good for you. But what this "middle-aged has-been" can teach you is how to bring truthfulness and honesty to your storytelling. I can arm you with the right tools to *survive* in this cut-throat, heartbreaking, wonderful business; talent alone is not enough. You need humility, patience, harmony . . .'

With an unabashed toss of her bouncy, shampoo-commercial

hair, Poppy collects her D&G tote bag, places her leather jacket carefully around her shoulders, and struts out of the grubby rehearsal room in her patent wedge boots, in search of celebrity and riches elsewhere.

'So if there are any more of you who are here just because you want to see your faces on the big screen or the cover of *Hello!* and are not willing to commit to hard work, sacrifice, and to embracing new challenges, then this is not the place for you,' says Portia, directing her words at each and every one of us in turn. 'Don't be afraid to speak up.'

The clock ticks loudly, a distant underground train rumbles below, feet pound the floor above, as the muffled strains of 'Dancing Queen' vibrate through the cracked ceiling.

According to Wikipedia, Portia has worked at The Royal Shakespeare Theatre, The National, and was even featured in a Ridley Scott movie. So why is she here? Is it the case that after a certain age the parts dry up? What hope is there for me? I'm a bit ashamed even to think this, but is there an element of truth in Poppy's outburst?

But there's too much at stake now even to contemplate giving up, so I must put my trust in Portia and the great Stanislavski's theory, that to be a successful actor you sometimes have to make an eejit of yourself.

'Okay, we have just ten minutes left,' says Portia, rummaging in her well-worn, Mary-Poppins bag and producing a small, multi-coloured ball. 'Let's see how many of those names you can remember. As you throw the ball, say the name of the person you're throwing it to and if you're right, the person catching the ball has to reveal to the group a secret about themselves – the deeper, the darker, the better. Aaand, Emily!'

It seems like everything is moving in slow motion, including my brain. The ball is heading this way . . . ooh, I can't think straight . . . Oh, God, oh, God, this is so embarrassing . . . What *am* I going to say?

'My name is Emily and . . . and . . . I once spent a night in a Middle Eastern jail.'

* * *

Being a Monday night, the Dog & Whistle, opposite Dramatic Ar s Centre, is deserted and we all pile around a long wooden table. Drinks in, we raise a glass to new adventures.

'So, Emily. Spill the beans,' says James, splitting open several bags of crisps to share. 'You can't leave us in suspense. How on earth did you end up in jail in the Middle East?'

I'm not entirely comfortable recounting the sorry tale as it's not something I'm proud of, and to this day I have never told my parents. The painful memory has been locked away for many years, but tonight, due to panic and a desire to impress, it was unleashed.

'I'd really rather not . . .'

'Come on!' they chorus, eighteen wide-eyed faces looking at me expectantly.

Even the barman is taking an unusually long time to wipe the table next to ours.

Riyadh, Saudi Arabia. I was fresh out of cabin crew training school. My second long-haul trip, in fact. I'd never travelled to such an exotic land before, and instead of lying in my air-conditioned room, I wanted to explore the narrow streets of the old heart of Saudi's capital; to smell the spices, the coffee, check out the colourful carpets and the ostentatious jewellery.

'Hey, girls, are you all nurses?' came a British voice behind us.

I don't blame them – the young expat geologists who invited us to their compound that night – nor do I blame my fellow crew who weren't strangers to Saudi and should have known better.

'Isn't alcohol illegal?' I'd asked feebly over the blaring music.

'Yeah, but you're on British soil here,' replied our host, handing me a glass of home-brewed wine. 'Cheers!'

What we naively and stupidly didn't bargain for was being stopped and breathalysed by the police on the way back to the hotel.

I don't blame the authorities either. We knew the laws of the land and we broke them. We were lucky we didn't end up being incarcerated for years, forbidden from entering the country again, or fired from our jobs.

I learned a hard lesson that night – to trust my own judgement and not be pressurised into following the herd.

If there was a prize for Most Shocking Secret of the Evening, then I can confidently say I would have won, but I feel cross with myself for having shared that most shameful of events with a bunch of strangers in order to be accepted, to be liked.

But then maybe daring to lay bare guilty secrets, disappointments, and desires is the key to being a good actor as opposed to a mediocre one.

Who knows, one day I might find myself tapping into the fear I felt on that terrible night to bring truthfulness to a role.

It's 1 a.m. by the time I turn off the light, having shared tonight's events with Beryl over a lukewarm Babycham.

It's early days, but tonight something shifted I think, and I got a tiny glimpse of where I'm headed – a fleeting confirmation that all of this will be worth it.

T. S. Eliot was right; it's all about the journey and not the destination.

Warning:

Babycham may cause over-sentimentality.

Chapter 2

I step off the crew bus, uniform, hair, and make-up immaculate. A homeless woman is huddled in the doorway of the hotel.

'Big Issue, Big Issue!' she cries. I open my purse and lean towards her, looking into her eyes. OMG! That woman is me.

I awake with a start to the blare of the alarm clock, hauling me out of my slumber, back to the real world.

It doesn't require a psychoanalyst to work out the meaning behind this recurring nightmare.

I simply cannot carry on living off the paltry proceeds from the flat Ben and I shared. This is supposed to be my emergency money, to support me after the course, during those 'resting' periods, in between theatre and TV contracts, daahling. Huh.

There's rent to pay, food, my credit card bill, and drama class fees.

How naive I was to think I could just sail into another job.

This afternoon's interview at Trusty Temps Agency is one of the few options left to me now . . .

* * *

'Are you familiar with PowerPoint?' lisps the recruitment consultant, running her French-manicured nail down my brief

CV.

'I haven't used it since school.'

'Excel?'

'Excel? Yes . . . I mean no.' (Lying v. bad idea, Emily.)

'Minute taking?'

'Sorry?'

'Not to worry. Any software skills?'

'Erm . . .' I bite my bottom lip.

Uncrossing her long, slim legs, she lets out a heavy sigh, and forcing her glossy lips into a smile, says with a hint of superiority, 'I'm afraid most of our positions are for people with these skills – but do keep an eye on our website, just in case an opportunity pops up for someone with your . . . abilities.'

'Of course,' I say with a careless toss of my head, trying to look self-assured and unconcerned, while inside I feel like a technophobic old bat. 'Thank you.'

I stuff my CV in my bag, pull on my coat and beret, then take the walk of shame from the back office, through the reception area, past all the busy, busy consultants, furiously tapping their keyboards, while holding terribly important conversations on the phone.

It's dawning on me with scary clarity that two decades of working in a metal tube have not armed me with the necessary skills to survive in the business world. I'm a dab hand at putting out a fire, boiling an egg to perfection at altitude, or serving hot liquids in severe turbulence without spilling a drop, but what use is all that in the wired-up world of desktop, data entry, and Teams?

Oh God, what is to become of me? Am I destined for a life of Pot Noodles and Poundland? What am I going to do? What in God's name am I going to do?

I trudge along the rain-soaked street. I can't face returning to Knick-Knack Corral just yet. I turn the corner, and there, like a safe harbour in a storm, are the twinkling lights of Starbucks beckoning me in. Yes, I know, I know I shouldn't be splashing out on a costly caffeine fix, but I am in the grip of a major confidence crisis, and a large caramel cream Frappuccino is cheaper than therapy.

Sinking into a squashy sofa, I take a sip of my coffee, draw a deep breath, and take out my notebook and pen.

Potential Job List:
~~Receptionist/Administrator?~~
Waitress?
Retail assistant?
Tour guide?
Cleaner?
Telesales agent?
Dog walker?
Market researcher?

Hmm. None of the above fills me with inspiration, but in my current financial state, I'd gladly don a baseball cap and serve greasy burgers from a catering van at a football stadium.

'Girl or boy?'

'Boy. Yours?'

'Same.'

My gaze is drawn to the next table, where a couple of well-dressed mums, accessorised with matching designer tots, sip cappuccino and cluck and coo . . .

'First baby?'

'Yes. You?'

'No. I've got a six-year-old and a nine-year-old.'

'Gosh, you look too *young* to have . . .'

My eyes mist over, and I am consumed by a sudden yearning to belong to that members-only club; to have a little person to dress up in spotty dungarees, to romp around the park with, and to read *Peppa Pig* to.

Next to them is a table of young, svelte businesswomen, sipping their skinny lattes.

'Let's go in there and show them what we're made of, girls. Here's to new clients!'

'New clients!' they all cheer, chinking coffee cups and giggling.

Busy people with busy lives . . . children to pick up from school, meetings and post-natal classes to attend, deadlines to meet. And me? No job, no prospects, no daily routine . . .

Adele's soulful voice filters through the speakers.

Well, I can either sit here crying into my coffee, or take hold of the reins, buckle down, and find myself work.

I know I'm hardly a suitable candidate for *The Apprentice*, but surely there must be a vacancy somewhere for a well-travelled waitress with first-aid and fire-fighting skills, who can say 'Welcome to London' in six different languages?

The earlier drizzle has now turned to torrential rain, so I dive for cover under the candy-striped awning of Galbraith's Jewellers. Row upon row of diamond rings blink at me through the glass. My chin starts to quiver and a huge tear sploshes down my cheek. Will I ever experience the thrill and romance of someone proposing on bended knee, before I reach the age of Hip-Replacement-Boyfriend? I had such high hopes when I was five, dressed in my mum's white nightie and high heels, clutching a bunch of buttercups in my grubby fingers, an old net curtain and crown of daisies on my head.

Through the blur of my tears I squint at a sign in the window:

RETAIL CONSULTANT REQUIRED
APPLY WITHIN

Before I have time to talk myself out of it, I press the buzzer . . .

Ms June Cutler, manageress of Galbraith's Jewellers, leans across the gleaming glass counter and peers at me over her half-moon glasses.

'Ideally, we are looking for someone with retail experience in the jewellery trade, as many of our items are *very, very* valuable,' she whines in a Sybil-Fawlty voice.

'I may not have worked in a shop as such,' I retort, 'but I have sold duty-free goods, and so I am . . . *au fait* with handling money and expensive items.' (Working in the first-class cabin taught me to always have a posh little phrase up my sleeve – preferably French – when dealing with supercilious, la-di-da people.)

'A bottle of Blue Grass eau de toilette is hardly a Rolex watch, is it?' she says, with a taut smile of her thin, red lips. I feel the hairs on the back of my neck bristle.

'We didn't just sell perfume and alcohol, but luxury goods as well – like gold and silver necklaces and designer watches: Cartier, Dunhill . . . and . . . and . . .'

Bloody typical! There was a time when I could have won *Mastermind* with 'The World's Leading Designers' as my specialist subject, but just when I'm under the spotlight, the names escape me.

Sybil, meanwhile, is scrutinising me as if I've just stepped off the set of some Tim Burton scary movie; then I catch sight of my reflection in the antique, gilt-framed mirror opposite, and do a double take. What the . . .? I have blood-red rivulets trickling down my face. Oh my God, the heavy rain must have caused the dye from my beret to run! (£3 from Primark, what do you expect, Emily?) I pull out a length of loo paper from my pocket, and a chewing gum wrapper falls to the floor.

There's a stony silence. Here it comes, another helping of '. . . but do keep checking our website' – not sure I can handle two rejections in one day.

'Very well,' she says with a sigh, holding out my damp, crumpled CV, like it's a snotty hankie. 'I have been left in the lurch rather, so you can start tomorrow at nine – sharp.'

'Thank you,' I reply, vigorously shaking her hand, sending the charms on her bracelet jingling.

Giving me a final once-over, she says pointedly, 'Just one more thing – dress code here is smart.'

I resist the temptation to tell her to stuff her job and her precious things, and head out onto the bustling street. I jump astride my bike, leaving drizzly, grey commuterville behind, and pedal towards the bright lights of Dramatic Ar s Centre.

* * *

'You bastard!' I mutter. 'How can you let me down like this on my very first morning?' As fast as I pump the air in, the faster it is released with a loud *hisssss*. I knew I should have caught the bus.

I fumble in my voluminous bag for my mobile and dial Galbraith's number.

'*You have used all your calling credit*,' comes the unsympathetic, recorded voice. Heavy rain starts to pound the pavement. Shit! Right, that's it! Wielding the pump, I unleash my pent-up anger and frustration on my bike, much to the sly amusement of early morning commuters, as they scuttle to the station, clutching their takeaway coffee, ears wired to hands-free.

Squelching and wheezing my way up the hill, I make a mental note to a) learn how to mend a puncture and b) invest in water-proofs.

'I'm *so* sorry I'm late, Syb . . . June,' I pant. 'I would have got here quicker if I hadn't had to wheel my bike and I wanted to call you, but my mobile was out of credit and . . .'

'You'd better clean yourself up,' she says, her steely gaze resting on my oil-stained hands. 'And may I remind you, Emily, you are on probation. If you are serious about working here, then you had better pull your socks up.'

Blimey, I haven't felt like this since Year 10, when I was hauled up in front of the headmistress for not wearing regulation gym kit.

'The stock room looks like a bomb's hit it,' she snarls, giving me a death stare. 'Health and Safety are visiting next week, so I'd appreciate it if you could tidy the place up, and ensure the fire exits are kept clear.'

'Sure,' I say in a sugary sort of way, jaw clenched.

(Another tip gleaned from years spent bowing to the whims of tricky passengers: whatever verbal abuse flies your way, DO NOT rise to the bait. Respond in an overly polite manner, and it will annoy the hell out of your antagonist.)

'"A bottle of Blue Grass eau de toilette is hardly a Rolex watch, is it?"' I mutter, giving my best JC impression from the top of the stepladder, as I fight with piles of slippery plastic bags that are refusing to stay on the shelf. Huh! I've sold Rolex, Raymond Weil, Piaget, Mont Blanc to Arab kings, I'll have her know.

'Emily! A customer!' comes a shrill voice from the top of the stairs.

God, five-thirty and seeing the girls can't arrive quick enough.

'Coming!'

* * *

As I chain my bike to the railing, I spy them through the dimpled glass, sitting in our favourite spot, by the open fireplace, and I smile inwardly.

My life may be starting to resemble a black comedy, but with a supporting cast like mine, I can just about deal with the fact that I've got Cruella De Vil for a boss, and that my acting dream is fast turning into a horror movie.

With abundant hugs and vats of wine, our gaggle of four have cried, advised, sympathised, and propped one another up through love, loss, and all sorts of drama, so what's a mere midlife career crisis and another broken heart in the grand scheme of things?

'Darling!' squeals Lily, jumping up and wrapping me in an Eternity-fragranced hug. 'We've missed you. How are you? You look . . . fantastic.'

'I don't,' I snort, pulling at my fluorescent-yellow sash,

suddenly conscious of my bare, rain-washed face and baggy, unflattering clothes.

'Come and sit down,' she says, patting a space on the banquette.

'*Chérie!*' says Céline, kissing me four times, as is customary in her native Paris. She is French *Vogue* personified: translucent skin, sculpted cheekbones, and a natural, wide-mouthed smile (something we see little of nowadays).

'Well, how's it going?' Lily asks eagerly, extricating my arms from my dripping-wet anorak.

'Fab,' I say with forced gaiety. They both look at me searchingly. 'Well, no, actually . . . awful.'

I feel someone tug my hastily tied, damp ponytail. I spin round, and there, brandishing a bottle of Sauvignon, is Rachel.

'Hey, how's our aspiring actress?' she says, stooping down to kiss me, her silky, chestnut hair tickling my cheek. 'Let's take a look at you,' she says, sloshing wine into my glass, as she studies me with her perfectly made-up eyes.

'You look more relaxed than when we last met, not long after you and Ben . . .'

'Ahem! To new beginnings!' Lily chips in, raising her glass.

'New beginnings!' we chorus, happy to be together once more.

'You're missing all the fun, you know,' says Rachel, rolling her eyes. 'The new first-class service means the darlings can now eat *whatever* they want *whenever* they want; one minute you're serving chicken chasseur to 5B, then 1E is asking you for boiled eggs and toast, while the group at the bar are crying out for crème de menthe frappé and canapés. Gaah!'

I pretend to wince, but the way I feel right now, I'd gladly serve a plane-load of raucous, drunk, demanding passengers single-handedly every day until I'm ninety, if it meant having my old life back.

'Now, who's for some houmous and warm pitta bread?' says Lily, heading for the bar.

'Me!' we chorus.

Turning to Céline, I ask dutifully, 'How's Mike?'

'On a ten-day Sydney/Melbourne,' she says, letting out a wistful sigh. 'But he's coming straight from the airport to stay at the flat for two days when he gets back,' she adds quickly, face lighting up.

I shoot her a knowing glance over the rim of my glass.

'Don't look at me like that,' she says in that to-die-for accent of hers.

'Like what?'

'That you-are-wasting-your-time look.'

I open my mouth to speak, but close it again and swirl my wine around my glass, eyes down.

'He's leaving after Christmas . . . next year,' she says, voice falling away.

'Why not this year, Céline? How many more Christmases must you wait?'

'The twins have their final exams this year and it's his wife's parents' golden wedding next June. So, I must be patient.' She smiles weakly, fixing my gaze from under the eyebrow-brushing fringe of her sleek, ebony bob.

Mike is a classic case of how a uniform with four gold bands and a peaked cap can transform a balding, paunchy, unsexy, middle-aged man into a *fairly* attractive, dapper specimen – hardly Mr Darcy material, but a darn sight more pleasing on the eye than off-duty Mike, believe me, with his high-waisted trousers and Concorde novelty socks.

'It's just that I know how important a husband and children are to you, and I worry that by the time he leaves – *if* he leaves – it will be too late.'

'*C'est la vie.*' She shrugs. 'Nothing in life is guaranteed. You were with a single man and . . .' She bites her lip and turns away. She squeezes my hand, shakes her head, and says softly, 'I am so sorry . . .'

'Hey, it's not your fault,' I say, resting my head on her shoulder. 'It's probably for the best,' I continue over-cheerily, blinking against the sting of tears.

Yet despite a string of disastrous relationships between us, we all remain silly, romantic fools, firm in the belief that Mr Right may yet appear – ETA as yet unknown.

That is all but down-to-earth Rachel; she called off the search some fifteen years ago, when she married her childhood sweetheart, Dave, who is a policeman. They keep our belief in love and romance alive.

The town hall clock is chiming twelve by the time we totter out onto the pavement and giggle our nighty-nights and must-do-this-more-oftens. I jam on my cycle helmet and pedal hard, head bent forward against the needle-sharp rain.

An aeroplane drones overhead, its tail-light blinking in between the squally clouds. I find myself gazing wistfully at it. My mood darkens in that instant.

Where is Ben right now? In mid-air, or sleeping in a king-size bed in some far-off, exotic land, a nubile twenty-something by his side? It doesn't bear thinking about. Does he ever spare a thought for me? What would he make of my new life?

'Minnie,' he used to say (Minnie – as in Mouse – was his pet name for me on account of my stick-thin legs and big feet), 'it's too late for all that showbiz malarkey. Stay home with me and let's make a family.'

Why did he only ever say those things after one too many wines? Had he really wanted children? Or had he been testing me, playing with my emotions? I'll never know now. What's wrong with me? Why can't I have a serious, uncomplicated relationship? Is that too much to ask?

An enormous articulated lorry thunders past, drenching me in filthy spray. From somewhere deep inside me, an animal-like scream bursts out, piercing the cold night air.

Come on now. Pull yourself together. YOU ARE A LIBERATED, INDEPENDENT, STRONG WOMAN WITH A GOAL. YOU ARE A LIBERATED, INDEPENDENT, STRONG WOMAN

WITH . . . waterlogged shoes and dripping hair plastered over your eyes.

I feel anything but independent or strong, and my goal now feels a world away. Have I been pitifully naive? No matter, as it's a little late in the day for doubt and uncertainty. Like it or not, I am now travelling down a one-way street, and the big question is, does it lead to a dead end?

Chapter 3

Diamonds Are a Girl's Worst Enemy

She should never have got mixed up in this assignment. Why didn't she walk away from the situation while she still had the chance and suffer the consequences? He was a stranger, after all. Too late for second thoughts. There's no turning back now.

She glances at her watch. 05:30. Just enough time to make contact, hand over the diamonds, and return to base. Mission accomplished.

No, sadly, I am not on the set of the latest Harlan Coben thriller; on the contrary, I am starring in my very own drama, entitled *Payback Time*. And my crime? Smugness – displaying sheer, unadulterated smugness. You know how it is: you dare to pat yourself on the back for a job well done, and next minute, a giant *Monty Python* foot appears from above and squishes you into the ground. That will teach you for being so damned pleased with yourself!

Determined to win over Cruella, who is on the verge of firing me on account of my poor sales record, I scrambled together an emergency marketing strategy, which happened to involve a bearded Scotsman and a one-thousand-five-hundred-pound diamond necklace . . .

'I'm looking for something a teensy-weensy bit special,' the unsuspecting browser had informed me as he entered the shop. 'It's my wife's fiftieth tomorrow, and she's feeling . . .' he looked around cautiously, checking he wouldn't be overheard '. . . *the change,*' he mouthed exaggeratedly. 'I'd like something with a wee bit of sparkle to cheer her up.'

'I see,' I whispered back. Here was my chance! Opening one of the cabinets, I said, 'How about this pastel gem-set bracelet? Notice how it shimmers with all the colours of the rainbow.' I tilted it back and forth, so the stones' reflection danced tantalisingly around the walls, like a kaleidoscope.

'I was thinking of something a bit simpler,' he said.

'Aah,' I nodded, undeterred. 'Well, in that case, how about this nine-carat gold pendant, hand-crafted in Italy?'

'Erm . . .'

'Or this eighteen-carat belcher-bar necklace? Its extra length means it can be worn as a belt, a choker, or a layered necklace,' I gushed, while demonstrating its many uses, just like I'd seen those shopping channel presenters do. 'Layered jewellery is featured on all the major catwalks this season, so your wife would be up to the minute with the latest fashion.' He bit his lip.

I could feel Cruella's x-ray eyes burning through my head from behind the two-way mirror in the back office.

Please, God, let me make a sale.

'Let me see now . . .' I said, brain racing, eyes darting wildly about. 'Aha, I know the very thing!' I launched into the window, swiping a fourteen-carat, white gold, diamond choker from the black velvet display stand. 'What woman wouldn't feel a million dollars wearing this?' I glanced at the clock – 5.26 p.m. – just four minutes to closing time; four minutes to save myself from the dole queue.

'. . . and . . . and Princess Diana wore the exact same style of choker when she took to the dance floor with John Travolta at the White House in the mid-Eighties,' I added quickly.

He toyed with his bushy beard.

'A high point in her short life,' I whispered sombrely.

'It's a wee bit more than I intended spending . . .' he said pensively, as he peered at the price tag.

'Reaching fifty is quite a milestone,' I replied, in a kind of cool, throwaway tone, shamelessly swaying the dazzling diamonds in front of his eyes, like a hypnotist's pendulum, hope hovering.

He glanced at his watch: 5.28. Beads of perspiration glistened on his forehead.

'I'm catching the red-eye to Edinburgh tomorrow, and I suppose a box of Milk Tray from WHSmith's wouldn't go down very well.' He sighed, fishing out his wallet, resigned.

'Absolutely not,' I squeaked, snatching his credit card before he had time to change his mind. I snapped shut the leather presentation case. Placing it carefully under the counter, I coolly sashayed over to the cash desk, struggling to quash my overwhelming desire to do a Highland fling right there, on the shop floor.

Transaction completed, I carefully gift-wrapped the box, not forgetting the Curly-Wurly ribbon effect with the scissors, which I did with a dramatic flourish.

'Thank you, miss. You've been very helpful. I cannae wait to see Morag's face the morrow when I get home.'

'I'm sure she'll be thrilled. Have a good flight home,' I said, opening the door.

He kissed my hand as he exited. Yesssssssss!

In buoyant mood, I waltzed around the floor with the vacuum cleaner, singing to myself as I went. Saved from the humiliation of begging for an overdraft increase – again. From now on Cruella would realise I was an asset to the shop and would be devastated when I inevitably had to give up my retail career for that of a West End star.

Then all at once Henry Hoover died. I spun round, and there

she stood, head shaking.

'Ah-hem! What is this, Emily?'

I shrugged. 'A jewellery box?'

'Correct. But this is no ordinary jewellery box, is it?' she snarled, face blazing, the veins in her swan-like neck pulsating madly. I stared at her, puzzled.

'This is a jewellery box that contains . . .' she said, milking every moment of her Wicked-Witch-of-the-West performance '. . . a very valuable item belonging to your customer!'

She dangled the choker in front of my eyes. OH-MY-GOD. I felt the colour drain from my face, my insides plummeting ten floors. I dropped the nozzle, realising with sinking horror that I had wrapped up the wrong box and sold nice, Scottish businessman one-thousand-five-hundred-pounds' worth of diddlysquat.

'Maybe we can trace him through his credit card? Or perhaps I could go to Heathrow tomorrow and try to . . .'

My voice fell away, as judging by Cruella's beetroot colouring, she was about to spontaneously combust.

So, that is how I come to be loitering around the airline check-in desks minus a ticket, a fifteen-hundred-pound diamond choker clasped tightly in my mitts.

The terminal is already abuzz with suited and booted businessmen on their way to Brussels or Belfast for a hard day's wheeling and dealing.

I scan the concourse, looking for a tall, wiry, bearded Scotsman, clutching a boarding pass and a beautifully wrapped box.

There's excitement in the air as loved-up couples prepare to jet off on romantic mini breaks to . . . Hang on a minute! My gaze lands on the Paris check-in queue. Eyes narrowing, I move in for a closer look. It can't possibly be. He's ten and a half thousand miles away . . . and yet . . . I'd recognise that sunburnt bald patch anywhere. (As a first-class galley slave, you can spend a lot of time gazing at the backs of pilots' heads, patiently waiting, steaming-hot tea burning your hands, while they finish prattling on to air traffic control and punching buttons on the instrument panel.)

It *is* him, I swear. And who's that woman he's got his arm wrapped around? It's not Beverley, his wife. She looks young enough to be one of his daughters, but she definitely isn't. I know this because I once served his family in first class when he took them on a working trip to Houston one Christmas.

Swiping my shades from my pocket and lowering my cycle helmet, I venture nearer and take up position behind a pillar.

'Paris? Two passengers?' says the check-in agent, switching on her *Stepford-Wife* smile. Taking their tickets, she taps furiously on the computer.

'Any chance of an upgrade?'

Oh, yes, that's our Mikey all right. The cheapskate, asking for an upgrade on his concessionary staff ticket. Bloody typical.

I'm tempted to walk right up to the desk, tap him on the shoulder and say, 'Hey, Mike, what happened? Céline told me you were in Sydney.' I'd love to see him try to wriggle out of that one. Talk about leading a double life – no, a *triple* life. How *does* he manage it?

'Would all remaining passengers travelling to Edinburgh on BA1430, please proceed to gate A8, where this flight is now closing. That's all remaining passengers . . .'

Oh, Lord! In all the drama I've completely forgotten about finding Mr Beardy Man – Mr Soon-to-Be-Divorced Beardy Man if I don't get my act together pronto.

Zipping my way in between trolleys and wheelie suitcases, I race towards the security gate. Standing on tiptoes, I spy him in the distance, collecting his coat, shoes, and a small gift bag from the conveyor belt.

'Boarding pass,' grunts the security officer.

'Please let me through. I need to give this to that gentleman down there – it's really important,' I plead, waving the box in the direction of the long line of travellers, waiting to be prodded and processed.

'If you don't have a boarding pass, then this is as far as you go,' he says firmly, darting me a scathing glare.

'*Please.* I'm ex-crew, so appreciate you have an extremely responsible and serious job to do, but if I don't get this to him . . .'

'Stand aside,' he growls, as a queue of travellers starts to form behind me, brandishing their boarding passes, impatient to proceed.

There's nothing else for it – filling up my lungs to maximum capacity, I push out my diaphragm and emit a rip-roaring, show-stopping 'WAIT!'

It's like someone has pressed the freeze-frame switch. All eyes swerve in my direction – all eyes but those of the one person whose attention I so desperately desire. He is now trundling along to gate A8, blissfully unaware of the brewing storm about to hit north and south of the border.

Back on the road, my mind is whirring with the thought of what I'm going to say to Cruella, and more importantly, do I tell Céline that Mike is not in Oz, but on a Parisian mini break with . . . with . . . another mistress?

* * *

'I'm afraid head office has taken the matter very seriously,' gloats Cruella. 'My hands are tied. I have no alternative but to let you go.'

'If you could just give me one more chance . . .' I grovel, panic rising.

'If I were you, I'd go back to what you do best – serving ready meals and selling novelty goods to tourists,' she says in a condescending, I'm-telling-you-this-for-your-own-good sort of way. 'It's a tough old world out there, and jobs aren't easy to find – even for the young.' Ouch.

She presses the door-release button; I draw a deep breath and exit the shop, cycle-helmeted head held high.

I am in a kind of daze, oblivious to the pushing and jostling of hurried passers-by. This is serious; I now have no job, my meagre savings are fast disappearing, my overdraft has reached its limit, and I am barely able to cover the monthly minimum payment on my credit card. An empty, lost feeling takes hold of me. Perhaps I should have stuck with my safe, familiar job and my secure life, instead of foolishly casting myself adrift without a set of oars. I used to be so focused, so positive that despite all the hardships, things would work out in the end. I feel like I got six winning numbers in the lottery and now I can't find the ticket.

Grabbing a mozzarella and tomato panini, I head for the river to think.

As I chain my bike to the side of the bridge, my thoughts turn to Céline. I pull out my mobile from my bag and scroll for her number. My finger hovers over the green button. Why am I hesitating?

As one of her closest friends, it is my *duty* to tell her, but how? Taking a bite of my sandwich, I rehearse what I'm going to say:

'Céline, are you sitting down? I'm afraid I have some shocking news for you . . .'

No, too dramatic.

'Céline, as much as it pains me, as one of your closest friends, I feel duty-bound to tell you . . .'

Nope, too convoluted – just cut to the chase.

'Céline, Mike's not in Australia. He's in Paris with another woman.'

Too abrupt.

Oh, God. The number's ringing and I haven't a clue what I'm going to say.

Voicemail.

'Hi, Céline. It's me. Emily . . .' Why has my voice gone up an octave? 'I was just wondering if we could meet. Soon. It's . . . it's important. Anyway, call me when you get this message. Thanks . . . Bye.'

* * *

36

THE SCENE IS THE WELL-FURNISHED LIVING ROOM OF A SEMI-DETACHED HOUSE ON THE OUTSKIRTS OF EDINBURGH. A SWEET, HOMELY COUPLE ARE SIPPING CHAMPAGNE AND GIGGLING.

MAN: Cheers! Many happy returns, pet. (HE TAKES A BEAUTIFULLY WRAPPED BOX FROM UNDER THE CUSHION.) This is just a wee something to show you how much I love and appreciate you.

WOMAN: Ach, you shouldnae have. (DABBING HER EYES AND SMILING, SHE KISSES HIM AND OPENS THE BOX. IT IS EMPTY. SHE BURSTS INTO FLOODS OF TEARS.) Is this some kinda cruel joke?

CUT TO AIRPORT. A BALDING, MIDDLE-AGED MAN AND AN ATTRACTIVE YOUNG WOMAN APPEAR THROUGH THE SLIDING DOORS OF THE ARRIVALS HALL. THEY ARE HOLDING HANDS, LAUGHING AND JOKING, PLAINLY HAPPY IN ONE ANOTHER'S COMPANY. A TALL, STRIKING FRENCH WOMAN IN AIRLINE UNIFORM APPROACHES THEM.

FRENCH WOMAN (TO THE MAN): How was Sydney?

MAN: I . . . er . . . what the blazes are you doing here?

FRENCH WOMAN: I could ask you the same question.

YOUNG WOMAN: Aren't you going to introduce us, darling?

FRENCH WOMAN PULLS REVOLVER FROM HANDBAG AND SHOOTS . . .

CUT TO A POLICE INTERVIEW ROOM. IT'S 2 A.M. DI JACK TEMPLETON PACES THE FLOOR.

A DISTRESSED WOMAN SITS AT THE TABLE, HEAD IN HER HANDS, SOBBING.

DI TEMPLETON: Don't lie to us. Your fingerprints are all over the necklace – and the box. As if that wasn't bad enough, you've got the bleedin' gall not only to gift-wrap the empty box, but to do the Curly-Wurly ribbon effect as well! Jeez, I've seen some callous, premeditated crimes in my time, but this. . . .

EMILY: *How many more times? I swear it wasn't planned – please, please, you've got to believe me . . .*

I awake in a knot of sheets and a cold sweat, heart banging wildly in my chest. Flicking on the bedside lamp, I peer at the clock – 03:45. I close my eyes tight and toss and turn. I wish I could sleep, but Céline's pale, tear-stained face and reddened eyes haunt my semi-consciousness. I replay her video message again:

Mike explained everything. We try again, because we love each other. Please . . . don't call me.

There's an iciness in her voice I've never heard before, and it chills me to the core. How can she take back that untrustworthy snake – *again*?

In my method acting class I'm learning about Stanislavski's 'magic if', which asks you to put yourself in the shoes of the character you are playing. *What would I do if I were in these circumstances?* What would you have done, Céline, if the roles were reversed? Would you have stood by and allowed me to be duped and ridiculed? I don't think so. And what about Mike's wife in all of this?

What a day! Not only have I succeeded in ruining a menopausal woman's milestone birthday, but tragically worse, I've also blown apart a precious friendship.

I seem to be lurching from one disaster to another; I've lost my job, one of my dearest friends, and at the grand old age of forty, am sleeping in a single bed in a home I don't own, an assortment of kitsch knick-knacks and an ancient moggy who hates me for company.

AARGH! In a fit of pique, I hurl my mobile at the wall. The Smurfs scatter in all directions, Action Man topples over onto Diana, who is sent crashing onto the tiled hearth, taking the Eiffel Tower snowglobe with her, which starts manically playing 'Jingle Bells'.

Horrified, I gawp at the shattered pieces.

Bzzz! Bzzz! Scrambling through the devastation, I grab my phone. New message: YES! Please, pleeease let it be Céline, telling me we shouldn't let a man destroy our friendship . . .

Ben: *I need to see you. Call me.*

* * *

Five days. I have just five days to prepare for the most important audition of my life. I was voted off first time round, but now I've been recalled; this is my one chance to prove that while I may not be the youngest or most glamorous contestant, I have got what it takes: that *je ne sais quoi*, the X-factor.

'It's only dinner,' I told Lily breezily. 'It's no big deal.'

'Please don't rush back into his arms. Promise me, hon,' she said, face darkening. 'You're just starting to resemble your old self again, and I don't want you going back to square one.'

'I give you my word. I won't do anything stupid,' I replied, secretly wondering if forty is too old to wear white . . .

* * *

I wipe the steam from my recently prescribed reading glasses and peer at my face in the bathroom mirror, in all its 3-D glory. Blimey. When did that happen? Those lines. When did they appear? And those grey hairs? And oh, my God, who stuck them there? Those gorilla legs?

I scrabble in my toiletries bag for a razor: there's a squashed tube of foundation, a bottle of Tesco own brand body wash, a few crumbs of blusher, and a blob of sticky lip gloss. Is this the same woman who, not so very long ago, thought nothing of spending $90 on mascara and a makeover at Macy's?

Having rejected every outfit in my wardrobe, I end up buying a classic little black dress from Autograph for £85. Now, before you throw your hands up in despair, I'll let you in on my shameful secret: I haven't cut the price tag off, and provided I don't spill anything on it, I give my word that I will return it to the customer services desk after D-Day.

* * *

'You look amazing,' says Ben, unusually nervous, as he pulls out a chair for me. (Wow! I can't remember the last time he gave me a compliment.)

'Thank you,' I reply frostily, as I surreptitiously shove my cycle helmet under the table and demurely pull the hem of my tight LBD below the knee. I take a dainty sip of water and pretend to study the menu. I mustn't make it too easy for him. It will take more than a curry and a dose of flattery to win me back.

'You've been on my mind a lot lately,' he continues in a low voice, pouring me a glass of wine.

Don't say anything. Play it cool. Let him do the talking. Dilemma: do I put on my reading glasses so I can actually read the menu, or do I order blind for the sake of vanity? If I am to spend the rest of my life with him, then surely I should feel comfortable being myself. After all, this is the man who held back my hair when my head was stuck down a toilet on *The Jolly Roger* in Barbados after one rum punch too many. (I still blush scarlet at the memory.) The same man who's seen me sans mascara, wearing a green face mask, a tatty towel on my head, and a brace on my teeth. But maybe that's the whole point: the very reason he left; maybe he wants a wife who's sophisticated, who looks her best all the time, not just when the occasion calls for it.

'Whenever I'm in LA I can't help thinking about our trips to Disneyland, and how we used to act like a couple of crazy kids,' he continues, swallowing hard. 'And only last week, I was on the Star Ferry in Hong Kong and remembered the time your scarf blew off into the sea, and how we'd lock ourselves away in my

40

suite and make love for hours, living on room service and Dom Pérignon. So many amazing memories. You will always have a special place in my heart – don't ever forget that.'

A huge current of relief and ecstasy surges around my body. 'Oh, Ben, I've been thinking about you too . . .'

'But I'm worried about you, Em,' he says, reaching for my hand. 'I heard you jacked in the job and are studying drama and living in a rented room. Don't you think you're a little too old to be changing courses? You've got to think of the future.'

'You only get one life and when you left . . .'

'But that's not my main reason for wanting to see you,' he interjects.

Stay calm. Play hard to get. Deep breaths . . .

'I've something important to tell you . . .'

'Yes?' I whisper, heart doing the quickstep.

'I thought it best to do the decent thing and tell you face to face before you hear it from someone else.'

My stomach does a backward flip. I feel the colour drain from my face. I twist the corner of the tablecloth tightly between my fingers, knees wobbling like crème caramel.

'First of all, despite what you might have heard, I want you to know that I didn't sleep with Maddie until we broke up.'

'What? Who's Maddie?' I say, sharply pulling my hand away from his.

'She's new . . . you . . . you don't know her. Anyway, nothing happened until . . .'

'Whooooa! So all that stuff about self-destruct buttons and "finding yourself" was a cover-up?'

'Not exactly . . . no. Let me finish, please. You don't know how hard this is for me . . .'

'You had me believing that you were having some sort of mental breakdown, when all the time you were in love with someone else. How could you?' I snap, throwing down my napkin, unsure of whether to fling myself on the floor or fly out of the door.

41

'Keep your voice down, Em, *please*,' he says through clenched teeth, nervously looking around at the other diners.

I stare at him in disbelief.

'Typical! That's all you care about: what people think of you. You are so damned self-centred! You invited me for dinner to relieve your guilt. Worried about me? Hah! Don't bother. I'll be *fine*,' I say, snatching my jacket, helmet, and bag.

Grabbing my wrist, he mumbles, 'I still care about you, Em. You're like family to me . . . I can only move on with my life if I know you're going to be okay. Maybe in time, we could even be . . .'

'Oh, pur-lease, don't say it! Let go of me! What an idiot I was to even *think* of getting back with you.'

I stagger out of the restaurant into the street, finding it hard to breathe. I unchain my bike from the lamppost, hands trembling.

'Don't be like this,' comes a voice in my ear. 'At least let me give you a lift home, Em, please.'

'Not necessary,' I hiss, jamming on my helmet and flicking on my lights.

'There's just one more thing you should know,' he blurts out, face ghostly in the silvery beam of the streetlight. 'Maddie's pregnant.'

Chapter 4

Looking for Lara

It's 5.30 a.m. I'm wearing rubber gloves and wielding a loo brush. How did my life come to this? I left Amy Air so full of hope and promise, now here I am, barely a year later, with my arm stuck down a toilet. I hate my job, I hate my life, and I hate myself for having got into this mess.

What was I thinking of? I should have carried on flying; okay, so it wouldn't have altered the fact that Ben left me and some other woman stole the life I should have had, but at least I would have been a comfortably off singleton. Thanks to some hare-brained idea that I could become the next Meryl Streep, I am now an impoverished perimenopausal woman without a place to call home, my life packed away in bubble wrap at a warehouse off the M4.

Who needs therapy or self-help books to mend a broken heart? All you need do is follow these three easy steps: a) Give up your well-paid, secure, and interesting job. b) Sell your comfortable home and move into someone's poky back room, complete with resident psychocat and knick-knacks. c) Forgo all luxuries and live from hand to mouth doing menial jobs.

Et voilà! You'll have so many majorly serious problems to

contend with (like SURVIVAL) that being dumped by your boyfriend will seem a minor blip by comparison.

My positive side tries to persuade me that jobs like this are all good, character-building stuff. Besides, should the Rovers Return or the Queen Vic be casting for a cleaning lady, my hands-on experience may just give me the edge over actors who've never operated a squeezy mop or emptied a Dyson.

Pah! Dream on. It's time I faced up to the fact that I'll never make it as an actor. The last few months have taught me that acting isn't just about remembering lines and moves; you have to let go of your inhibitions, be vulnerable and daring. Something always holds me back – fear of making an idiot of myself, I guess, and the harder I try, the more awkward and nervous I feel.

'Stop thinking so much,' Portia keeps telling me. 'Thinking about how we sound or look makes us self-conscious. Be brave, go with your instinct, and don't analyse situations. It destroys the magic.'

I shudder when I think of the huge sacrifice I've made – and for what? I squirt another dollop of Toilet Duck and scrub furiously, tears plopping into the bowl.

'G'day!'

Startled, I wheel around, toppling over onto my bucket of cleaning stuff.

'Sorry, I didn't mean to scare you,' says the tall, young stranger, crouching down and handing me my grubby J-cloth and can of Mr Muscle. His Pacific-blue eyes hold my gaze.

'I'm Dean. New night security. I must have been on patrol when you arrived.'

'Emily,' I sniffle, proffering a yellow, rubber-gloved hand. 'The cleaner . . . in case you were wondering.'

'Well, Emily, nice to meet you,' he says, treating me to a dazzling smile. 'Maybe see you around tomorrow.' And with that he is gone.

* * *

That evening, as I climb the steps of Dramatic Ar s for the very last time, I stop to admire the full moon.

I close my eyes and centre myself, breathing deeply. Lily believes this is a time for cleansing, for new beginnings, for emotional and spiritual growth. She told me to make a wish out loud in front of the moon then visualise it coming true.

She also said it's a time for looking in the mirror and saying nice things to yourself. I draw the line at that one though.

I came to drama school to learn how to make sense of Shakespeare, how to walk in a bustle and corset without keeling over, to flirtatiously flutter a fan, and to sing and dance simultaneously without getting breathless. No one warned me that you had to take part in a tabloid-type reality show before you were allowed to pass 'GO'. If they had, I think I would have stuck to serving chicken and beef at thirty-two thousand feet.

Maybe it's time to put stability back into my life. I should forget my dream, wake up, and behave like any normal middle-aged woman, by getting a proper job with a pension scheme and Christmas bonus.

'You've had twenty-four hours to think about this, and now you're telling me that your motive, the event that's going to get those anger juices flowing, that's going to *fuel* your performances in time to come, is the fact that you had a puncture, were late for your first day at work, and your boss was mean to you?' says Portia, scrutinising me with a look of despair in her kohl-rimmed, piercing green eyes.

Here we go again. I must be some kind of masochist, to have spent the last nine months putting myself through this kind of torture.

I'm realising that the optimist in me has been telling lies – encouraging me to keep on keeping on, because any day now I'll find the key to that secret door that leads to the actor's holy grail; that special place that separates the truly talented from the merely mediocre. But let's be realistic for once: I'm never going to find the key, am I? With no Plan B, where does that leave me? I swallow hard, blinking against the threat of tears. God, please don't let me cry. My toes clench together in my jazz shoes, my face and neck flushing the colour of a strawberry smoothie.

'Come on, Emily, surely you can do better than that? Haven't you ever been accused of something unfairly or had your heart broken in two?'

'Sure, but . . .'

'Well then, how did that make you feel?'

'I . . . I . . .' I murmur, shrugging my shoulders and casting my eyes downwards, wishing I could silently slither down a gap between the floorboards.

'Didn't you feel betrayed, wounded, bloody furious?' she probes.

'Of course, but . . .'

'Well then, now's your opportunity to break through those emotional boundaries and tell us what's in your heart. No one's going to laugh at you. If you're serious about becoming an actor – a *good* actor – then you have to live on the edge, bare your soul. Acting is all about trust, Emily.'

'I know, I know,' I reply sheepishly. 'It's just that, well . . . I'm not entirely comfortable with all this *touchy-feely* stuff. Please don't get me wrong,' I add quickly, desperately searching for the right words, 'I . . . I'm not exactly the stiff-upper-lip type . . . far from it . . . I mean, I cry at nature programmes and . . . Richard Curtis movies . . . but . . . well, it's just that . . .'

'Do you want to be one of those actors who believes they've done a good job so long as they remember their lines and don't bump into the furniture?' continues Portia, a hint of exasperation in her voice. 'Or would you rather be the type of actor who *inhabits* a role, who sets the stage alight, who can hold an audience in the palm of their hand, make them squirm in their seats, move them to tears, or cause them to laugh uncontrollably?' Her eyes are flashing now, as her amethyst ring catches the light, sending a whirlpool of lilac light around the room, like a glitter-ball.

'But isn't acting all about pretending?' I say weakly. 'Don't tell me you have to have committed murder before you're eligible to play the villain in an Agatha Christie.'

All eyes hit the floor, and an uncomfortable silence hangs in the air. I flush even harder.

'Acting is about finding the truth in imaginary circumstances,' says Portia matter-of-factly.

I know she's right. All the same . . . some things are personal. How I wish this were over. I can't carry on just staring at the floor though. It's humiliating. Got to do something . . . oh well, here goes . . .

'Those years we spent together, the plans we made – did it all mean nothing to you?' I say, quietly, haltingly. '*You* were the one who brought up marriage and children, not *me*, and then when I said I was ready, you kept me hanging on. And all that stuff about "finding yourself" . . . what a joke! You didn't even have the decency . . . no, let me finish . . . you didn't even have the decency to tell me what was *really* going on.'

All the bottled-up emotions swirling around inside me since that hideous night come flooding out, filling my words with anger and sadness. A big tear slides halfway down my cheek, attaching itself to my nostril, and my legs turn to Plasticine. I grab the corner of the chair.

'Why couldn't you have sat me down and told me the truth? That you'd fallen out of love with me and met someone else? But no . . . you wanted me to think you were having some sort of mental breakdown, when all the time you were sleeping with *her*. And I was too in love to see through you . . . even blamed myself. Hah! You're nothing but a coward and a liar . . . Come back! Don't walk out when I'm talking to you! Why must you always bury your head in the sand? Come back . . .!' I cry, my outstretched arm flopping limply by my side.

Moments pass.

'Are you all right?' asks Portia gently, handing me a tissue.

'I'm fine, really I am,' I say, giving my nose a vigorous blow. I'm not faking it; I really am all right. In fact, I'm more than all right; I'm elated, in a strange sort of way. I did it, and it feels great – liberating – like this huge, tangled mass of poisonous emotions wrapped around my heart has been hacked away and has finally lost its stranglehold. I wasn't just saying those words; they came from somewhere deep inside me.

'At last! It took you to the very end of the course to get there, but I *knew* you had it in you,' says Portia, treating me to a beaming smile. 'Now, file those emotions away, under *ANGER*, *HURT*, and *DISAPPOINTMENT*, ready to be unleashed as and when the part calls for it,' she continues, squeezing my arm.

I rejoin the group, sitting in a circle on the floor. I suddenly feel as if everything has fallen into place. Up to this very moment I have been stumbling, muddling my way through, putting on a brave face to the world, pretending to myself that I'm better off without Ben. It's now rapidly, brilliantly dawning on me that I truly had been clinging to a lost cause, and I'm free at last.

Thank you, Stanislavski. I think I've finally got it.

* * *

It's Karaoke Nite at the Dog & Whistle. James and Sally take to the stage to give their Dolly and Kenny rendition of 'Islands in the Stream'. My mind rewinds nine months and that first awkward meeting. What a long way we have all come: the emotions, the secrets, the triumphs and failures we have all dared to share.

'To you all and the great adventures that lie ahead!' announces Portia, popping open another bottle of prosecco.

'To us!'

I look around at our merry band, so full of hope and anticipation. I wonder how many of us with dreams of becoming actors will become Hot Property, and how many will end up scraping together a living as market researchers or living statues.

My tyres hiss as I weave along the rain-drenched road home. I freewheel down the hill, feet off the pedals, head tilted back, face cooled by the sudden downpour. I feel lighter somehow, as if at any given moment my bike and I might soar up into the black night and fly across the moon, just like in *E.T.*

I have no idea what the future holds or how I'm going to survive, but tonight, for the first time since embarking on this mad journey, I feel I'm taking tentative steps towards reclaiming the confidence and self-esteem I lost during Bengate, and I'm filled with – not sure what, but this much I do know: I am no longer afraid of being alone.

Goodbye and thank you, Dramatic Ar s, for showing me that though life may be difficult at the moment, I refuse to be brought down by cheating, critical lovers or unforgiving, bitter bosses. Sure, there will be more bumps along the way, but I have a choice; and I choose to keep following my dream, no matter where it leads.

* * *

My love affair with Russia began at the age of fourteen, when they showed *Doctor Zhivago* on the telly one Christmas. We were studying the Russian Revolution at school, and this epic film brought those dry History lessons to life, and was the reason I got an A* that term.

While most of my friends were drooling over Jason Donovan or Tom Cruise, Yuri Zhivago was the object of my adolescent desire. I would backcomb my hair into a bouffant up-do, just like Julie Christie, wear oversized sweaters and my mum's faux-fur hair band, her pale coral lipstick completing the Lara Look.

I even bought a second-hand balalaika with my pocket money and tormented my parents and the dog by playing 'Lara's Theme' over and over. I begged Mum and Dad to book Russia for our annual summer holiday instead of Spain. (Needless to say, Spain won the majority vote.)

Some twenty years later, when my flight schedule took me to Moscow, I channelled my inner Lara once more, as I skated in Gorky Park, fantasising as I fell over that I might one day be scooped up by a handsome Russian doctor who would write me beautiful poems.

The only person who ever came to my rescue was an ice marshal called Zoya, who reminded me of Miss Trunchbull and could lift you up with one arm. I decided then it was high time I grew up and left my Russian romance in my teenage past.

But today I am required to dig deep and channel my inner Lara once more, as my first professional audition, two months after leaving drama school, is to play Olga in Chekhov's *Three Sisters*.

How I'd love to say it's an epic BBC costume drama, involving three months' filming in grand palaces and sumptuous ballrooms, but the truth is it's a 'profit-share', pub-theatre production. I may have been awarded a D– in Maths, but even I am able to calculate that 40 seats @ £10 ÷ 14 cast members + 5 crew = very little profit (and that's assuming it's a full house every night). But then I'm not in this business for the money, rather 'to do interesting work that challenges me' – isn't that what actors always say on chat shows?

With only travel expenses guaranteed, you'd imagine there wouldn't be much competition. Apparently seven hundred actors applied to audition for the fourteen roles, as the venue's prime location means you might get spotted by agents and casting directors. It's an opportunity to hone your acting chops, playing the kind of roles awarded only to star names in the West End.

* * *

Ignoring the stench of beer and the odd peanut, I slither around the stained and grubby floor of the Red Dragon pub, going 'sssss.' I want to stand up and shout, *Could somebody please explain to me what this has got to do with Chekhov?*

'Right then, that's the end of the warm-up, and in a few moments we'll be calling you into the room one by one, so please have your audition pieces ready,' says someone called Rocket, with dreadlocks and a clipboard.

I pace up and down, quietly practising my speech – again:

"'Sir, I desire you do me right and justice, and to bestow your pity on me; for I am a most poor woman, and a stranger, born out of your dominions, having here . . . having here . . ."'

Oh, God, what comes next?

'Emily Forsyth!' calls Rocket.

A queasy feeling floods my stomach. I'm ushered into a poky back room, where I'm introduced to the creative team.

'Now, Emily, what audition piece are you going to do for us today?' asks Hugh, the director.

'I'd like to do Katherine . . . Queen Katherine from *Henry the Eighth*.'

Casting me a sympathetic glance, he nods. 'In your own time.'

With four pairs of expectant eyes upon me, I draw a wobbly breath.

"'Sir, I desire you do me right and justice, and to bestow your pity on me; for I am a most poor woman, and a stranger, born out of your dominions, having here no judge indifferent, nor no more assurance of equal friendship and proceeding . . ."'

With my audience just inches away, and crates of mixers, packets of assorted crisps, and pork scratchings occupying almost every available space, it's hard to imagine I'm a sixteenth-century queen in a grand hall, begging my husband not to force me into a quickie divorce.

"'. . . in God's name turn me away, and let the foul'st contempt shut door upon me, and so give me up to the sharps't kind of justice."'

I lift my eyes from my kneeling position.

'Thank you,' says Hugh, breaking the long silence. 'Now we'd like you to read part of Olga's speech for us.'

The script starts to quiver as I take it from him.

'Turn to page two, beginning from the top please.'

I try to channel my nerves into capturing Olga's mood of despair.

'"Don't whistle, Masha. How can you! Every day I teach at the Gymnasium and afterwards I give lessons until evening, and so I've got a constant headache and my thoughts are those of an old woman . . ."'

PSSCHH hisses a toilet from above. GERDUNG, GERDUNG go the pipes.

'"I've felt my strength and my youth draining from me every day, drop by drop. And one single thought grows stronger and stronger . . ."'

I play the speech distractedly at first, but halfway through find myself relaxing into it and actually enjoying it.

Then suddenly it's over: my one and only chance to make an impression. I wonder if they'll let me do it again . . .

'Okay. Finally, what do you feel you can bring to the role of Olga?'

'Hmm. Well, like Olga, I used to be dissatisfied with my job, felt I'd missed out on marriage, felt old before my time, longed to be somewhere else. The difference is I did something about it. But I can still remember how that feels, and I could draw on those emotions.'

'Interesting,' says Hugh, rubbing his chin. 'Thank you for coming. We'll let you know on Monday.'

Monday? That's a whole three days. But hang on! What am I fretting about? I can't afford to take the job even if they do offer it to me. So it's for the best if I don't get it. Just put it down to experience.

* * *

I glance at my watch: 5.30. Humph. That's it then. The deadline has come and gone. Their loss. Not for them, a *thank-you-*

for-my-first-break mention when I collect my BAFTA, so bollocks to them.

Half an hour later, the *Sex and the City* theme tune comes drifting across the landing into the bathroom. Jeans at half-mast, I stagger and stumble to the bedroom, and swipe my mobile from the dressing table.

'Emily, it's Hugh.'

I hold my breath for a moment.

'Oh, of course, the audition. Hi,' I say in my best I'm-a-very-busy-person voice, heart leaping into my throat.

'Good news . . . we'd like you to play Olga for us. What do you say?'

My tummy does a double somersault. I open my mouth to speak, but catch myself in time. I want to grovel with gratitude and swing from the chandelier (or in this case, the wire-framed fabric light fitting with rayon fringe), but I mustn't appear too desperately keen. I count to three, then say coolly, 'I'd love to – thank you – I'd love to.'

'Great. Rehearsals start next Monday. Rocket, our deputy stage manager, will email you all the details. Good to have you on board.'

'Thank you,' I say again, trying to maintain my composure until he hangs up.

'YESSS!' I whoop, punching the air and landing with a thud.

'Emily, is that you?' calls Beryl from downstairs.

Hastily zipping up my jeans, I screech over the banister, 'Beryl, I got the job!'

'Fan-bloody-tastic, darlin'! Let me just turn *Pointless* off an' I'll crack open that bottle of Asti Spumante in the sideboard. I've been waiting since Christmas for an excuse to drink it.'

Three glasses of tepid Asti Spumante later, and my euphoria has turned into sickly panic. With daytime rehearsals for three weeks, how am I going to earn any money? Why didn't I think this through more carefully? *Look before you leap*. Will I never learn? My self-esteem may well have had a bit of a boost, but the same can definitely not be said for my bank balance. There has got to be a way . . .

* * *

"'Masha will come to Moscow for the summer . . . *aargh!* . . . for the *WHOLE* summer . . . Masha will come to Moscow for the whole summer . . .'" I repeat, as I wind my way in between the desks, flicking my duster with one hand, balancing my script with the other.

'Hello again!'

I spin around, tripping over computer cables and a wastepaper bin.

'Sorry, I've gotta stop freaking you out,' says Dean, grabbing my elbow, his piercing gaze meeting mine. My heart gives a little flutter.

'Glad to see you looking cheerier than last time we met.'

'Yes, sorry about that,' I reply, glancing at him sideways.

'Guy trouble?'

'That, and one of those where-the-hell-is-my-life-going moments.'

He looks at me blankly. He must only be in his twenties, so I guess this concept is about as alien to him as TikTok is to me.

I glance at the clock. 'Sorry, I don't mean to be rude, but I've got to be at my next job in less than an hour, and I haven't started the vacuuming yet.'

'Sure thing. You know, we should . . .'

'Sorry?' I bellow over the roar of the hoover.

He shakes his head and mouths 'Goodbye.'

* * *

I pedal through the damp, chill, early morning air, chanting, 'Aleksandr Ignatyevich Vershinin, Aleksey Petrovich Fed . . .

54

Fedotik.' Gaah! Why is no one in Russia called Bob Jones or Jim Smith? I glance at my watch: 7.15. 'Aleksandr Ignat . . . Ignatyevich Vershinin, Aleksey Petrovich Fedotik . . .'

My other morning job is at the Red Dragon, which is very handy, as we rehearse here.

Using all the female charm I could muster, I persuaded the landlord that good beer and Sky TV alone were not enough to lure the clientele. What the place needed was a woman's touch: a splash of bleach here and a squirt of air freshener there. (That was the polite, edited version.)

Anyway, it worked. So from 7.30 a.m. I'm Mrs Overall, picking chewing gum off bar stools and replenishing paper towels. Then, fast-forward three hours, and I'm Olga Prozorova, schoolteacher and eldest sister to Masha and Irina, dreaming of marriage and Moscow.

There's even a shower I can use. The pipes gurgle and rattle a bit when I turn it on, and it splutters and drips freezing cold water, but at least I don't arrive at rehearsal smelling like a compost heap.

By the end of the week, I'm sleepwalking my routine:

04.30: Alarm goes off. Hit snooze button.
04.35: Alarm goes off. Roll out of bed.
04.45: Down a bowl of Special K.
05.00: Grab bike and pedal like the clappers.
05.15: Arrive at Office 1. Clean.
07.15: Leave office for pub. Clean.
09.30: Shower, change, wolf down Beryl's BLT breakfast and flask of coffee.
10.30–15.00: Rehearse. Discuss.
15.30: Home, revise scenes we did today, learn lines for tomorrow, supper.
18.00: Arrive at Office 2. Clean.
21.30: Bed, in order to be up with the lark and repeat all of the above.

In between times, I am also sending out mail-shots to agents and casting directors:

Please cover my performance as Olga in 'Three Sisters' at the Red Dragon Pub Theatre, Lady Jane Walk, Richmond. 17th December – 31st January at 7.30.

Even if only four or five turn up it will be worth it – won't it?

* * *

TONIGHT AT 7.30
THREE SISTERS
BY
ANTON CHEKHOV

I feel my stomach lurch as I glance at the sandwich board outside the pub. This is it. No more 'Sorry, what's my next line?' or 'Should I be sitting at this point?' After three weeks' rehearsal, I *think* I'm pretty solid on my lines and moves, but there is always that fear lurking somewhere in the shadows, of stepping out in front of an audience and thinking, *Who am I? What the hell am I doing here? Who* are *these people?*

I make my way upstairs to the cramped, communal dressing room. Where, oh where is the star on the door and the mirror with light bulbs all around it?

I am the first to arrive and bag myself a wee corner. With fourteen of us in the cast, it's going to be a tight squeeze. I lay out my make-up, hairbrush, bottle of water, and lucky elephant charm (a treasured gift from the cleaner at the crew hotel in Mumbai). I then distribute my First Night cards.

One by one, the others start to drift in, and nervous, excited chatter and vocal warm-up exercises soon reverberate around the room.

There is a rap at the door and Hugh enters, pushing eighty-year-old Betty, playing Anfisa, the nanny, into the lap of Vershinin (he's the lieutenant, who's in love with Masha, my sister, but they're both married, his wife's suicidal and . . . well, it's complicated).

'Break a leg, everyone. Unfortunately our audience tonight is *slightly* thin on the ground, but please don't let that put you off. I want you to act like the place is full – which I'm sure it will be once the reviews are out.'

Another knock on the door and Rocket calls breathlessly, 'Act One beginners, please!'

As I wait in the pitch blackness behind the stage, I wonder if there's anyone out there at all. No excited chatter or rustling of sweet wrappers. I find a tiny hole in the masking drapes, close one eye, and peer through, just as the door at the back slams shut. A solitary cough fills the silence.

The lights go down and the opening music, by some Russian composer whose name I can't remember, let alone pronounce, crackles through the speakers. I clear my dry throat, fumble my way through the leaden darkness five steps to the makeshift stage, and take up position. The music fades and the lights snap on, burning my face, blinding me with their glare. Here goes . . .

'It's exactly a year since Father died . . .'
So far so good . . .
'Don't whistle, Masha.'
A phone rings.
'Hello?'
'How could you?'
'It finishes around ten-thirty, I think . . . I hope . . .' (snigger) . . .
'I end up with a perpetual headache . . .'
'Okay, darling, see you in the bar. Hmm?'
'. . . Today I'm free, I'm at home, and I have no headache . . .'
'Ooh, I know . . . make it a vodka and orange . . . a double . . . I'll need it! Byee!'
'Shh!'
We haven't even reached the end of Act One and I am consumed by an overwhelming sense of despair. Marvellous method acting?

57

Would it were true.

A car alarm goes off.

What in God's name is that guy doing?

'. . . Andrey, don't go off . . .'

I don't believe it. He's getting up. KER-CHUNG! goes the seat as it flips up. EEEEEEAK! creaks the door. A shaft of light streams through from the bar.

'He has a way of always walking off. Come here.'

'GOAL!' comes a collective, triumphant cry from the bar, just as the door swings shut.

I guess Chelsea must have scored against Sheffield then.

We brazen it out to the interval – somehow. Acts Three and Four go a little better, and apart from the odd cough, our meagre audience seems to settle down. Maybe they're actually getting into it. On second thoughts, judging by the lukewarm applause as we take our curtain call, maybe they were comatose.

It wasn't meant to be like this; I didn't expect a standing ovation and flowers to be thrown at our feet, but I wasn't prepared for this: to be in a production where the actors outnumber the audience. Is this what I have sacrificed my job and everything for? This is not my dream. I had such high hopes. Things are just not panning out as I expected. My bubble has burst already. My nails are chipped and dirty; my knees are bruised from pushing and shoving desks around the office and scrubbing stone steps at the pub. I wouldn't care had I had one reply from a casting director or agent; even a *WE REGRET TO INFORM YOU* would have been nice, courteous.

'Well done, everyone!' enthuses Hugh, giving us the thumbs-up as we trudge up the stairs. 'The drinks are on me.'

I'm about to make the excuse of having to be up at the crack of dawn, when Susannah, who plays Masha, as if reading my mind, says, 'Come on, sis, shall we show our faces and have just one?'

'Why not?' I say flatly, forcing a smile.

'Ladies!' calls Hugh, waving us over to the bar.

'Hugh's a sweetie,' whispers Susannah. 'I've worked for him before, and not only is he a brilliant director, but he really values his cast. The theatre is his lifeblood. He should be at The National – but then shouldn't we all, darling?'

Despite early success (she was plucked from drama school at the age of nineteen to play Rumpleteazer in *Cats*), Susannah tells me she has struggled since, doing the odd commercial and bit part on telly.

'The only way I get to do the juicy, classical roles is on the Fringe, in productions like this, with a couple of students or maybe a pensioner or two for an audience at matinées. But who knows, one of these days, Sam Mendes may be out there scouting for new talent,' she says brightly. 'Top-up?'

She's right, and I feel ashamed for harbouring snobbish thoughts about the lack of dressing room space, the non-existent set and having to cobble together our own costumes. This cast has great talent with TV, film, and West End stage credits and, despite the lack of money, they are dedicated and determined to make this production the best it can be. I need to learn to be more realistic and patient. They are an inspiration to me.

I will not give up. NEVER.

* * *

Poor Dean. I don't imagine for one moment that a long, dreary Russian play about three miserable sisters is his cup of tea. Nevertheless, desperate for a paying public (fewer than ten in the audience and performances are now threatened with cancellation), I cajole, chivvy, then bully him into coming along – and to bring as many of his mates as he can muster.

'Okay, you win,' he says eventually, holding up his hands, mouth breaking into a wide, toothpaste-ad grin. 'I'll come. I seem to remember I saw the movie with Whoopi Goldberg when I was a kid, and I quite enjoyed it.'

I look at him quizzically. Movie? Whoopi Goldberg doing Chekhov?

'Aah,' I say, cruelly amused. 'I think you may be mixing it up with *Sister Act*.'

'Hmm,' he says pensively. 'But it's funny, right?'

'Er . . . not exactly.'

His eyes bore into mine. 'All right, I'll come, and I'll bring some of the guys as well – but on one condition,' he says, folding his arms as he leans against a desk.

'And what's that?' I enquire breezily, scooshing some anti-static cleaner onto a computer screen.

'That you'll let me take you for dinner one night.'

Unaccustomed as I have become to being asked out on dates (let alone by a guy who looks young enough to be my son), and particularly when I'm looking like Gollum in Marigolds, a blush creeps into my cheeks.

'Well?' he says expectantly, fixing me with a challenging look.

'I . . . but . . . well . . . you don't have . . .' I say guardedly. 'Okay . . . but no fewer than six friends, agreed?'

'Yay! Gimme five!' he says.

'What? Oh . . . yay!' and we slap palms. Please don't laugh.

* * *

'How old?' splutters Lily over afternoon tea the next day, looking at me agog.

'You cradle snatcher, you!' says Rachel, slamming down her cup.

'We need an audience, so what choice do I have?' I say innocently, teeth sinking into my scone.

'Maybe he has a fetish for rubber gloves?' says Lily.

'Or he's got an Oedipus complex,' adds Rachel.

'Hey, I take offence at that,' I say, screwing up my face. 'You're all just jealous.'

'Damn right we are,' says Lily. 'So when are we going to meet this antipodean hunk?'

'Whoa, not so fast! He's only asked me to dinner, not to walk down the aisle with him. And I never said he was a hunk.'

'No, but I bet he is,' says Rachel, eyes twinkling mischievously, desperate for details.

'Okay, so he is tall and looks like he works out, but what has that . . .?'

'I knew it!' she says, thumping her fist on the table. 'Isn't life funny? Cabin crew fly all over the globe, rarely meeting anyone, and you work as a cleaner at the crack of dawn, when the only people around are milkmen and all-night garage attendants, and quick as a flash – oops, excuse the pun – this gorgeous, young guy from the other side of the world sweeps you off your feet!'

'Hold on a minute, girls. You're reading too much into this. I never said he . . .'

'You know, when I was a teenager, I watched classic English films like *The Airport Affair*, and read novels like *Love in the Skies* and *Captain of My Heart*,' says Lily, taking a sip of tea. 'I was sold a dream of a flight attendant's life: stolen glances in the cockpit and romantic, candlelit dinners overlooking the Taj Mahal. And the reality? "I didn't have a starter so knock five dollars off my share of the bill."'

'The people who wrote this stuff should be sued for misrepresentation. They should tell it as it is,' chips in Rachel, toying with the sugar. 'That you're more likely to meet your Mr Right cleaning toilets than on board a plane bound for Rio.'

'Somehow I don't think *Love in a Broom Cupboard* or . . . *Kiss of the Cleaner* would exactly fly off the shelves,' I remark. 'Now, talking of dishy, charming pilots, which we weren't, any developments in the Mike/Céline situation?'

'Don't ask!' they groan loudly, in unison.

'The latest thing is, he and his wife are now moving to a bigger house with land and stables so the kids can have horses. I mean, honestly, are these the actions of a man who is about to leave home?' says Rachel, shaking her head wearily.

'Why she stays with him, I'll never know,' I say. 'Such a lovely girl, with so much to give.'

'She once said to me, "What if there is no one else out there for me?" As if, and anyway, surely being on your own is better than this constant heartache?' says Lily.

'I guess things are never black and white. I mean, he must have something, mustn't he?' I say feebly. 'Maybe I should have kept my dislike of him under wraps though. She never returns my calls or texts. Does she ever mention me?'

There is a thick silence between them as they stare into their empty tea cups.

'I only told her about Mike because I care, you know,' I continue defensively. 'She would have done the same.'

'Shit! Is that the time?' says Rachel, gesturing for the bill and pulling out her purse. 'I've got to check in soon and I haven't packed yet.'

'My treat,' says Lily. 'Now, go! You know what the M25 can be like at this time of day.'

'Thanks, angel. I'll see you both at the play. Sooo excited! Break a leg, Em!' she says, grabbing her car keys and blowing a kiss.

I look at Lily searchingly.

'You okay, hon?' she asks, a frown creasing her forehead.

'Why do I get the feeling you're both hiding something from me? I'm not asking you to take sides. I'd just like to know why you look uncomfortable whenever I mention . . .'

'Céline knew.'

'Well there's a surprise. She's obviously in denial . . .'

'About Ben,' Lily blurts out.

'Sorry?'

'Mike told her about Ben and . . . Ms Mile High, but made her swear not to breathe a word.'

'What? You mean she knew all the time and didn't tell me!'

'Yes.'

'How long?'

'About six months.'

'Six months! And did *you* know?'

'No – neither of us knew until you told us you were splitting up.'

'I can't believe it. Six months! And she just stood by and watched . . .'

'Mike put her in an impossible situation. She feels awful about it.'

'Yeah, but then to add insult to injury, she takes out her guilt, anger, hurt, and whatever else on *me*!'

'I'm not excusing her, but according to her therapist, it's a common reaction.'

'She's in therapy? But she always comes across so confident, so comfortable in her own skin, so . . .'

'Many of us do, sweetie, but underneath . . .' Lily shrugs, tapping her PIN number into the hand-held machine. 'Please don't let this cause an even bigger rift between you. Give her a call. *Please.*'

'I don't see why I . . .'

'Please, hon. She's not in a very good place right now.'

'I'll think about it,' I reply.

Arm in arm, we stroll over to the bike rack. As I lean forward to release the padlock, I flinch.

'Darling, you've got to give up this cleaning lark,' Lily says, rubbing my back gently. 'Surely there's something else you could do – less physically demanding and better paid.'

'I know. I promise once the run is over, I'll hang up my Marigolds for good.'

'I'm glad to hear it,' she says, sliding elegantly into her car. 'Now go home, get some rest, and oh, do something about those nails, please. I can hardly believe that this is the same Emily Forsyth who was once awarded a distinction for Cabin Crew Grooming.'

I peer at my distorted reflection in the bicycle bell, ghostlike face, sunken eyes, and messy hair poking out from under my helmet. Was that woman really me? The one who had monthly manicures, pedicures, and facials? The one who was photographed for the in-flight magazine, gracefully pouring tea into a china cup, and gently tucking in a sleeping passenger with a tartan blanket?

I pedal through the park, my tyres scrunching on the crisp, frosty carpet. A startled stag bounds out of the bushes and off into the distance, a garland of pine trailing from his battle-scarred horns. An unexpected rush of contentment floods through my veins. There's definitely something to be said for this spartan life. Sometimes, like now, it gives me a fresh view of the world. I must have driven through this park hundreds of times in my nifty little sports car. Did I ever notice things like this back then? Did I ever smell the damp undergrowth, or stop to watch the heron balancing on one leg in the rushes?

Despite being flat broke, exhausted and spotty, I wouldn't swap my life now. It's a small price to pay to be allowed to act on a professional stage (albeit four wooden pallets shoved together, barely twelve feet long). No one ever said it was going to be easy. Most good actors start from the bottom, don't they? It's not as if I have dreamy aspirations of becoming the next Kristin Scott Thomas; but so long as I can keep myself financially afloat, who knows what opportunities may come my way.

As for the Céline situation: it's taught me I can't change others, only myself. If she chooses to be with Mike then that's her business. I did what I thought was right and it backfired on me, but I refuse to beat myself up about it, have a stand-up row, or allow bad feelings to fester. Am I going to allow Mike and Ben to destroy our friendship? No way. I will rise above the hurt and anger by sending her an invitation to a performance of *Three Sisters*.

This doesn't mean I excuse her behaviour, or that I'm a walkover; it means I want to move on. I'm tired of playing the blame game and carrying a grudge. It's weighing me down and is not good for the soul. If I am to survive in this crazy, turbulent, wonderful business, then I need all the inner calm and strength I can find.

'Is that the excited chatter of an audience I can hear?' says Susannah in disbelief.

'OMG! Did someone say the word *audience*?' splutters Ed, playing Chebutykin, cocking his ear.

'Darlings!' says Hugh, bursting into the dressing room, beaming expansively. 'Now don't let it throw you, but we have a full house! I knew that review in *Time Out* would do the trick. Good luck, everyone, and oh, this is your five-minute call.'

I take up my starting position and draw a deep, steadying breath. The atmosphere tonight is warm and vibrant, yet I'm the most nervous I've been throughout the run. Dean and his young friends, my friends, who regularly see the hottest Broadway shows, wouldn't come to see an old, serious Russian play in a shabby pub had I not sold them the idea.

I think I can hear Lily's laugh. I dare to look through the spyhole in the drapes. My eye scans along the rows. In a space not much bigger than Beryl's front room, having the audience in glaring proximity can be distracting enough when you don't know them, but . . . there they are: Rachel, Lily, and . . . an empty seat. Disappointment floods my veins. I should have resisted the temptation to look. I mustn't let it throw me. Concentrate.

All at once the door at the back is flung open. Bright light spills down the aisle. The silhouette of a female figure. She hesitates.

'Over here!' hisses Lily.

'We have clearance,' whispers the stage manager.

'She came,' I whisper.

He looks at me blankly. 'You okay?'

I give him the thumbs-up.

The lights go down; the music starts.

What a difference an audience makes; hearing reactions to what's said on stage lifts everyone's spirits and performances. Everything is heightened, and the lines ring out earnest and true.

Instead of the usual, muted interval break, the atmosphere in the dressing room tonight is lively and buzzing.

'You know the bit where I say, "Your clock is seven minutes fast"? Well, I got a reaction! Woohoo!' says Nick, playing Kulygin. 'They've actually picked up on my psychoneurosis – that I'm more concerned about the clock than the fact that my wife may be sleeping with another man. Bitch!'

'I do love you really, darling,' says Susannah, blowing him a kiss in the mirror.

'This calls for a celebration. Tea all round,' I say, flicking the kettle switch and collecting everyone's mugs.

As Act Four unfolds, we have the audience in our grasp – not one shuffle or yawn or mobile phone menace.

'"If only we knew, if only we knew!"'

The music fades. The lights go to black and there is silence. Lights up, and we join hands for the curtain call. Thunderous applause cracks the air, accompanied by cheering, whistling, and stomping.

Soon the whole audience is up on their feet. We all look at one another in astonishment, savouring the atmosphere. Dean was true to his word, and his rent-a-crowd has come up trumps.

'See the effort I made to persuade you to have dinner with me?' he says later in the bar, handing me an enormous glass of wine. 'We really enjoyed it, didn't we, guys?'

'Aw, you're just saying that,' I reply with a self-deprecating shrug.

'Nope, but what was the big deal with Moscow?'

'Darling! Well done!' A familiar, cultured voice cuts through the raucous babble, and I turn to see Portia walking towards me, arms outstretched, theatrical in her long, burgundy velvet coat and fedora.

'Is this the same woman who, not so long ago, was embarrassed to lay bare her emotions?' she says, clasping me to her. 'You shone tonight, Emily. I'm proud of you.'

'Really?' I say, secretly thrilled, though my insecure side is telling me she's only being polite.

'*Really*. Your performance worked. You breathed life into Olga, and my heart went out to her. I wept at the end.'

'I didn't come across too whingeing, too bitter?'

'Not in the slightest. You got the balance just right.'

'It's just that some nights, I feel my insecurity infects the audience and I lose them altogether. The more I think about it, the worse it gets.'

'If you're worrying too much about the audience, then you're not concentrating. Believe in yourself more, Emily,' she says, placing her hands firmly on my shoulders. 'Never forget Shakespeare's words in *Measure for Measure*: "Our doubts are traitors, and make us lose the good we oft might win by fearing to attempt."'

She takes out a pen and jots the quote down on a Post-it note, then places it firmly in my hand.

I look deeply into her face. She hasn't just taught me about acting; she has taught me so much about myself, more than any therapist could have done, and I feel a stronger person for having known her.

'Thank you, Portia,' I say, hugging her, tears teetering on my lashes. '"Our doubts are traitors" will be my mantra from now on.'

'Are you up for Waltzing Matilda's karaoke bar later?' yells Dean, resting his elbow on my shoulder.

'Erm, yeeeah,' I say with an uncertain smile.

A pair of hands cover my eyes, a whiff of expensive scent wafting in the air.

'You were fab!' chorus Lily and Rachel.

'Girls!' I screech, spinning around. 'Thank you for coming. It means the world to . . .'

'*Chérie*, I am *so* proud of you,' Céline whispers, kissing me tentatively on both cheeks.

For a long moment we just stare into one another's startled eyes.

'I wasn't sure you'd come,' I say, biting my bottom lip, my tone perhaps a tad too cool.

'Portia, these are my friends . . .'

I scan the bar, looking for her, but she is gone.

'Over here!' calls Hugh from a dimly lit booth. 'Bring your friends. There's more than enough prosecco to go round!'

'Sis!' cries Susannah, patting the space next to her. 'This is Lionel, my agent . . .'

It's almost closing time before Céline takes me aside for a few quiet words.

'I'm so sorry for . . .'

'Look,' I say firmly, determined not to dredge up the past, and especially tonight, of all nights. 'I don't want to fall out with you. You had your reasons and . . .'

'"*Le cœur a ses raisons que la raison ne connaît pas.*"'

I look at her inquisitively.

'"The heart has its reasons, which reason knows nothing of." This does not excuse my behaviour, but . . .'

'I've moved on, Céline, and if you and Mike are happy, then . . .'

'It's finished,' she mumbles.

'Excuse me?'

'It's over.'

'Really?'

'Yes.'

'For good this time?'

She bites her trembling lip and nods.

I look deeply into her sad, blue-lagoon eyes. I want to say I'm sorry, but I'm not. Setting down my glass, I impulsively put my arms around her and hold her tight.

'Eleven years of my life . . .'

'I know.'

A huge tear rolls down her cheek and splashes into her wine glass. I rummage in my bag for a tissue, resisting the temptation of telling her she's better off without that lying, narcissistic, serial cheater. After all, it's not so long since I was in her shoes, and I know only too well how irritating those well-meaning break-up clichés are, and how they can make you feel even worse. You have to find your own way through the break-up maze.

Corny though it may sound, I'm now discovering the power of one and no longer feel lonely when I'm alone. I wish I could make her see that there's a world of opportunity and adventure out there, just waiting to be found, but she has to have the courage to work it out for herself. As Céline is quick to point out, I have a passion for something that drives me and isn't dependent on a man's love. *I'm* the one responsible for making my dream come true. For Céline, the beautiful, hopeless romantic, her dream of becoming a wife and mother relies on finding a husband – and soon.

'Drink up. You're coming to Waltzing Matilda's with us,' I tell her. 'I seem to recall we once made an awesome Agnetha and Frida at Kirk's Karaoke Bar in downtown Dallas, did we not?'

'*Mon Dieu!*' she groans, cringing at the memory. Running the tissue carefully under her lower lashes, she downs the last of her wine. 'Let's go.'

Nothing like a bit of 'Dancing Queen' to reseal a friendship and lift the spirits.

* * *

It seems I've only just drifted off, when I am woken by Rod Stewart belting out 'Maggie May'. I open one eye: 04:30. Slamming the OFF button on the radio alarm, I raise my head from the pillow. I feel like I'm drowning in a swirling, green, psychedelic sea. I fall back, holding my head in agony. The thought of overflowing bins and disinfectant makes me want to throw up. I stagger to the bathroom, one hand grimly holding my head, the other my stomach.

The road approaching the office is riddled with bumps and potholes, and normally I manage to avoid the majority of them, but this morning, with my eyes half shut, I cycle headlong into each and every one, rattling my bones and jarring my nerves.

As I push the Dyson to and fro, gradually, agonisingly, fragments of last night seep into my fuzzy consciousness, torturing my mind. Last night I truly believed our rendition of 'Voulez-Vous' was worthy of a part in *Mamma Mia!* Now, in the cold, sober light of day, it's dawning on me that Céline and I must have sounded like a pair of wild dingoes.

That night, and for the remaining ten performances, we are back to an audience of sleepy pensioners, uninterested GCSE students, and the odd drunk from the bar. We now know how it feels to have an appreciative crowd, and so the remainder of the run is an anticlimax – a bit like getting upgraded to first class once, and then having to revert to flying economy.

But I have been given a taste of how it feels to play a multi-dimensional character in front of an appreciative audience, and it's made me hungry for Hedda Gabler, for . . . okay, maybe I'm a tad too old to play Hedda. I could play the likes of Lady Macbeth though, or Shirley Valentine. But how do you land that kind of role, unless some maverick director takes a risk on casting an unknown?

* * *

Dean turns up on the last night for our dinner date decked out in an ill-fitting, rumpled suit. He confesses he watched Scene One then retired to the bar.

'The table's booked for ten-thirty,' he says, planting a slobbery, beery kiss on the side of my neck.

I stare at the floor, my gaze immediately drawn to his feet, which are sporting a pair of five-toed trainers that make him look like . . . Amphibian Man. Try to ignore this, Emily.

Pressing his hand firmly into the small of my back, he steers me unsteadily towards the door. Why am I already starting to feel this is a bad idea?

The dainty waitress nods graciously and leads us through the closely packed tables to a dark corner of the restaurant.

By the time our tom yum soup arrives, I *know* this was a mistake. I should have insisted we just go for a drink. I vaguely remember Susannah telling me that night at Waltzing Matilda's that she's joined a dating app, and that you should only agree to a coffee or drink on the first date. Then if you discover you haven't got much in common, you don't have to endure an interminable and costly meal. Why didn't these pearls of wisdom register in my brain? (Probably because at the time it was otherwise engaged in ABBAville.)

'Are you on TikTok?' asks Dean, slurping his soup.

'Nope,' I reply, eyes ghoulishly transfixed by the blade of lemongrass hanging from the end of his damp chin.

'Pity,' he continues, throwing down his spoon and pointing his phone at me.

'What are you doing?'

'Now my mates and Mum and Dad can see my Mrs Robinson in the flesh.'

'Sorry?'

'That's what Mum and Dad call you. You know, older woman seduces younger man.'

'Whaaat?'

He lurches forward, phone held high as he pulls me into frame, sending the basket of prawn crackers into orbit.

'Hi, everyone! This is the British lady I've been telling you about. Say "Hi," Em.'

I wriggle out of his grasp and dive under the table.

'Put the phone away!'

'Aaw. Don't be shy.'

'I said, put-the-phone-away!'

'Gotta go, guys. That's the typical British reserve I've been telling you about. Catch yawl later!'

As I resurface and scramble back onto my seat, I wonder how I am to survive beyond the green curry.

I sneak a look at my watch and stifle a yawn. This is *so* embarrassing.

'Some of my mates are going to that new nightclub in Kingston later. I said we might meet them there,' he says keenly, his glassy-eyed stare glued to my breasts.

'Look, Dean, I'm really sorry, but nightclubs aren't my thing,' I mumble, covering my chest with my napkin.

'Cool. We could go somewhere quiet for a drink – just the two of us.'

'I really don't . . .'

'Hey, Siri! Any good bars in this area?'

'It's been a long day.' I squirm. 'I don't mean to be rude, but do you mind if I give it a miss?'

His face clouds over and an awkward silence falls between us.

The evening has got to end NOW. I stand up and fish in my bag for my purse.

'Oh, my God! I just remembered, I promised to feed my landlady's cat while she's away. Poor thing will be starving. Please take this towards the meal,' I say, clumsily shoving a twenty-pound note into his hand.

'No, please, this is my treat. Look, if your landlady's away let's buy a bottle of wine and have it at yours.'

Subtlety is obviously getting me absolutely nowhere, so there's nothing else for it: Emergency Evacuation Procedure to be deployed pronto . . .

'Great idea, but not tonight, eh?' I say, giving a staged yawn. 'Now I really must go. Thanks for the meal. It was lovely.'

'But what about your main course?'

I hesitate, then spying a taxi, I leg it out the door and do a death-defying dash across the road. As I jump into my getaway car, I heave a sigh of relief, not daring to look back.

* * *

72

I push the living room door open a fraction.

'I'm home, Beryl.'

'Nice time?'

'So-so. Glass of wine?'

'No, thanks, dear, I've got my Johnny Walker,' she says, shaking her tumbler of scotch, ice clinking.

'Okay then, goodnight.'

'Goodnight, sweet'art.'

Flopping onto the bed, I take a huge gulp of wine, pop in my earbuds, break into a tube of Pringles, switch off the light, and close my eyes. Ah, bliss!

Mobile rings. It's Lily.

'Hi, hon. Sorry, I didn't expect you to pick up. I was going to leave a message. Don't want to interrupt your hot date.'

'It's okay. I'm lying on the bed with . . .'

'Sorry, sorry. I'll ring tomorrow.'

'. . . Sam Smith and a tube of Pringles.'

'What? No Dean? What happened?'

'Aargh, don't ask. It was a disaster. I left him at the restaurant.'

'Why? Look, I know we've pulled your leg unmercifully about the age thing, but who cares? If you both . . .'

'Apparently his parents think I'm a cougar. It's not funny, Lily. And that's not the only reason. We don't have anything in common and truth is, I only agreed to go out with him because we needed an audience and yes, I was flattered to be asked out by someone so much younger – gave me a bit of an ego boost after Ben. But, eeuw! He dribbled his soup and spilled wine everywhere.'

'Give the guy a chance, Em. He was probably nervous, poor lamb. How sweet of him to offer to pay for dinner, when he probably doesn't earn much.'

'*And* not only did he try to introduce me to his TikTok followers, but he was wearing these strange trainers which made him look like . . . he had webbed feet.'

Lily stifles a giggle. 'So?'

'I know, I know, I'm being judgemental, but he's made me realise how much I like being single. Ironic, isn't it? I used to be like Olga – desperate to marry – but if only the Olgas of this world could see you don't have to have a man in tow to prove to the world how special or wanted you are.'

'But what about romance, Em?'

'I've got a more realistic approach to romance these days, Lily. I don't buy all that fairy-tale nonsense.'

'It's early days yet, hon. Never say never. Mr Darcy may be just around the corner.'

'I'd forgotten what a minefield the dating game is. All that wondering what to wear, what to say, trying to be someone you're not; I'm getting too old for all of that. Besides, I'm focused on my career now. Enough of me. What about you?'

The ensuing silence is charged with emotional intensity.

'Lily, it's been seven years. Nick wouldn't want you to spend the rest of your life alone.'

'I know, I know,' she says, a slight tremor in her voice.

Lily was a supernumerary on her first flight to Mombasa. Nick was a cameraman on an assignment for a wildlife programme. The moment their eyes met over the crushed Coke cans and empty nut packets of Lily's drinks trolley, they were smitten. Before long they were living together, and one year later, they tied the knot in a private ceremony in the place where they had met.

A chill still goes through me as I remember the night I got the call, telling me that Nick and his crew had gone missing on an expedition to Alaska.

Despite the heroic efforts of the rescue teams, their search was hampered by severe avalanches and they were never found.

Lily says she's grateful to have known such tender, respectful, kind, mutually supportive love just once in her life, as some people – even married people – don't ever experience that.

And that's the only kind of love I would like: not to settle for someone because time is running out, but the type of love Lily and Nick shared; someone who's my friend first, my equal, and accepts me for me and doesn't set out to change me. But I know that kind of love is hard to find, so if it never comes my way, that's okay, because I'd rather be on my own and look after me, instead of trying to rescue and fix the man in my life, which can be, quite frankly, exhausting.

'Is there any truth in the rumour that you went on a date with a certain LA journalist?' I venture.

'Might be,' says Lily coyly. 'But don't get excited. He's just for fun – not husband material, before you ask.'

'And? Are you seeing him again?'

'Uh-huh.'

'When?'

'I've got a three-day LA next Thursday.'

'What's his name?'

'Randy.'

'Randy. That's very . . . American. Attractive?'

'Yeees . . . in a kind of Action-Man-doll way.'

'You mean he has bendy arms and legs?'

'Naturally. *And* swivelling head.'

'Chiselled cheekbones? Dimpled smile? Designer scar on his left cheek?'

'Yep.'

'Muscular torso?'

'Of course. This model also comes equipped with detachable designer shades.'

'Fuzzy, GI haircut?'

'*And* plastic, moulded pants.'

'So, not detachable then?' I quip, choking on a Pringle.

'Absolutely not!'

Chapter 5

Little White Lies

I confess. I am a coward. There, I've said it. But how else was I supposed to avoid the embarrassment of seeing Dean again? And depending on which way you look at it, my sudden allergy to Mr Muscle could be considered a legitimate excuse for not being able to return to work. Besides which, what hope do I have of securing a decent acting role with a posture fast resembling the Hunchback of Notre Dame?

So, job centre, here I come! Then it hits me like a slap in the face with a wet flip-flop: I have made myself unemployed and am therefore not eligible for benefits; unless chipped nails, and an embarrassing liaison with a security guard young enough to be my son, qualify as extenuating circumstances. Oh, God, why do I never think things through?

I spend the next three weeks see-sawing between positivity and a nervous breakdown. I fall into bad habits: going to bed late, getting up at lunch time, and horror of horrors, get hooked on *Loose Women*, frequently shouting at the telly when one of them says something outrageous.

The rest of the time I'm checking my phone and email, making sure I haven't missed that life-changing message from the casting director who was blown away by my performance in *Three Sisters*, and wants to cast me in their next project. I try unsuccessfully to resist looking at X, Facebook, and Instagram, which are full of '#busydayonset' and '#blessed'.

Lily tells me I'm caught in something called a 'ludic loop' and need to break this addictive cycle if I am to have a clear and focused mind, so invites me over to hers for some green tea and meditation.

Whatever life throws at Lily, she always manages to radiate positivity (though not in a smug, #grateful way). She's walking proof that yoga, chanting, and meditation by candlelight really do work. (I tried this once, but fell asleep and the candle dripped wax onto Beryl's furry rug, so decided not to risk it again.)

'So,' she says, handing me a mug of steaming tea and a freshly baked cupcake, 'it's, what, a month now since *Three Sisters* finished? That's no time.'

'I know. I don't understand why I'm having a wobble. I wasn't expecting scripts to fly into my inbox, but I hate all this uncertainty, not knowing where the next pay cheque is coming from, if I'll ever work again . . .'

'But that's part and parcel of being an actor, isn't it? I'm sure even Helen Mirren goes through dry patches.'

'Yeah, but I doubt she has rent to pay,' I say, wiping green icing from my chin.

'So, do you want to walk away and go back to hoiking a trolley up and down an aisle for the rest of your working life, or sit behind a computer from nine to five? You needn't answer that. If you're going to stay the course, Em, you need to train yourself to have positive thoughts. That way you'll attract positive energy.'

'I hear you, Lily. But how long should I give it? Another year, five? And how am I to survive in the meantime?'

'Where's your fighting spirit, Em? How much do you want this?'

'How much do I . . .? I've given up *everything* for my dream.'

'Yes, but you've got to keep on keeping on. If parts are so hard to come by, then write your own play and cast *yourself* in the leading role.'

'Great idea, but . . .'

'If you want this enough then you'll find a way, that's all I'm saying. Now, sit!' she says, taking my mug and indicating her reflexology chair in the conservatory. 'I want you to concentrate on your breath,' she soothes, pressing hard on the soles of my feet. 'That's it. Now imagine you are breathing in white light. Shut your eyes and concentrate on the sound of your breath. Now visualise what it is you want, and repeat after me, *I am opening myself to new possibilities.*'

'I am opening myself to new possibilities.'

'Good. Now, whatever it is you want, start *believing* that it will happen. Imagine yourself in that situation, and it will have a positive effect on bringing about your heart's desire. It is possible for our thoughts to control the universe. What do you want from life, Emily? Visualise it . . .'

* * *

NURSE (PLAYED BY EMILY FORSYTH): *You do realise, don't you, that I could be dismissed for getting involved with a patient?*

PATIENT (PLAYED BY BRADLEY COOPER): *Look me in the eyes and tell me you don't feel it too? I love you, and if I make it through the operation, then I want you to promise me we'll spend the rest of our lives together.*

NURSE: *But if the Medical Council finds out . . .*

PATIENT PULLS NURSE TOWARDS HIM. THEY KISS . . .

'Delivery!'

I am hauled from my romantic reverie by the thud of the front door and a faint charcoaley, tomatoey, cheesy aroma.

'Supper time,' whispers Lily.

'Blimey, how long have I been asleep?' I say, rubbing my eyes.

Lily resumes slicing up the pizza. 'Only an hour or so. You looked so peaceful and happy, I didn't want to wake you. How do you feel?'

'All kind of . . . floaty, more calm . . . less like I want to crawl under a stone.'

'Good. You'll find the corkscrew in the top drawer.'

On the bike ride home, I give myself a good talking-to and decide it's time to take control and not wait for something to happen. Time to start thinking positive thoughts, do yoga, and create the life I want.

Lily's right; if opportunity won't come to me, then I need to devise a way of getting to it.

To my surprise, it doesn't take long (five days to be precise) for the visualisation technique to work its magic. I found the ad in *The Stage*, just below *POLE DANCING OPPORTUNITIES IN JAPAN* . . .

PRESENTERS WANTED
FOR NEW SHOPPING CHANNEL

Many actors would probably pooh-pooh the idea, but women on the verge of bankruptcy cannot be choosers.

So I emailed the channel, and after a brief Zoom interview, where I presented a Puff the Magic Dragon ornament (borrowed from Beryl's china collection) to an imaginary audience, they offered me a trial slot.

And who knows, today, shopping channel presenter, tomorrow, heaving-bosomed, bonnet-wearing BBC period-drama heroine – okay, so period-drama heroine's mum/maiden aunt.

* * *

'There's nothing else for it – lift up your dress please,' commands George, the no-nonsense sound engineer, as she strides purposefully towards me, swinging a transmitter and clip-on microphone, like a lasso. Whatever possessed me to wear my tattiest knickers, the ones with the elastic showing, on today of all days?

A receiver is poked in my ear.

'Emily, can you hear me?' comes an anonymous voice.

'Yes.'

'Say something please, so Gary can check the sound levels.'

'Erm . . . she sells seashells on the sea . . .'

'No need to shout, and mind your sibilants. Now, if I speak to you while we're on air, whatever you do, do not acknowledge me, okay?'

'Okay.'

'Ignore the camera, and direct all your comments to Annabelle. Take your lead from her. Remember the presenter's mantra: P-R-N. Personalise, Romanticise, be Natural. Imagine you're having a chat over the garden fence. Okay? Aaand five, four, three, two, one.'

'Good afternoon, and welcome to our brand-new Victorian lifestyle programme,' gushes the oh-so-glam Annabelle, switching on her glossy-lipped, Hollywood smile, bang on cue. 'Joining me today is Victorian *expert*, Emily Forsyth, who is here to talk to us about an *exciting* new range of home products, inspired by the Victorian era.' Leaning towards me with an outstretched, perfectly manicured hand, she continues in her saccharine timbre, 'Hello, and welcome.'

'Hello.' I force a smile, lips sticking to my teeth.

'Now, Emily, do tell us, when did this passion for Victoriana start?'

I wrestle with my mind, which is ordering me to tell the truth: *six days ago, when I got this job.*

'It began at school, Annabelle. I always loved History, and the Victorian era in particular has always held a special fascination for me.'

'Lovely! Now let's start with this beautiful little Victorian figure. But it's not just an ornament, is it, Emily? When we lift up the lady's crinoline, we see it is in fact a beautifully crafted trinket box,' she says prissily, holding the hideous thing up to camera.

I nod earnestly, thinking that it wouldn't look out of place on a shelf in Poundland.

'Yes, Annabelle, as you said, beautifully crafted – a work of art, in fact.'

'Personalise!' comes The Voice in my left ear.

'I . . . I remember when I was a wee girl, my great-grandmother had one of these on her dressing table. I've lost count of the number of beads on her dress . . .'

'Show us the dress in more detail,' cuts in The Voice again.

Startled, I look up and spy myself fleetingly in the monitor. I've never seen myself on screen before – apart from the time our school was featured on the regional news because Miss Farquharson, our PE teacher, was picked for the first women's caber-tossing team at the Highland Games.

'Don't look into the camera,' snaps The Voice.

I grab the lady in my clammy hands and indicate the beading with my trembling finger.

'Erm, notice the . . . the detail, yes, *detail* on the dress,' I stammer, swallowing hard. 'Each bead is painstakingly stitched on by hand.' (*What the hell am I saying?*) 'These are called bugle beads,' I continue knowledgeably, 'and these teeny-weeny ones are seed beads, measuring just two millimetres . . .'

No sooner have the words left my mouth, than several of the beads fall off and roll across the table and onto the studio floor. I freeze.

'Forget the beads!' barks The Voice.

Annabelle swiftly comes to the rescue, indicating the next item. 'Now, what have we here, Emily?'

'Aah, yes, the pitcher and bowl. This is my favourite

piece from today's collection, and in my opinion, the best value for money.'

'Romanticise!'

'Both the, er . . . jug and the bowl are made of porcelain and are . . . hand-painted. Of course nowadays we would use this purely for decoration, but in early Victorian times before indoor plumbing . . . erm . . . yes, before indoor . . .'

What in God's name is she doing?

I find myself talking to Annabelle's behind, as she crouches down on the floor, head under the table.

'Ignore Annabelle – she's off camera. Just keep talking!' orders The Voice.

With unprecedented enthusiasm I jabber, 'Notice the . . . the . . . scalloped, gold-reaf lim . . . erm, gold-leaf rim – of the jug. This is, erm . . . *complemented* by the bowl.'

'Personalise!'

'. . . I have one just like this on my dressing table at home. The lovely, floral design symbolises love. In the Victorian era flowers spoke a secret language . . .'

Annabelle triumphantly holds up the misplaced information card, calmly resumes her seat, adjusts her skirt, flashes her gleaming smile to camera two – and proceeds to cut me off mid-flow. 'Well, that's item number 1653, the Victorian pitcher and bowl at an unbelievable price of £24.99. Ooh, I'm hearing the phone lines are very busy, so hurry to avoid disappointment. Now, Emily,' she says, moving over to the mock fireplace. 'Tell us about this charming Victorian fire-screen.'

Oh shit. Nobody mentioned anything about standing up and moving about. Guess I just follow her lead. Look relaxed, natural. No sudden, jerky movements. The camera tails me, past the fake bookcase and plastic aspidistra, to the hearth. Ignore it. Look natural. Pretend you're having a chat over the garden fence. Personalise. Romanticise. Be Natural.

'This is typical of the kind of fire-screen you would have found in the front parlour of a Victorian home. I have one just like this that hides a nasty electric heater. The design is hand-painted' (*is there no end to my lies?*) 'and notice the stunning scroll design,' I gush, stooping to indicate this feature, while ever so subtly showing off my new, stick-on nails. I think I'm starting to get the hang of this now. The key is to stay calm and cool, be persuasive, yet not too pushy – none of that hard-sell stuff. P-R-N, P-R-N . . .

'Tell us, Emily, how is this *distressed effect* achieved?'

Straightening up, I feel a sudden twang.

'Hmm?' I say in a high-pitched tone, glued to the spot.

Annabelle is looking at me quizzically. I see her mouth moving, but her words are washing over me. Yep, the inevitable has happened, and I am about to disgrace myself in front of the entire British Shopping TV nation. The transmitter, which is attached to my ancient, washed-out knickers, is now hanging by a thread, dangerously dangling somewhere around the knee area, like a bungee jumper about to plummet to the ground at any moment.

Panic surges through me. I haven't a clue what Annabelle means by a *distressed effect*, but one thing I know for sure: several thousand viewers will suffer the distressed effect if the elastic snaps. Oh, shame! Oh, earth-swallow-me-up shame! The phone lines will be jammed with complaints, and I will be a national laughing stock. Just when I thought I'd broken into the glamorous, lucrative world of television, my career, just like my knickers, is in tatters before it's begun. Oh, God, oh, God, why am I such a calamity?

Meanwhile Annabelle is chuntering on and on, and I nod intelligently, trying to hide the fact that I am experiencing a major technical hitch. Dear Lord, when will this be over?

At last she wraps up the half hour with, 'Well, I'm afraid we've run out of time for this, our first Victorian special . . .' (*And probably our last*, I almost hear her say.) 'Coming up next is Tracey with her *Pampering for Pets Hour*. My thanks to Emily, and to you, the viewers at home, for joining us. Bye for now. Byee.'

'Well done!' says Annabelle with an unconvincing smile. As she turns her attention to the crew, I seize the opportunity of hoisting up my knickers through my dress. Scary George appears out of the shadows, and I am unceremoniously unplugged. Now what? How do I make it out of the studio and along the corridor to the safety of the loo, without shedding my last scrap of dignity?

'I've got another presentation in studio three in fifteen minutes,' says Annabelle, consulting her watch. 'Would you like me to take you back to the green room?'

'*NO!* I mean, I'll be – fine. Thanks,' I say in a falsely bright tone.

She looks at me expectantly. I rootle in my bag, pretending to look for my Oyster card. Please just go, *please*.

'Well,' she says, shrugging her shoulders, 'maybe see you again some time. Don't forget to hand in your pass to security.'

'Yeah, sure,' I say, pausing mid-rummage to give her a little wave. 'And . . . thank you.'

I look round and survey the scene. A couple of cameramen are winding up cables, while a studio assistant is setting up for *Des's DIY Show*. I seize my chance, and keeping my knees tightly together, shuffle out into the long, long, brightly lit corridor, past the photo gallery of perfectly groomed presenters, their twinkling-toothed smiles beaming down at me.

Never has the sight of the little skirted figure on the loo door been so welcome.

Phew! I've made it. Safe inside, I let the offending briefs drop and hastily chuck them in the bin.

I travel home in a shameful, knickerless state, promising myself that when that pay cheque finally arrives, it's off to M&S for me.

* * *

Should any of you be considering a career as a presenter, here are some of Emily's handy, on-camera tips for ladies:

Wear trousers or a skirt – something with a *firm* waistband.
If you simply *must* wear that floaty little Monsoon number,
NEW knickers with REINFORCED elastic obligatory.
NEVER use words like *unbreakable, shatterproof* or *sturdy*
– you're asking for trouble.
Whatever happens (product malfunction or comet colliding
with earth), KEEP TALKING!!

* * *

Over the next few weeks, I gulp, perspire, flounder, and fly by the
seat of my pants through a variety of guest presentations, extolling
the virtues of owning exercise bikes and Elvis commemorative
plates. I tell myself to give it time, and I may yet become the
next Lorraine Kelly.

But that was before the nylon, foldaway-bag fiasco, which
firmly puts paid to any aspirations I may have of reporting showbiz
gossip from a breakfast sofa.

It had worked so well in the bedroom mirror that morning,
but of course, come the live show, it all went horribly wrong . . .

'This handy, nylon bag folds away to next to nothing. Its clever
three-in-one design allows the bag to *grow*, so to speak, by unzip-
ping the compartments, like this. Ahem . . . like *this* . . .' At first
I try the softly, softly approach, then yank it hard, the nylon
bunching up as the zip's teeth refuse to let go. 'It has a drawstring
for added security,' I say, dry-mouthed, grabbing nervously at the
toggle, which promptly comes off in my hand.

Meanwhile, back in the studio, you can hear a bead drop. The
cameraman's head rises slowly from behind the lens. The floor
manager is gesticulating wildly with her clipboard, mouthing,
'Go onnnn!'

Say something, tolls a voice in my head . . . *anything.* But it's
of no use; my brain and mouth refuse to communicate with
one another. Initially, fear spreads through me; then, all at once,

another, louder voice cuts through the mental chaos, calmly saying, *Why have you allowed yourself to be sidetracked into this wow-factor world of easy payments and on-air testimonials? This is ludicrous. An actor is what you want to be, not Sir Alan Sugar's next business partner.*

I've got to get out of here – now. Calmly placing the bag and the toggle on the mock kitchen counter, I commit the TV presenter's cardinal sin of walking off set.

Making a quick, recuperative pit-stop at the ladies, I then march along the corridor, heels clacking decisively along the tiled floor, eyes focused straight ahead. I can almost hear the laughter echoing behind me from the Barbie and Ken lookalikes on the gallery wall.

Where did *they find her?*

She's obviously never been to a tanning studio in her life.

And those teeth! Has she never heard of veneers?

She couldn't sell hair extensions to Kim Kardashian on Celebs Get Hitched *even if she tried.*

No, I do not belong to their world.

I've had enough of appearing calm when zips get stuck, buttons pop off, lids refuse to open, and garden fairy lights fuse. Despite not having a job to go to, I need to come up with a convincing get-out plan pretty damn quick, as I'm down to demonstrate hand-held turbo steamers the day after tomorrow.

As I enter the green room, there's Prue from Production pacing up and down, one hand on her hip, the other clasping her mobile to her ear.

'What happened, Emily?' she says tetchily, snapping the phone shut and ushering me into the ladies' dressing room. My stomach clenches. 'I accept things go wrong sometimes, but we expect our presenters to carry on regardless, not freeze up and leave the crew, the viewers in the lurch.'

'You're absolutely right, Prue. In fact I've decided that . . .'

'Sales were very poor, I'm afraid. The client's been on the phone already. He's not very happy, as you can well imagine.'

'Of course. I really feel that I'm not . . .'

'We can't run the risk of losing valuable business in this way.'

'Quite. I'm just not cut out . . .'

'I'm sorry, I know it's short notice, but I've decided to take you off the Turbo Steam Cleaner slot – in fact, I won't be assigning you to any more presentations in the future.' Voice softening, she continues, 'Many actors find they simply aren't suited to this type of work, so don't lose any sleep over it, will you?'

Oh no, Prue, I won't. In fact, had you come up for air and listened to what I had to say for just one moment, I would have told you that I'd already decided that you'd have to find someone else to promote your turbo steam cleaners, rotary choppers, and electrical foot warmers because I QUIT!

'Oh, just one more thing,' she continues. 'You do realise, don't you, that your microphone was still live and caught your bathroom break on your way over here?'

Whaaat?!

The glass lift can't deliver me quick enough to the steel atrium of Homeworld TV. I sign out and return my pass to the uniformed receptionist, putting on a self-assured air, head held high.

As I stride along Southwark Street, it starts to rain. I don't have an umbrella, but I don't care. And I don't care that I've embarrassed myself again live on air or that I've been fired, because I feel free, free to carry on looking for what it is I *really* want. Okay, so the presentation was a bit of a train crash, but it's given me a TV credit for my CV, it's paid off a chunk of debt, and they say failure is the key to success, right?

The old me would have skulked back to Beryl's, retreated to the sofa in my PJs, and binged on chocolate and old episodes of *Friends*. The new me sweeps into Carluccio's, orders spaghetti carbonara, a glass of house red, and toasts the future.

The old me wouldn't have eaten alone in a restaurant, because people would think I was lonely and sad. The new me doesn't care what people think and is happy to be alone.

I order a macchiato, grab my pen and notebook, and begin to write. Lily lent me a book called *Write It Down, Make It Happen*, which shows you how writing down your goals can focus your mind and help you achieve them.

Had I written my Wish List a couple of years ago, it would have read something like this:

> Marry Ben.
> Live in a big house with a garden and pool.
> Have kids.
> Get a dog.
> Be happy.

Today it reads:

> Find an agent.
> Do interesting work that fulfils me.
> Write and perform my own play.
> Learn to live in the moment.
> Find inner peace.

I have no idea how long it will take the universe to get back to me, so in the meantime I will clear my head of negative thoughts, practise yoga and meditation, begin writing my play, and relieve financial stress by finding a bread-and-butter job while waiting for THE CALL.

Chapter 6

The Italian Effect

Today is the day I will find a job. *Any job.*

I scan the parade of shops as I pedal by – heaps of possibilities: there's the bakery, off-licence, newsagent's, cut-price bargain store, chemist, the kebab shop – then a hazy memory of Rachel's birthday, and being served a dodgy doner on the way home by someone resembling Hannibal Lecter's brother pings into my brain. Maybe not.

Panting like a dog, I arrive at the top of Richmond Hill and notice the dry cleaners, which has been closed for months, now boasts a green, white, and red awning with 'Il Mulino' and a windmill emblazoned across it.

I peer through the window, and spying someone inside, tap on the door. It is opened by a small man with a weatherworn face and crinkly-kind eyes, a stripy apron accentuating his barrel-like girth.

'*Sì?*'

'*Buongiorno!* Do you have any vacancies for waiting staff?'

'Do you have experience?' he asks in his thick accent. I nod.

'*Prego,*' he smiles, raising his heavy eyebrows and beckoning me inside.

I am immediately transported to some little corner of Italy. The spine-tingling tones of Pavarotti percolate through the coffee-filled air. The rustic furniture is covered with red and white gingham tablecloths, and behind the bar sits one of those old, 1950s Gaggia espresso machines.

'Luigi,' he says, warmly shaking my hand.

'Nice to meet you, Luigi. I'm Emily.'

'Coffee?' he asks, tipping beans into the grinder.

'Mmm, please.' I smile, squinting at a sepia photograph of a little urchin boy standing next to an old windmill.

'Do they have windmills in Italy?' I ask.

'*Sì*,' he replies. 'No many. This windmill, it is in Sicily. *Allora*, you want to work in my restaurant . . .'

One cappuccino later, and I am officially a member of Luigi's substitute team, starting tomorrow. He prefers to employ native Italians, but I manage to persuade him by promising to learn a little of the language (at least enough to enable me to pronounce the names of the dishes correctly, like *talliatelli* and not *tagliatelli*, which caused Luigi to crack up when he asked me to read the menu aloud).

I believed my waitressing days were well behind me, but needs must; it's either this or the dole queue, and the hours will fit in with my busy audition schedule. Hah!

* * *

Tonight is my debut at Il Mulino, and the restaurant's first preview night, ahead of the official opening next month. Luigi introduces me to Carla, his daughter, a soprano singer, who's helping out her father in between classes and auditions. With her jet-black hair, flashing eyes, and hourglass figure, she was born to play Carmen.

'Come with me, *cara*, I show you the kitchen,' she says, sweeping through the double doors, hips swaying like a pendulum.

She and the chef exchange some words in Italian, then with

sleight of hand, he tosses fresh herbs and brightly coloured peppers from a giant, sizzling pan high into the air, like a conjurer, performing his very own brand of magic.

'Bravo!' I cry, and immediately wish I hadn't. He grunts something tetchy under his breath and angrily sloshes more red wine into the sauce. Not a good start.

'Don't mind Sergio,' says Carla over the hiss. 'He just likes everyone to know he's the *capo* – the boss. And this . . . is Nonna Rosa,' she says fondly. A bird-like lady all in black sits on a stool in the corner, long ribbons of potato peel falling from her knife into a huge, dented, aluminium pot on the floor. Her face creases into a wrinkle-etched smile. '*Ciao.*'

Luigi enters, and they all start babbling at once, their voices becoming louder and higher, their gestures more vehement. There's soon enough passion and melodrama unfolding to rival any opera, and I half expect a brawl to break out among the colanders and carving knives. Every word is fuelled with passion and sounds to me like the Italian equivalent of *Eh, show some respect. You work for this family now. If you have anything to say, say it to Don Cannelloni.*

'What was all that about?' I ask Carla, as we head back to the dining room.

'*Allora*, my father,' she says with a careless shrug of her shoulders, 'he just wanna know why Sergio put cannelloni back on the specials menu. *Benvenuti!*' she calls, breaking away as six more customers materialise through the door.

The bell rings furiously. 'Table four!'

I spin around full circle and then back again. Carla's busy taking coats, Luigi is deep in conversation with a customer, and the rest of the team are uncorking bottles of wine, pouring drinks, taking orders, and gliding in between tables with steaming dishes.

'*Pronto!* Quickly!'

Oh, well, I can't hang around looking like a nun at an Ann Summers party, so taking a deep breath, I head towards the kitchen. Sergio darts me a surly glare and nods towards the counter. I scoop up the two plates of steaming minestrone soup, then pirouette back out through the swing doors.

As I approach table four, the lady in the group is in mid-conversation, gesticulating wildly. I stand there patiently waiting for her to finish, but I'm invisible.

'*Scusi*,' I whisper, fingers now burning. I attempt to navigate my way around and aim for the empty space in front of her. But just as the plate is about to make contact with its target, she waves her arms again, and it smashes to the floor, the warm roll shooting across the table, hot minestrone soup flying everywhere: over her, me, the tablecloth, the wall. '*Scusi*,' I say, grabbing her napkin, frantically plucking cubes of celery and carrot from her doubtless designer suit.

I feel every pair of diner's eyes drilling through me. A concerned Luigi emerges from behind the bar.

'*Mamma mia!*'

I've poured countless glasses of red wine and cups of hot drinks through tropical storms and clear air turbulence without spilling a drop, but I am to learn that there's a certain knack to negotiating one's way around the arms of animated Italians.

Luigi rescues the situation by offering the table complimentary wine and an invitation to the opening.

My proud ego is telling me to run out of the door, never to return. Mindful me is telling me to let go of who I used to be: the super-efficient, confident purser, in charge of a 787 cabin. The rules are different here, and I must give it time and be open to learning new skills.

With the final customers gone, and the tables cleared, Nonna Rosa shuffles in from the kitchen, bearing a huge casserole dish, and beckons for me to sit down. Luigi opens a bottle of red wine, and Carla places a basket of warm bread on the table.

Sergio sits scowling in the corner, long legs crossed, chewing on a cocktail stick.

'*Mangia!* Eat!' says Nonna Rosa, nodding to me as she drizzles olive oil onto the bread; and more and more food keeps appearing.

Carla recalls that Nonna Rosa used to make the main dish every Sunday for the family when Luigi was a little boy living in Sicily. The *Agnello All'Albertone* is the best lamb I have ever tasted, and the Montepulciano slides down deliciously, making me feel all warm and cosy inside.

As air crew I'd wolf down my food, standing up in the galley, eye on the clock, frequently interrupted by demanding passengers. Tonight I savour the flavour of each mouthful, happy to be here, in this moment – even if I don't understand most of what's being said, or why the chef has taken an instant dislike to me.

Pedalling home, I stop on the bridge and look out over the river, the moon and the lights from the bars and hotels reflected on the glassy water. I breathe in the cool air. A train rumbles in the distance, a flock of Canada geese honks as they fly low over the river, disappearing into the black distance.

For the second time tonight I'm aware I'm living in the present, appreciating what's going on around me, instead of allowing things to pass me by unnoticed, because my mind is tied up elsewhere. Could this be the effect of the Montepulciano, or am I at last learning to slow down and let go of the past?

* * *

Now with some cash to spare, I invest in new publicity photographs, a showreel, and a voice demo. I make calls and send emails every day to agents and casting directors. Replies are rare and mostly negative: too old, too young, too tall, too short, too fair, no TV/film credits. It's pointless griping about the situation; frown lines are ageing, and besides, no one's listening. So I immerse myself in drafting my own play, practising yoga every day, and whispering *I am opening myself to new possibilities* whenever I am out of earshot.

I now know my conchiglie from my tortellini, and when I'm waiting to take orders, I'm honing those all-important character observation skills, which Portia taught us are crucial to becoming a truthful actor.

When the mood takes him, even the ice-cold Sergio is starting to thaw a little now and manages to crack the odd smile.

My favourite part of the night is when the last customer has left – my cue to flip over the *CHIUSO*/CLOSED sign. Luigi calls, '*A cena!*' and we all gather around the table.

My spoken Italian may not be up to much, but I'm learning to eat like one: i.e. slowly and a lot. The courses may be many, but the portions are smaller, tastier, and leave you wanting more. No mounds of soggy spaghetti here, topped with sauce from a jar and a shake of cheese powder, but home-made pasta cooked *al dente*, served with sauces made from sweet, buffalo tomatoes, rosemary, basil, ricotta, aubergines, and oregano, sprinkled with shavings of fresh parmesan.

* * *

*OPERA CABARET 16 JUNE at 19:30
JOIN US AT IL MULINO FOR WINE,
SONG & HOME-COOKED, TRADITIONAL FOOD.
A TASTE OF THE WARM SOUTH BROUGHT TO
RICHMOND-UPON-THAMES.*[/S]

'*Perfetto!*' Luigi says with a beaming smile as he smooths the local newspaper out on the table. '*Allora*, is everything ready for tomorrow? Sergio, I need your final shopping list by the end of tonight, *d'accordo?*' Sergio loosens the collar of his chef's jacket and gives a bad-tempered shrug.

'Carla, the piano tuner will arrive at five o'clock. Have you made a final decision about the music?'

'*Sì, babbo.*' She sighs, her long, curling lashes almost touching her eyebrows as she looks up to the ceiling.

Carla and her fiancé, Luke, a dentist (they met and fell in love three years ago, when he serenaded her during painful root canal treatment), have been rehearsing tirelessly at the community centre, putting together an eclectic programme of popular Italian songs and various arias from well-known operas; nothing too high-brow, just something to complement the Italian dining experience, and to hopefully set Il Mulino apart from the many other, well-established restaurants in Richmond. If this goes well, it could also provide the duo with the ideal platform to showcase their musical talents.

'*Allora*,' says Luigi, rising, 'the flowers and wine will arrive in the morning. If there are no further questions, then I see you all this evening.'

* * *

I'm in the changing room at Zara during my break, trying on black dresses for the opening, when my phone rings.

'Emily? Lionel of LB Management.'

'Sorry? Who's this?'

'Lionel. Susannah's agent. We met at *Three Sisters* a few months ago.'

'Hi. Yes, I remember now,' I say, heart quickening.

'I realise this is short notice, but I've got a free slot for a commercial casting. A client let me down at the last minute, so I was wondering if you'd like to go in her place?'

'Er, sure. When?'

'This afternoon at three.'

'Erm, but it's one o'clock now.'

'Up to you. Just thought I'd run it by you. It's for a pasta sauce commercial and the fee, minus my commission, is two and a half grand.'

Two and a half . . . I glance at my watch again.

'Where is the casting?'

'Dean Street, Soho.'

'Okay, I'll do it!'

'Great! Give me your email address and I'll send you the details.'

* * *

It's bang on three by the time I reach Alpha Advertising in rain-washed Dean Street.

'I'm here for the tomato sauce casting,' I pant, a puddle forming around my feet.

The receptionist scrutinises me with her oh-I'm-so-bored expression, and mumbles through her Angelina pout, 'Fill in this form and take a seat.'

'Where's the ladies'?'

'Emily Forsyth and Ninian Moncrieff!' calls a shrill voice from the corridor.

A middle-aged, Bertie-Wooster type in cords, checked shirt, and squeaky Church's brogues places *The Times* under his arm, scrapes a comb through his slicked-back, greying hair, and swaggers over to the young woman with headphones slung around her neck.

'Emily Fors . . .!'

'Just coming!' I cry, nervously unbuttoning my dripping-wet mac.

The studio door slams shut. At the far end is a long, leather sofa, crammed with young, trendy advertising executives, sipping their takeaway Starbucks.

'This is Ninian and Emily,' says the woman with the headphones.

'Okay, you've read the blurb,' says a man with a goatee beard and small crucifix dangling from his left ear. I'm about to explain I haven't yet had the opportunity to read the blurb, on account of being late, due to signal failure on SW Trains (again) and not being able to run very fast in my new wedge shoes, but he ploughs on without pausing for breath.

'Now . . . Emma . . .'

'Actually, it's Emily.'

'Let's have you first. Stand on the white cross please, and when you're given the nod, say your name and agent's name, profiles and hands to camera. Just leave your things on the floor. Okay?'

Profiles? Hands to camera? And do I give my details deadpan, or do I smile and say them with feeling, thereby conveying my warm, sincere personality and versatile acting talent? Never having been for a commercial casting, I don't know the protocol.

'When you're ready please.'

I plump for a bit of both – not too serious, not too gushing. Ninian opts for the cool, I-do-these-all-the-time approach.

'Thank you,' says Goatee, leaping up. 'Now, just to recap – the scene is a small, intimate Italian restaurant. If you'd like to sit down here, please,' he says, propelling us over to a metal table and chairs.

'In front of you is a plate of pasta cooked in Pino Pinuccio sauce. I'm afraid it's cold, but I assure you it was freshly cooked this morning. Now, I want a bit of improvised chit-chat to begin with, and then as you start to eat, you, Emma, go into wild raptures at the taste,' he says, clicking his fingers while simultaneously stamping his foot, like he's about to launch into a paso doble. 'You, hubby, on the other hand, carry on eating, oblivious to the stares and sniggers from the other diners. Okay?' He claps his hands, then leaps backwards onto the arm of the sofa, eyes boring into me, chin cupped in his hand.

'Camera rolling . . . and . . . action!'

Looking around me at the stark, white walls, I say in a thin voice, 'I'm so glad you brought us here for our anniversary, darling. What a lovely surprise.' Ninian looks at me expressionless.

I poke the oily pasta with my fork.

'Mmm, this pasta is really delicious,' I say through a mouthful, resisting the urge to gag. Goatee jumps up, tugging at his beard, crucifix swinging wildly back and forth.

'No, no, no! We want a bit of va-va-voom! Let us feel our mouths salivating, let us *taste* that pasta sauce, let us be *swept* along with the sheer enjoyment, the *passion* . . . think *When Harry Met Sally*, think . . . think . . . *orgasmic*!'

He flops back down, eyes twirling in annoyance. Ninian sighs and fires me a withering look. I've a good mind to chuck the bowl of pasta over his perfectly coiffed head. I know he isn't supposed to say anything, but God almighty, it's like sitting opposite a tailor's dummy.

I wonder if he works much; perhaps *MORTUARY CORPSE* is his speciality, and he has a string of enviable TV credits to his name: *Silent Witness*, *Sherwood*, *Line of Duty*, *Unforgotten*, *Casualty*, *Midsomer Murders*; the possibilities are endless.

'Now let's try it again, please,' hisses Goatee, chewing gum furiously as he glances at his watch. I glimpse the panel: a stony-faced woman with half-shaved hair yawns, a young guy sporting a man-bun and grungy jeans waggles his trainer-clad foot, while the cool rock chick in denim skirt and cowboy boots plays with her iPhone.

Okay, you arty-farty advertisers, you want va-va-voom? I'll give you va-va-voom!

Two and a half grand may be a drop in the ocean to Ninian Moncrieff, but to me it's a fortune. And that cheque with my name on it is just within my grasp. All that stands between it and me is a few moments of humiliating myself in front of a bunch of strangers. That's not so bad, is it?

I close my eyes, draw a deep intake of breath, and fling my head back, diving into a frenzied attack on the mound of pasta, stuffing it into my mouth with both hands, covering my face with Pino Pinuccio sauce, panting and moaning.

'Mmm. More . . . more . . . Yes, yes, YESSSS!'

Ninian looks at me, open-mouthed, eyes wide.

'Thank you!' booms Goatee eventually, jumping to his feet, a mocking smile playing across his lips. 'Well, what can I say? Meg Ryan, eat your heart out! We'll be in touch.'

Ninian scarpers, doubtless terrified he may end up having to escort me back to the tube. I am left to pick up my bag, coat, and last morsel of dignity in stunned silence. I fumble in my pocket. Where's a tissue when you need one? Head held high, I exit, leaving behind a blob of pasta sauce on the door handle.

I enter the crowded waiting area, woefully aware of the other candidates' eyes boring through me as they pretend to read their casting briefs.

I clear my throat. 'Where's the loo?' I ask the receptionist.

'Second door on the left,' she mumbles, without lifting her eyes from her screen.

Dammit, it's engaged, so I about-turn and make a break for it, leaving behind a trail of bloody devastation.

* * *

I pedal up Richmond Hill that evening, shouting into the wind things like, 'You can keep your two and a half grand and your disgusting sauce!' and '"Like Mamma used to make"? Er, I don't think so!'

By the time I reach Il Mulino I'm feeling much better, though after today, how can *When Harry Met Sally* still be my go-to film when I'm feeling blue?

On the plus side, Lionel considers me 'a prospect' (thank God he wasn't witness to this afternoon's performance) and has agreed to take me on his agency's books. He may not be the crème de la crème of agents, but he has far more contacts than I do, and unrepresented actors are taken less seriously by casting directors. So despite another ego-bashing, something positive has come about to balance things out, and will be toasted in red wine at the end of the shift.

* * *

I wish I hadn't decided to break in my new black heels tonight. With a full restaurant, I'm multi-tasking like a woman possessed: meeting and greeting, hanging up coats, taking multiple orders from large tables, uncorking wine, answering the phone, making reservations, clearing and laying tables.

Since that unfortunate mishap with the minestrone, I have now ditched my tentative Britishness when faced with large tables of vociferous, gesticulating customers, and have adopted the Italian serving technique. It can best be described as a kind of simplified cha-cha-cha and goes like this: holding the dishes high, take to the floor, approach the table, step forward, step back, step forward, side-together-side, side-together-side, aaand place the plates on the table (carefully), turn, step forward, and return to the kitchen. Mission accomplished.

The bell rings furiously. Juventus lost to Manchester City in the Champions League earlier, and there's been a lot of banging and crashing coming from the kitchen tonight, accompanied by lots of angry Italian swear words, which even Pavarotti at full pelt is unable to drown out.

Drawing a deep breath, I straighten my skirt, smooth my hair, and enter the lion's den with a wide smile.

Sergio tuts and waves his hand at the two starters. '*Vai!* Go!'

This is all I need after the afternoon I've had. Thank God this is the last order.

Grabbing a knife from the wall, he starts furiously chopping up parsley.

'*Vaiii!*'

Okay, Gordon Ramsay! I'm going, I'm going. Ugh. How much better this place would be were he not around.

Blinking back hot tears, I pick up the starters and am just reversing through the doors, when Sergio lets out a blood-curdling howl. My plates smash to the floor, sending tomatoes, mozzarella, and basil hurtling through the air. I spin round to see thick liquid, the colour of claret, spurting from his hand, splashing the white-tiled walls. A waxy, grey hue floods his skin; his strangely wide eyes roll back as he drops to the floor like a stone.

'Luigi!' I scream. Oh God, oh God, what's the first-aid procedure? Something about elevation? Is that right? Grabbing two vegetable crates from under the sink, I remove his blood-splattered clogs and raise his legs.

The door swings open. '*Madonna mia!*' exclaims Luigi, horror sweeping across his face.

'*Ambulanza! Pronto!*' I cry, a stab of panic piercing through me.

Now what? Control the bleeding, yes, control the bleeding – but how? Nonna Rosa appears at my side clutching a tea towel and kneels by Sergio, mumbling in Italian, tugging at her crucifix. I grab the towel and his slippy, blood-soaked hand. My stomach lurches as I notice one of his fingers dangling like a broken twig. I feel sick and giddy. Please God, this is not a good time for me to pass out. I bind it tightly with the towel and raise his arm above his head, pushing his hand hard against my chest. Blood trickles through my fingers, dripping onto my crisp, white shirt. I must keep my cool, practical head on until the ambulance arrives.

'Rosa, ice! Erm . . . *gelato*?' (No, no, that's ice cream.) '*Glace!*' She looks at me, bewildered. No, that's French. '*Ghiaccio?* Yes, *ghiaccio!*'

Sergio's eyes flicker open and he twists his head sideways, moaning like a wounded animal. The sound chills me. I gently squeeze his other hand and we hold one another's upside-down gaze. The pain in his expression slices through me. I want to tell him he's going to be okay, but can't think of the right words.

'*Ambulanza* – here soon. *Tutto bene. Tutto bene.*'

I look towards the door. Where *are* they?

'*Dio mio!*' cries Carla, appearing at my side, face blanched with shock.

'Carla, we must keep him warm. Get his coat.'

Where the hell are they? Please hurry, *please*.

A siren screams, and like a scene from *ER*, two paramedics burst through the swing doors wheeling a stretcher.

'We've got you, mate,' says one of them, kneeling as he opens his medical bag. 'I'm just going to give you some morphine to relieve the pain and steady that racing heart of yours, okay?' I look away as the needle is produced. I feel Sergio's body judder.

'You can let go now,' says his colleague, laying a reassuring hand on my shoulder. 'Ready? Three, two, one. There we go.'

I stagger to my feet and look down at Sergio's face, his eyes wide with shock and fear.

'*Tutto bene*,' I whisper, as he is whisked out to the waiting ambulance. '*Tutto bene*.'

I just stand there, staring at my blood-drenched shirt and hands. There's a swimming sensation in my head as my legs buckle beneath me and I slump down onto the floor.

* * *

I jog past the bins and piled-up garden furniture early next morning, entering the restaurant through the gleaming, pine-scented kitchen, where Nonna Rosa is by the sink, chopping onions, humming and crying at the same time.

'*Ciao*, Rosa,' I pant, pulling out my earbuds and kissing her on both cheeks.

'Any news about Sergio? Er . . . *notizie da Sergio*?'

These three little words unleash a torrent of Italian, of which '*aeroporto*' is the only word I understand. I just do my customary nodding routine, interspersed with the odd '*sì*' or '*no*', then escape to the dining room with a '*mi scusi*' the moment I'm able to get a word in edgeways. It's empty and silent. I put on some *Madame Butterfly* to soothe my frayed nerves. Grabbing a stiffly starched tablecloth from the pile, I start laying up.

A retro flower power van mounts the pavement. A woman in dungarees jumps out.

'Let me give you a hand,' I say, propping the door open. Back and forth we go, until all the floral arrangements are inside.

'Twenty individual centrepieces, three large,' she says, handing me the consignment note and a pen. 'Hope it all goes well.'

'Wine order for Il Mulino,' comes a voice behind me.

'Ah, yes, that's us,' I reply, chewing on a fingernail as the delivery man negotiates his trolley around the obstacle course of rosemary, white freesias, and red roses.

'Twelve cases of Valpolicella, Chianti, Lacryma Christi, Verdicchio, Pinot Grigio, and prosecco,' he says, unloading. I begin to check the boxes off against his inventory, but with so much more to do, I skim through the list and pray that nothing's missing.

Help! Where are the other servers? Has Luigi found a sous-chef? Where's Carla? I can't run the show on my own. The evening hasn't even begun and I have this horrible sense of foreboding. I feel panic rising inside me, mixed with guilt about Sergio's accident; just moments before, hadn't I wished him gone? Next minute, bam. He was lying on the floor in a pool of blood. My visualisation powers have taken on a telekinetic life of their own, like in some Stephen King horror film.

'That's your lot. Sign here please,' says the deliveryman, thrusting his clipboard into my hand. 'When's the party?'

I sigh heavily. 'Tonight, believe it or not.'

His eyebrows shoot up and he gives a low whistle. 'I'd get the white in the chiller as soon as you can.'

'Sure,' I say with a hint of sarcasm, scooping up a handful of cutlery. Now, will that be *before* I've laid up twenty tables, folded eighty napkins into birds of paradise, put fresh towels in the loos, sliced up the lemons, polished the wine glasses and filled the butter dishes?

'Good luck!' he says cheerily, shutting the door behind him.

I flop into a chair, surveying the war zone: boxes of wine, flowers, glasses, tablecloths, bread baskets, bunting, cutlery everywhere. I feel exhausted and emotionally drained, and have absolutely no idea how I'm going to get through the day, let alone the grand opening. With local press invited, the future of Il Mulino could be riding on the success of this one night. It's going to take an Oscar-worthy performance to pull this off. I haul myself to my feet, turn up the volume of the MP3 player, and resume laying up.

This is my favourite bit of *Madame Butterfly*: the finale, where I'm told she reads the inscription on her father's knife: 'Who Cannot Live with Honour Must Die with Honour'. She stabs herself just as that two-timing love rat, Pinkerton, is heard calling out her name. (He wasn't worth it, love.)

Cutlery in hand, I surrender to the stirring score, belting out my very own (culinary) aria.

'*Conchiglie, tortellini,*

'*Lasagne alla bolognese,*

'*Tiramisù? Tiramisù? Tiramisù?*

'*Pizza margherita. Amore mio!*'

'Emileeee!'

The music dies.

'*Fettucine alfredo . . .*'

My voice disintegrates as I feel a hand gently touch my shoulder.

'Emily, this is my nephew, Francesco Rossi,' says Luigi, the ghost of a smile drifting across his face. 'He will be in charge of the kitchen until Sergio returns.'

'Zio Luigi, you tell me in the car she is British, but she can sing like an Italian,' says the dark stranger, the corners of his mouth twitching.

'Pleased to meet you,' I say, flushing to the roots of my unwashed hair as we shake hands.

'You dropped this,' he says, bending down and handing me

a knife.

'*Grazie*,' I say in a low voice, averting my gaze, sorely tempted to do a Madame Butterfly and die with honour then and there.

Chapter 7

Curtain Up!

As the crowd starts trickling in, we take coats and serve drinks while Luigi mingles with the guests. Once they've settled in with appetisers and wine, he taps a glass with a knife and the lively chatter dies down, a sea of expectant faces turning to meet his.

'Welcome, friends!' Pointing to the sepia photograph of the windmill behind the bar, he recounts in halting English, how as a small boy, he would spend his summer holidays at his grandparents' in Sicily and play in the disused windmill next door. He believed its spinning blades were wings. He'd sit inside the tower and fly to far-off lands, encountering giants and mystical creatures along the way.

But as soon as the church clock struck six, he would race home in time to wash his hands, comb his hair, and lay the table for Nonna, for he knew if he were late, there would be no supper, and a day without Nonna's cooking was like a day without play.

'*Allora, basta!* Enough!' he says, wiping his moist brow. A warm smile and a look of unmistakable pride spread across his face as he announces, 'Now I go back to the kitchen, and I leave you with my beautiful daughter, Carla, and my future son-in-law, the future Luciano Pavarotti!'

Spontaneous laughter and applause break out, swiftly followed by a series of oohs and aahs as Carla, in a sizzling red, floor-length, off-the-shoulder gown slinks down the stairs, through the tightly packed tables, followed by Luke, in a crisp, white, wing-collared shirt sans tie, and dark waistcoat, his thick, golden hair (more beach boy than dentist) sleek and shiny.

The clapping dies down as he takes his place at the piano, opens the lid, straightens his back, and flexes his fingers. (Blimey, he can perform root canal on me any day of the week.) Carla's diamante earrings sway gently back and forth, catching the light. He nods his head towards her, and with a toss of her tumbling ebony tresses, the lyrics to some heart-fluttering aria spill from her sumptuous, painted mouth.

I haven't a clue what the words mean, but I assume it's about yet another tragic heroine about to snuff it.

Throughout the night I zigzag in between the tables, topping up red and white wine, sneaking a little sip for myself when no one's looking.

I know it's mean of me, considering Sergio's lying at home minus a finger, but with Francesco in charge, the kitchen is a different place. The interaction between us all is easy and humorous, and the food's just as good – no, *better*. And the positive vibe flows out into the dining room.

You never know what mood Sergio is going to be in, and if you don't understand him right away, he either mumbles something you just know is derogatory, or raises his voice and waves his arms about. (I have him to thank for my extensive knowledge of Italian expletives.)

Then I remember the look of fear in his eyes less than twenty-four hours ago, and despite everything, I can't help feeling sorry for him. Beneath that fierce Italian bravado, he can be just as vulnerable and scared as the rest of us.

The kitchen now closed, I pour myself another glass of Valpolicella and cram a stuffed courgette flower into my mouth – whole.

'I am serious about what I say before,' shouts Francesco, straining to be heard above the enthusiastic clapping and singing of '*Funiculì, Funiculà*'. 'About teaching you Italian.' His warm breath tickles my ear.

'Great!' I say, hand covering my mouth to avoid showering him with bits of batter.

'*Allora*, tomorrow at Tamino's coffee shop, next to the station? Two o'clock, *sì*?'

I give a cool nod, keeping my eyes ahead, but biting back a hamster-like grin as I sway in time to the music.

'*Sogni d'oro*,' he says, swinging his jacket over his shoulder.

'Excuse me?' I say, turning to face him.

'This means, "Golden dreams." *Ciao!*'

'Right. Goodnight.'

From the corner of my eye I watch his tall, broad-shouldered frame weaving swiftly through the revelling crowd and out of the door.

It's gone two before the last few customers are persuaded to leave and past four by the time the tables are cleared and re-set, chairs stacked, floor swept, dishwasher loaded, and tips divvied up.

I whizz down a deserted Richmond Hill, the wind at my back, my heart beating in time to the mambo from too little sleep, too much wine, caffeine – and perhaps a little too much excitement.

* * *

When I arrive at Tamino's the next afternoon Francesco is already there, perched on a high stool, sipping coffee and reading the Italian newspaper, *Corriere della Sera*.

The chef's garb of white jacket and checked trousers has been replaced by faded Armani jeans and a pale blue, collarless shirt, with a navy cashmere jumper casually draped around his shoulders.

'*Buongiorno, principessa!*' he says, rising and pulling out a chair. 'What do you like?'

'A macchiato please,' I say, launching myself up onto the stool.

He smiles, then strides over to the counter.

I peer at the book lying on the table and lower my glasses onto my nose – *Italian for Beginners*.

I flick through the pages. BICYCLE. '*Una bicicletta,*' I whisper.

Francesco returns with the coffee, sits down opposite me, and crosses his long legs.

'*Grazie.*'

As we talk, I dare to study his face close-up: aquiline nose, square jaw, deep-set eyes, teeth slightly out of kilter, dark, wavy hair, tinged with grey; not handsome, in a smooth, Tom-Hiddleston way, but more of a Tom-Hardy type – rugged, raw yet charming; the type of man who'd protect you in a street brawl . . .

'*Allora* . . . shall we begin?'

'What?' I feel the heat rising in my cheeks. 'Oh . . . yes, of course.'

Pushing the book across the table, I say, '*Ho una bicicletta.*'

'The "h" is silent – like "o". O *una bicicletta*. Please try again.'

Taking a slurp of my macchiato, I repeat – with confidence this time, '*O una bicicletta.*'

He fires me a bemused look over the rim of his coffee cup.

'What?' I say awkwardly.

He indicates my mouth. Is he making fun of me?

'*O – UNA – BICICLETTA,*' I repeat, louder this time.

'You have some . . .'

'What?' I rummage in my bag for my compact mirror, my face flushing pomodoro-red at the sight of my frothy coffee moustache. I'm sure there's a tissue in here somewhere . . .

Francesco leans across the table and hands me a freshly

laundered linen handkerchief, a smile flickering across his lips. My heart speeds up.

'*O una bicicletta*,' I blurt out.

'*Bravissima!*' he exclaims, high-fiving me.

* * *

And so two afternoons a week I buy Francesco coffee and he teaches me Italian.

If I get stuck and break into English, he puts on his teacher face, shakes his head, and waggles his finger.

I don't ever remember language learning being so much fun. But back when I was a gawky, pigtailed schoolgirl, my Modern Languages teacher was a short, dour-faced Glaswegian, sporting shabby clothes and halitosis. And now? Now my heart flips over at the sight of my teacher's smile, the tilt of his head as he listens patiently to my attempts at grammar, sentence construction, and pronunciation, the way he says '*E*-milee' and calls me his '*piccola studentessa*' in that make-your-knees-go-weak accent of his.

* * *

Isn't life strange? It seems to me the moment you stop wanting something so badly, it comes and bites you on the derrière . . .

'I hope you're sitting down, darling,' gushes Lionel in a rare phone call some two weeks later, 'because I have got you a casting for an eight-week run with the Jeremy Hart Rep Company in Branworth by the sea!'

'What? Where's Branworth?'

'Oh, somewhere up North. Anyway, I've got some bits of script that I'll email to you, darling, and Jeremy will see you tomorrow at The Spotlight Studios at three. Okay?'

'Tomorrow?'

'Got to dash. Three pantomime dames to find before Friday. Byeee!'

CASTING BREAKDOWN:
To play a mermaid, German secretary, bride and Cockney maid.
To assist stage management as required.
Good team player, flexible, versatile, good at accents.

A mermaid? A bride? Me?!

But Lionel is having none of it and reminds me that my reward at the end of the season would be the much-coveted Equity union card – a little plastic card that is my proof that I am a proper professional, and which gives actors discounts on everything from theatre tickets to hair removal.

I don't know why I'm getting in a tizzy. I probably won't get it.

A few weeks ago I'd have jumped at the opportunity, so why the sudden uncertainty, the negativity? Could it be anything to do with a certain Italian gentleman? No-ho! Of course not.

I suppose it will be good audition experience, and I can't risk being dumped by my one and only agent, so pushing all thoughts of loyalty (and brewing romance) aside, I download the relevant sections of script onto my iPad.

Italian lessons now temporarily on hold, Francesco slips into the role of supporting actor with surprising ease and comedic enthusiasm.

* * *

It is a truth universally acknowledged, that a casting director will only get in touch if you got the job.

Nevertheless, after three weeks of radio silence, I confess to feeling a niggle of hurt.

Having recently watched Audrey Hepburn in *Roman Holiday*, it dawns on me: there's something that's sure to give me an instant shot of dopamine . . .

Studying my pixie cut with highlights in the mirror, I see a rejuvenated me; lighter, more fun, more positive, and the sparkle in my eyes has returned.

I exit the salon fifteen minutes later than arranged. Francesco is nowhere to be seen. Taking out my phone, I scroll for his number.

Someone taps me on the shoulder.

'Excuse me. Can you help me? I am looking for my friend.'

'Francesco, I'm so sorry . . .'

'*Mamma mia!* She look just like you – but a little older, maybe.'

'Excuse me?' I say, giving his cheek a playful slap.

'You look even more beautiful,' he says, ruffling my spiky golden hair. Meeting his intense gaze, I feel the colour rising in my cheeks as he takes my hand.

'I booked us lunch at Sarastro in Drury Lane. Okay?'

'Perfect.'

All at once my mobile springs into life. As usual, it's worked its way to the bottom of my cavernous bag, and not until my purse, a half-eaten tube of extra strong mints, my mini Italian dictionary, a Tampax, a bottle of water, keys, my Oyster card, a scrunched-up tissue, lip gloss, and satsuma are spewed all over the pavement that I am able to locate it.

'Emily, darling, it's Lionel,' he says in a singsong voice I've never heard before. 'Terrific news – you got the job!'

'What? You're kidding. It's been so long I assumed . . .'

'Turns out their first choice was offered a last-minute contract to play Maria on a six-month tour of *The Sound of Music*, so has left them in a bit of a pickle. You start on Monday.'

As he rattles off the terms of the offer my mind goes into overdrive. Monday? I can't possibly start on Monday! What about the restaurant? And Beryl? I've paid next month's rent in advance. What about my yoga class, my Italian lessons?

'So pleased for you, darling. Firing that email off to you right now. Toodle-pip!'

Francesco looks at me enquiringly. 'Good news?'

'Yes . . . and no.'

Where has my ambition, my drive, my self-belief gone? Over ninety per cent of actors are out of work. I should be jumping up and down and swinging round the lamppost with joy.

Francesco hands me the rest of my scattered belongings, including a yellow Post-it note.

Our doubts are traitors, and make us lose the good we oft might win by fearing to attempt.' Remember! Love & luck, Portia xx

* * *

CHIUSO/CLOSED. Turning over the door sign for the last time, a feeling of melancholy swells my heart.

'*A cena!*' calls Luigi. Francesco slips into the empty space beside me on the banquette. There are a couple of bottles of prosecco chilling in an ice bucket by the side, and a little pile of gifts by my place: a box of my favourite Baci Perugina chocolates, a bottle of Montepulciano, and a notebook in which Nonna Rosa has written several of her recipes.

'Thank you,' I say, swallowing hard, looking at them all through a sudden mist.

These people have become like family to me. Il Mulino has given me a sense of belonging, and they have taught me so much: the importance and enjoyment of the simple things life has to offer; good food, wine, conversation, music, friendship, and family.

Luigi leans across the table and pinches my cheek.

'It is not goodbye, *cara*, just *arrivederci*. There is always a job here for our *piccola inglese*.'

'*Grazie*, Luigi,' I say, swallowing the lump in my throat.

'And if you need anything, anything at all, you just call your

Zio Luigi. *D'accordo?*'

'*D'accordo,*' I say, giving each of them a hug in turn. 'Now I really should be going. My train leaves in six hours.'

Francesco picks up my bag of goodies and opens the door. '*Prego.*'

Our footsteps reverberate along the deserted pavement. He stops suddenly, gazing up at the low-hanging, milk-bottle-top moon.

'Look! Orion and here, the Great Bear.'

'Where?'

He stands behind me and guides my hand towards the jewel-filled sky. My heart quickens.

As we reach the bicycle rack, he places my bag in the pannier while I put on my helmet and flick on my lights.

'Good luck,' he says, holding my gaze with his dark, soulful eyes.

'Thank you. Goodni . . . I mean, *sogni d'oro,*' I reply, smiling up at him, doing my best to sound Italian and cool.

As I go to peck his cheek, he leans towards me. I close my eyes, hoping to feel his lips on mine.

'Eiii!' he cries as his forehead bashes against the peak of my cycle helmet.

My eyes ping open and I let out the breath I've been holding. 'Are you okay?'

Rubbing his head, his mouth breaks into a wide grin and we collapse into howls of laughter.

'May I?' he asks eventually, his hand unclipping the strap of my helmet and throwing it in the bicycle basket.

I nod, heart beating so fast I think I might faint.

He runs his fingers through my hair, tilts my head up to meet his soul-searching gaze and gently kisses my lips.

Stop this now! yells my subconscious. *You're getting sidetracked again. It will only lead to heartbreak.*

Hands cupping my face, he looks at me intently. 'I will miss you, Emily Forsyt . . . Forsythhh.'

I stifle a giggle.

'This is correct, no?'

'Perhaps just a *little* less stress on the "th"?'

He shakes his head and sighs. 'My English teacher, she is no good. I must look for another.'

I stretch onto my tiptoes and lean in for another kiss.

'And I will miss you too, Francesco Rrrrossi.'

Chapter 8

Flying by the Seat of My Pants

'Branworth Station, Branworth Station, next stop,' cuts in the guard's muffled voice over the Tannoy. I put *Miranda* away with the other three scripts – the other three, untouched, UNLEARNED scripts.

I swing my rucksack onto my back and feel a twinge.

I wonder if I'm capable of learning four parts in almost as many weeks, when I have difficulty memorising passwords.

The Jeremy Hart Repertory Company is one of the few left of its kind. Nowadays most actors have the luxury of at least three weeks of rehearsal; not so here, with a new play to learn every week. The audiences are made up of the local community and regulars, who plan their holidays around the play season. Many of the actors have appeared here year after year and have a huge local fan base.

When I'm not required to rehearse, I have to hunt for props, help paint the set, assist the wardrobe department, beg shops and restaurants to display our posters, and keep tea, coffee, milk, and biscuit supplies replenished.

'Eight pound sixty, duck,' says the taxi driver, as we draw up outside Gloria's Hollywood Apartments – reputedly the best theatrical digs in town.

I push a tenner into his hand. 'Keep the change,' I say distractedly, looking upwards.

'I'll look for your name in lights!' he calls, beeping his horn as he pulls away from the kerb.

I press the buzzer. Through the frosted glass I can make out a figure descending the stairs. The door opens and I am face to face with a lady sporting a dated beehive, tight, velour top, leopard skin, stretchy ski pants, and black satin slippers with fluffy feathers.

'You must be Emily. I'm Gloria. Come in, love, and I'll show you your apartment,' she says, beckoning me inside. 'You're in the Bette Davis Studio,' she announces proudly, as she bustles up the flock-wallpapered stairway in a vapour of 4711 cologne and nicotine, gold pendants jingling. Framed, black and white, signed photographs of Gloria with various celebs whom I vaguely recognise from old sitcoms and soaps cram every square inch.

'Would you like a cuppa?' she asks.

'Mmm, yes, please,' I reply, dropping my rucksack to the floor. She disappears in a swish of bamboo curtain, through to the galley kitchen.

'How about a Gypsy Cream as well?' she calls. 'You must be starving after your journey.'

'That'd be great.'

I take in my surroundings; the living room-cum-bedroom is spotlessly clean, with a standard lamp, crushed velveteen settee, and sheepskin rug. There's a giant television in one corner and a single bed in the other, covered in a paisley-patterned eiderdown. The walls are Artexed, giving them that rough, Seventies, faux-farmhouse effect. Off the corridor is the burgundy bathroom suite, with matching, twisted-loop pedestal mat and loo seat cover.

'You know, I always fancied being an actress myself,' says Gloria, handing me my tea and biscuit. 'When my mother died and left me the house, I decided to convert it and take in theatricals. They've all stayed here: the Roly Polys, Hinge and Bracket, Cannon and Ball, the Krankies, Dottie Wayne, Joe Pasquale . . . and last week I had the cast of *Saturday Night Fever*. If you could pay me on a Friday, please – and I prefer cash. Oh, and don't forget to sign my visitors' book before you leave. Don't hesitate to knock if you need anything,' she says, handing me my key, then clip-clopping down the stairs.

After unpacking, I wander down to the beach, and out to the end of the deserted pier. I look out at the heaving ocean and draw a deep breath. So, this is the life I've dreamed of – the life of a jobbing actor – how will it pan out? What will the rest of the cast be like? What if I can't remember all my lines?

I head back towards the shore, buffeted along by the strong wind, whipped up from the sea. As I draw closer, I notice the lights are on in the chippy. I order a haddock supper, which I devour with greasy fingers on a bench in a draughty, graffiti-covered shelter while listening to the playlist of Italian songs Francesco compiled for me.

With the light now starting to fade, I find my way to the little repertory theatre.

SEE TWO PLAYS IN ONE WEEK! boasts the poster pasted outside. And there's my name in tiny print at the bottom of the cast list. No backing out now. I look down the list of plays, and the scary thought of all those lines hastens me back to Gloria's for an early night.

* * *

Next morning, heart racing, I climb the stairs to the rehearsal studio. I pause momentarily as I turn the door handle and suck in a deep breath. The room is full of actors talking in loud, confident voices, laughing, squealing, hugging, and air-kissing one another.

'Darling! How *wonderful* to see you again – can't believe it's been a year . . .'

'Been working much?'

'Oh, this and that – a bit of voice-over work and one episode of *Coronation Street*.'

'I hardly recognised you – the Botox takes years off you . . .'

'. . . that soup commercial will pay my mortgage for the next three months . . .'

The door opens and Jeremy, the director, whom I recognise from the audition, appears, followed by his creative team.

'Good morning, everyone, and welcome to The Civic Theatre for this, our fortieth anniversary season. Gather round,' he says, indicating the circle of chairs. 'Now, for the benefit of those who haven't been here before, to my left is Babs, who's in charge of wardrobe; Lesley, set designer; Ellis, lighting; Rich, sound; Kris, stage manager; and his second-in-command, Abi, our deputy stage manager.'

'Hi!' says Abi, who is crouched on the floor, marking the layout of the set with white tape.

Jeremy looks anxiously at the door, then his watch. 'Well, we'd better get started. Let's go round the room, introduce yourselves, and then tell us the name of the character you'll be playing in our opening production.'

The door flies open and a well-preserved actress I vaguely recognise from an old sitcom sweeps into the room, a long, red PVC raincoat draped around her shoulders, clutching what looks like a meerkat with hair extensions.

'So sorry I'm late, Jeremy darling. You know how I *hate* early mornings.'

'Margo darling!' gushes Jeremy, leaping to his feet and kissing her on both cheeks. 'Let me grab you a pew.'

Scooping up a chair, he announces, 'Ladies and gentlemen,

she doesn't need introducing, but put your hands together please, and give a warm welcome to our leading lady, Margo Dalziel!'

Margo smiles graciously, gives a regal wave and says, 'Aren't you forgetting someone, darling? This is Phoebe, everyone,' she says, proudly holding up a scrawny paw. 'You see, she's saying "Hello,"' she gushes, smothering the yelping meerkat in kisses.

'Right, let's crack on, folks,' booms Jeremy over-brightly, eyes studying the ceiling. 'Here are your rehearsal schedules. Please take one and pass them on . . .'

As my eyes run down the schedule, my stomach twists and my heart quickens. I am perfectly prepared to earn my thespian wings by working my socks off, but I can't help feeling a tad panic-stricken when I realise that after opening night, we begin rehearsals early the following morning for the next production, while performing the play we rehearsed the last week every evening, with matinées on Thursdays and Saturdays.

At the end of each run, I have to pack away all the props, help 'strike' (take down) the set and put up the new one, which I have to dress with the curtains, pictures, rugs, books, ornaments, etc., I have somehow miraculously sourced in time for the full dress rehearsal at 2.30.

At the risk of appearing a diva, when exactly am I to learn my lines, let alone eat, sleep, wash my smalls? I raise my hand gingerly.

'And so to our first play, *Miranda*,' says Jeremy, pulling a file from his bag. 'Emily, our latest recruit, is to play our mischievous mermaid.'

Jeremy motions for me to stand up. All eyes swivel in my direction. I slowly lower my arm, tugging at my recently cropped hair, wishing it would magically grow back.

'This isn't *Phantom of the Opera*,' grumbles Babs that afternoon at my wardrobe fitting. 'We simply don't have the budget for wigs. Why Jeremy cast you, I have no idea. He should have consulted *me* first.'

I open my mouth to speak but think better of it.

A long, blonde wig is eventually found scrunched up in a Tesco carrier bag from a 2001 production of *Les Liaisons Dangereuses*, and after a gentle soak in some Dreft, it is grudgingly met with Babs's approval.

* * *

My very first scene is with Charles, the chauffeur, who has to carry me on stage and around the room, while I marvel at the furnishings and paintings.

According to the script, Charles is *broad and tough-looking*, so don't ask me why five-foot-five, skinny-as-a-rake Vincent Crumb has been cast in this role. I may not be Victoria Beckham, but the way he wobbles and wheezes as he carts me around makes me feel less like a delicate mermaid and more like a beached whale.

'We haven't time to spend on this now, so please can you work on this scene in your own time?' says Jeremy, clutching his forehead. 'Right, moving on . . .'

* * *

Miranda – Opening Night

'Everyone got their personal props?' calls Abi, standing in the doorway, scanning her clipboard.

'I've lost a glove!'

'Anyone got any hairspray?'

'Can you call Babs? A button's just come off my jacket.'

'Has anyone seen my cigarette holder?'

Excited chatter from the auditorium blares through the speakers. Every seat sold. I feel sick.

During the dress rehearsal this afternoon I forgot my lines three times, and my wig got caught in the zip of my tail during a quick scene change.

I close my eyes and inhale deeply, to steady my frazzled nerves. I breathe in the sweet perfume of the two bouquets of flowers on my dressing table: freesias from Mum and Dad, and pink roses from Francesco. I glance at the card and smile a private smile.

Good luck, cara! Fx

Mamma mia, if he could see me now, I think as I stare at the Donatella Versace lookalike in the mirror.

'Act One beginners, please.'

I'm not on for nine pages, but set off early to allow myself time to waddle down to prompt corner in my fishtail. I also need to have a practice-run in the wheelchair, which only materialised half an hour ago.

I scoot up and down the backstage area, heart going da-dum-da-dum-da-dum.

'We have clearance,' announces Kris, giving the thumbs-up. 'Break a leg, everyone!'

The lights go down, and the curtain goes up on Act One, Scene One.

'Fade music. Cue telephone . . . go!' whispers Abi into her mic.

Vince swigs water from one of the bottles on the props table, his eyes darting about nervously.

The green light comes on. Knees bent, he scoops me up into his bony arms, and we veer onto the shaky set of the doctor's Bloomsbury flat.

Under the glare of the lights, it's as if I am watching someone who looks and sounds like me moving around the stage and saying the lines.

'Am I heavy?'

'No, miss . . . quite the contrary.'

'You look so very strong.'

'Do I, miss?'

'What wonderful muscles!' (Snigger from the stalls.)

'I do a bit of amateur boxing, miss,' groans Vince, as he chucks me onto the sofa, one page early, which means I have no alternative but to cut my line, 'Carry me round the room, will you, Charles?'

Civic Theatre stalwart, Vanessa Morrell, playing Clare, the doctor's wife, swans on upstage right, saying, 'You can put Miss Trewella down, Cha . . .' and glowers in my direction.

I am dumped in the offstage darkness after my first scene, and fumble my way to the quick-change area, where Babs is standing by with my long dress and pearls, in preparation for Act Two, Scene One.

'Breathe in,' she commands through a mouthful of safety pins, yanking the waistband of the tail tighter around my midriff.

Meanwhile, Rocky Balboa is pacing up and down stage right, in preparation for round two . . .

If adrenaline gives a person the superhuman strength to lift a car, then please God, can it not do the same for Vince?

'Ah, here she is. Put Miss Trewella on the settee, Charles.' And my prayer is answered.

Our first-night nerves gradually vanish as Doctor Theatre works his magic, shifting the action up a gear, giving the lines punchiness and pace.

We are now just one scene away from the interval, and my favourite bit of the whole play, where I have the stage all to myself – the pivotal moment, where the audience realises for the first time that Miranda is not disabled after all . . .

I flop into the wheelchair; Babs fusses with the ribbon of my négligée, and the jewelled clasp in my hair, then tucks the tartan blanket tightly around my legs and under my feet, so the tail doesn't poke out.

Margo, playing the nurse (looking for all the world like she's starring in one of those old *Carry On* films), pushes me on stage.

'Why did you never get married, Nurse Cary?'

'I never wanted to,' she replies, her gin-infused breath wafting over me.

'Don't you find men attractive?'

'No . . . nor they me . . . which makes it easier.'

'I'd take you out any night of the week, sweetheart!' comes a voice from the gods. Several guffaws echo around the auditorium.

Coquettishly batting her false eyelashes, Margo cries, 'See you in the bar afterwards, darling!' which prompts several wolf-whistles.

'I love men.' I yell this line, determined to get us back on track.

Margo thumps the back of the chair and eventually says, 'Well, well . . .' This is not in the script, and therefore slightly worrying. She then proceeds to cut the next page of dialogue.

The lights slowly fade and the set is bathed in greeny-blue light. Thunder rolls, lightning flashes, the rain lashes against the windowpanes, and the haunting wisps of 'Fingal's Cave' by Mendelssohn drift through the air. Cellos and bassoons gather momentum; Miranda, trance-like, removes her négligée. (Bit of a barney with Jeremy and Babs about this stage direction, due to my refusal to bare my assets to an audience of elderly holiday-makers – or any holidaymakers for that matter. Two large shells, strategically super-glued to a flesh-coloured, strapless bra save the day.) She lets down her flowing locks and flicks her scaly tail high into the air. Lightning, thunder, gasps from the audience, curtains, wild applause. This is what is *supposed* to happen . . .

'Goodnight. Turn on the wireless, will you; and switch off the lights as you go out.'

'See you in the morning.'

'Don't forget my scallops.'

'There are just as good fish in the sea as ever . . . Goodnight.'

MIRANDA MANIPULATES HER CHAIR OVER TO THE FRENCH WINDOW.

Why won't the bloody thing move?

MIRANDA MANIPULATES HER CHAIR OVER TO THE FRENCH WINDOW.

I push the wheels with all my might, but . . . NOTHING. I

lean forward . . . if I could just reach the door handle . . . oops . . . nearly. The chair rocks back and forth. Nervous whispers come from the auditorium.

'Release the brake!' hisses Abi from the wings. Aha! How stupid of me. I grab the lever and flick it to the down position; the chair starts to roll backwards on the raked stage, towards the orchestra pit. The audience holds its collective breath. I push the wheels forward with all my might and hurtle towards the French windows, crashing into the table. The goldfish bowl wobbles precariously.

MIRANDA LOOSENS HER HAIR SO THAT IT CASCADES DOWN OVER HER SHOULDERS.

My trembling hand, now slippy with sweat, can't get the hair clip to undo. I tug at it, and the wig moves precariously to the side, so decide to abandon that bit of business.

I'm trapped, unable to move, the négligée and blanket now tangled up in the wheels.

Please bring the tabs in and end the agony. Pleeeease.

The curtains come in slowly, jerkily, and our first-night audience is left at the interval, doubtless believing that *Miranda* is a horror story, with the central character bearing a scary resemblance to Norman Bates's mother in *Psycho*.

*NB: no goldfish are harmed in this production. They are played by mandarin orange segments.

* * *

Just as we are getting into our stride, the run reaches its end and it's on to play two.

Thank the Lord I haven't a part in this one, so can relax a little and focus on finding props and painting the set.

But then at the dress rehearsal, Jeremy drops a bombshell:

'Darling,' he says in a low voice as he places a suspiciously reassuring arm round my shoulders. 'We have a bit of a – situation

125

on our hands . . .'

'What kind of a – "situation"?' I ask tentatively.

'It's nothing to worry about . . .'

I swallow hard.

'Rich has a last-minute meeting in London tomorrow afternoon and our budget doesn't stretch to a freelance sound engineer, sooo, as the only spare member of the stage management team, the duty falls to you, my sweet.'

My stomach plummets like a drop tower. He CANNOT be serious.

'Oh, Jeremy, please let's get one thing straight,' I say with pleading eyes. 'I may be a dab hand at splashing a bit of paint around, or knocking a couple of bits of wood together, or finding props for you, but operating a sound desk?!'

'You'll be *fine*,' he says with feigned conviction. 'You can shadow Rich tonight, and the systems here are all manual, not a computer in sight, so you see, you'll be fine, trust me. Okay, everyone, let's start from where we left off – the top of Act Two, please!'

I now know what ASM *really* stands for: A Stupid Mug.

* * *

Ahoy There! A Farce (What an Understatement)

Here I am in a tiny, hot, soundproof box at the back of the auditorium. It's airless, rank with sweat (where's a Jo Malone scented candle when you need one?) and has a deck of dials and switches that reminds me of the cockpit of a 787.

The door opens and Kris's head peers round.

'Good luck!' he says, giving me the thumbs-up.

'House lights, down. Cue music . . . go!' crackles Abi's voice through my headphones (or 'cans', as the techies call them). My quivering finger depresses the switch, and the theme music from *Desert Island Discs* swells the theatre.

'Fade music. Sound cue one . . . go!' cuts in Abi's voice again. The tinny sound of rolling waves and the screech of gulls sifts through the speakers, setting the scene. Phew. I wind the reel-to-reel tape to the next red marker. There are several pages of dialogue before my next cue, so daring to relax a little, I take a swig of water and look down onto the set and my, dare I say, *impressive* handiwork. The balsa wood palm trees look surprisingly realistic (as long as no one leans against them), although my last-minute brainwave of dressing the stage with real coconuts (two for one at Morrisons) is proving to be a bit of a safety hazard.

The play is a three-hander, and as the only female in the cast, Margo is in her element, playing a *femme fatale*, shipwrecked on a desert island with her husband and her lover. This week she is wearing a skimpy, low-cut, raggedy tunic, held together with angel breath. Her character is supposed to be in her twenties, but I'm learning that being top of the bill here has its perks – other than financial – one of them being you get to choose your own parts and costumes.

'Cue music . . . go!' calls Abi. 'Well done, Emily, you made it to the interval. Fifteen minutes, please.'

Blimey, maybe I'm not such a technophobe after all. Who knows, if this acting lark doesn't work out, a career as a sound engineer might not be beyond the realms of possibility.

There is a knock at the door and Ellis enters, carrying a mug of tea and a Kit Kat.

'Hey, well done, you! Rich had better watch out – we have a budding sound engineer in our midst.'

'Please don't tempt fate.' I smile through my slug of tea.

'Just do exactly what you did in the first half and you're home and dry.' He winks reassuringly, shutting the door behind him.

The three bells ring out.

'Ladies and gentlemen, please take your seats as this evening's performance of *Ahoy There!* will continue in two minutes. Two minutes please.'

Only three more sound cues to go until we reach the end of the play. Whey hey! I can almost taste that glass of chilled Sauvignon waiting for me at the bar.

'Rupert, I think I can see something in the distance. Could it be . . . could it be a ship?' proclaims Margo.

I slowly wind the tape forward manually, in preparation for the ship's siren, two pages of dialogue hence. Hmm. Strange. Can't see the marker. Rewind the tape using the switch this time, and look again. No red marker. Maybe I didn't wind it on far enough. I press the fast-forward switch. Whirr. Nothing. I press rewind. Whirr. Nothing.

I've found a red marker on the tape but which sound effect is it?

'Cue ship's siren . . . go!' instructs Abi. Heart knocking against my chest, I depress the switch, keeping everything crossed . . . and the screech of monkeys echoes around the auditorium.

'Rupert, Geoffrey, it is a ship!'

'We have one flare left, thank God,' says Rupert. 'They are bound to see us.'

Terror floods through my veins. It's like watching a train about to crash in slow motion, and not being able to do a thing about it.

'Cue sound of flare . . . go!' says Abi, the tiniest hint of exasperation in her usually super-cool voice.

Nothing.

'Cue flare . . . go!'

Nothing.

'What was that noise?' ad-libs Margo, cupping her hand to her ear.

'What noise?'

'I think I heard the flare.'

'Flare?'

'The-one-Rupert-set-alight-just-now,' she says loudly.

The three actors look at one another with fear in their eyes.

When will this end? After what seems an age, they start jumping up and down half-heartedly, calling, 'Ahoy there!'

'Cue ship's siren . . . go!'
Silence.

* * *

Week Five: Murder on the Tenth Floor – **A Thriller**

This week I'm murdered in the first half of the play, thank God. A few lines at the beginning, followed by twenty-five minutes' dead acting, until the interval. During the break, I have to change into my 'blacks' and take up the stage management duty of chief lift operator.

The play is set in a multi-storey office block. The 'lift' is a wooden, sliding door, painted silver. I have to squeeze in behind the scenery wall before the start of the second half and wait for the red cue light to turn green. At Detective Inspector Lord and Sergeant Cooper's entrance, the light comes on, and I pull the string attached to the top of the door as smoothly as I can. Then I'm stuck there until they exit, almost at the end of the play.

'The door must positively gliiide, Emily,' Jeremy had said. That's all well and good, but he's not the one squashed in there with practically no room to manoeuvre, let alone breathe.

The play is completely sold out – nothing like a good, juicy whodunnit to pull in the bored holidaymakers from their B&Bs on a dull, drizzly night in Branworth.

'Stay right where you are!' orders Vince, as this week's villain, Jack Spencer. He flicks on the torch and trains the beam onto my face. 'I'm afraid you know too much,' he continues, pulling a gun from the inside pocket of his overcoat.

'Don't be a fool, Jack. The police won't buy your story. But I can help you . . .'

Vince pulls the trigger. I know the routine now: grab the corner of the desk, clutch chest with other hand, squeeze blood capsule, fall to knees, open mouth slightly as if to speak, glazed look, fall on my side, back to the audience (so they don't see me breathing), and remember what Jeremy said: 'Don't overact, darling – remember, less is more.'

But hang on, where's the bang? The trigger clicks again. Nothing. Vince shoots me one of his customary, bug-eyed Mr-Bean looks.

No good relying on him to get us out of this. He spouts his lines verbatim, but as I discovered in *Miranda*, throw the unexpected at him, and he clams up.

A mega-dose of adrenaline rushes around my body, and I find myself backing away, ad-libbing like mad.

'You won't get away with this, you know. No, you won't. No, siree! The police will be here soon. There's no way out – unless you'd care to try the window. But the windows are double-glazed, so you won't be able to break them . . . even with a chair . . . nope . . . no way . . .'

My back is now pressed against the 'lift' door, blood trickling through my fingers onto my shirt, for no apparent reason. Vince is rooted to the spot, doubtless petrified of what I may say or do next. There's only one thing for it . . .

In a last-ditch attempt to rescue the situation, I feign prising the door open and fall in backwards, as if into the lift shaft (a black masking curtain). I then spin around once (less is more), crying 'Aaaaaaaaaaah!'

Abi looks at me flabbergasted from prompt corner, as I snatch one of the cast-iron stage weights and drop it to the floor with a thud, signifying my sticky end.

A good bit of improv, I think, until it dawns on me horribly as the plot unravels, that all references to the shooting (of which there are many) have now to be changed on the hoof, and the two local am-dram enthusiasts, cast in the non-speaking roles of ambulance men, don't get to come on stage at all.

* * *

Week Six: Another Op'nin', Another Wig

Strike a match within three feet of my head, and I will combust. Yet despite the half can of hairspray and ton of kirby grips, my mangy hairpiece keeps falling off.

'Could we do away with the hairpiece altogether, Babs?' I beg, as she spears my head again.

'You're supposed to be a nineteen-year-old virgin bride, Emily, and without it . . .' she says, casting a critical eye over my spiky pixie crop, 'well, I'm afraid there's no nice way of putting this, you – you look like Mrs Tiggy-Winkle.'

'What about my *Miranda* wig?'

Judging by Babs's reaction, you'd think I had just suggested wearing my birthday suit and a pair of Doc Martens.

'I beg your pardon? Did you say your *Miranda* wig?'

I nod, smiling weakly.

'You can't possibly wear that wig! Our regulars would recognise you right away from *Miranda*. No, you have to look completely different. There!' she says, standing back and studying my reflection. 'As long as you don't move your head around too much, it'll stay put, and on matinée days you'll have to keep it on in between shows.'

It was bound to happen sooner or later – and tonight it does . . .

'Oh, Archie, you do love me, don't you?'

'Of course I do, Shirl. You're the only girl for me.'

'Oh, Archie!'

'Oh, Shirl!'

Archie takes me in his arms and spins me around. As I come in to land, I notice a blonde, ferret-like thing sitting on his shoulder.

'I can't – wait – until – we're – married, darling,' I squeak. I know I have another line, but my concentration is broken. Unaware, Archie/Vince looks at me intently through his Coke-bottle spectacles, eyes hugely magnified, drops of perspiration glistening in the furrows of his terrified brow. I can't think what to say. Remember what they drummed into us at drama school? If your concentration goes, stop and momentarily focus your attention on something very familiar to you, and this will jog your memory . . .

'Oscar Charlie, got a pick-up from Station Road . . .'

We look at one another open-mouthed.

'Oscar Charlie, are you in the vicinity?'

I bite down hard on my lip, fighting a laugh. The Branworth taxi service is mysteriously filtering through the speakers! I ad-lib my way to the end of the scene, but try as I might to retain a sense of professionalism and carry on regardless, my dialogue is expelled in short, sharp bursts, like machine gun fire. The curtains come in, and we all drop to the floor, rolling around in a fit of uncontrollable laughter.

* * *

Week Seven: Salad Days

No part to learn, no technical responsibilities, just a million props to find, including four of those old-type mobile hairdryers; you know, the ones on castors, with giant hoods?

Have been into almost every hairdresser in Branworth. They are all very trendy places with staff of an average age of twenty-three. With their brightly coloured hair, body piercings, tattoos, funky clothes, and waif-like figures, I feel about ninety-five next to them.

'Do you have any old hairdryers I could borrow for a play?' I yell over blaring rap music. 'You know, the old-fashioned type with a hood . . . and wheels . . . no?'

My request is usually met with blank looks or mild amusement. I chicken out from asking them to display our poster and flyers. I get the feeling that neither they nor their cool clientele are likely to want to spend their Saturday night watching Timothy and Jane dancing and singing 'Oh, Look at Me!', accompanied by

Minnie, the magic piano.

Footsore and hairdryerless, I start to wend my way back to the theatre, wondering if it may be at all possible to adapt the whole thing to the present day. Problem is, we're back in that *frightfully* nice world where *gay* means happy, and people go to *marvellous* parties and drink *lashings* of beer, and say things like *gosh* and *he's a thoroughly decent chap.*

I'm ravenous, and an illuminated 'Fish 'n' Chips' sign lures me up a little side street. As I'm waiting in the queue deciding whether or not to have mushy peas, reflected in the mirror, I spy a board outside the pebbledash house opposite . . .

HAIR BY MADGE
SHAMPOO & SET HALF-PRICE
FOR PENSIONERS WEDNESDAYS

Now that looks just the kind of place . . .

'Yes, love?' says the lady behind the counter, fish slice at the ready.

'Sorry, gotta go,' I say, flying out of the door. Forget jumbo sausages and mushy peas, there's more pressing business at hand.
[insert line break]

'If you can manage to get them downstairs, then you're welcome to borrow them,' says Madge, opening the stock room door. 'Can I leave you to it?' she says, consulting her watch. 'My lady's colour should have come off five minutes ago.'

'Sure, thank you, and here's the poster, and oh, I'll drop off the tickets for Thursday night's show tomorrow morning.'

Isn't life weird? Not so long ago, I was pushing a trolley through a metal tube, and now here I am, proudly propelling a dusty old hairdryer with wonky wheels through a shopping precinct. Oh, the glamour!

* * *

'No, no, no, Emily! You pop up from behind the sofa *after* the telephone rings, not *before*,' booms Jeremy's voice from the darkness of the dress circle. 'Now let's go back to the top of the scene from the bishop's entrance.'

In an ideal world we would have rehearsed this for three weeks, ensuring that the slick co-ordination of lines and moves is imprinted on the brain. But in this drama production line, you've barely time to erase the previous character and plot from your memory before you're twenty years younger than last night and are speaking in a Cockney accent as opposed to 'Received Pronunciation' (or 'RP', as it is called in Thespian Land). The art of ad-libbing is a must here, to be pulled out of the hat whenever the playwright's words elude you.

So, to the play itself: vicar, vicar's wife, bishop, gardener, and ditsy maid (typecasting?). Lots of diving under beds, popping in and out of cupboards, and toe-curling double-entendres like, 'Ooh, put that away before somebody else sees it!'

No unruly wig this week, thank God, just a mobcap and an Eliza-Doolittle accent.

'Good evening, bishop. May I take your mitre?'

'Thank you, Edith. Is the vicar at home?'

'Yes, your 'oliness. 'e's in the library and is expecting you.'

BISHOP EXITS UPSTAGE RIGHT.

'Edith! Edith!' *(FROM OFFSTAGE.)*

'Lawks, that's Bill, the gardener!'

I bob down behind the sofa.

Silence.

'Hold it! Emily! Emily!' calls Jeremy tersely.

'Yes?' I say, peering dubiously over the top.

'Is there a problem?'

I stand up, shielding my eyes from the glaring lights. 'No. You told me not to appear until the telephone rings.'

'That's right, but Rich's cue for the telephone ring is your line, "He must have seen me come back from town," is it not?'

'Sorry, I . . . I was concentrating on when to appear and clean forgot my line. Sorry,' I mumble sheepishly.

'Okay, everyone, let's go back to the top of the scene once more, thank you!'

Last night I dreamed I was naked on stage, it was my turn to speak, and I had absolutely no idea what play I was in. I will never pull this together by tomorrow night. There is nothing else for it: forget all that terribly useful stuff Portia drummed into us about Stanislavski. There simply isn't time to explore the inner self. The only technique I'm interested in is survival, and if that means strategically placing bits of the script under the bed, behind the sofa, and in the cupboard, then so be it.

HOW TO SURVIVE WEEKLY REP
by
Emily Forsyth

This actors' manual is to be my project while waiting for my next job. The headings so far are:

Chapter 1
Emergency Stage Evacuation
(procedures to be followed when you have absolutely no idea what your next line is)

Chapter 2
Violent Convulsions
(aka 'corpsing')

Chapter 3
How to Survive Farce
(after not enough rehearsal and avoid having a nervous breakdown)

I will have to amend Chapter Three, as the procedures are not watertight, as I discovered tonight – to my cost . . .

Act Two, and I am within touching distance of the finish line. A couple of pages of dialogue, in which to catch my breath after my leap over the back of the sofa, swiftly followed by energetic dive into the cupboard, to avoid being found by the vicar and his young (ahem) wife. Vince is playing the role of Reverend Pritchard and Margo, Mrs P.

So here I am, crouched down in my usual spot, having a quick slurp of my water and a sneaky look at my script, in preparation for my final scene. My ears prick up as I hear Margo deliver my cue line – two pages early.

Before I have time to shift my brain into gear, the cupboard door is flung open and I am revealed, like a rabbit caught in the headlights. In one hand I am clutching my script, and a bottle of Evian in the other; but worse than this, my skirt is hitched up over my knees and my nasty pop-sock secret is out. I rise slowly, staring into the black void, frantically scanning my memory for my line – nothing. My improvisation skills too let me down, as I find myself saying, 'I'll just pop upstairs, ma'am, and see if her ladyship requires anything.'

'Her – *ladyship*?' enquires Margo, eyes wide, a slight tremor in her voice.

'Yes, her ladyship, your mother . . . who has been upstairs . . . bedridden these ten years since,' I reply, tripping up the stairs. 'God love 'er.'

'But *we* require you to pour the tea,' says Margo firmly, grabbing the hem of my skirt through the spindles. '*Nowww*.'

'Begging your par-don, ma'am,' I continue, wrenching myself free, 'but I shan't be a moment.' And I disappear out of sight, onto 'the landing'.

'Pssst! Abi!' I hiss, waving my arms in the direction of prompt corner.

Abi looks up, removes her cans, and says in a loud whisper,

'What are you doing up there? Get back on stage.'

'What's my line?' I mouth exaggeratedly.

'What?'

'What's – my – line?'

'How should I know?' she replies, frantically flicking through her script. 'You're in a different play to the rest of us.'

Part of me is tempted to climb down the backstage scaffolding and retreat to my dressing room, leaving my fellow actors to it. After all, this is Margo's fault for skipping two pages of dialogue in the first place. But then Portia's words ring out in my head: 'Acting is all about teamwork and being a supportive company member.'

With this in mind, I come to Vince and Margo's rescue by hysterically screaming an improvised exit line: 'Lawks! Sir, madam, come upstairs right away! Her ladyship is . . . DEAD!'

They scuttle upstairs and we huddle together on the tiny 'landing' until Abi has no alternative but to bring the curtain down.

* * *

I emerge from the stage door and thread my way through the hordes of eager autograph hunters waiting for Margo. Someone taps me gently on the shoulder.

'Excuse me, please will you sign our programme?'

I turn forty-five degrees and promptly burst into tears, as Lily, Céline and Rachel, arms outstretched, shroud me in a group hug.

'Hey, don't cry,' says Lily, wiping my cheeks with her thumb. 'It was supposed to be a *nice* surprise.'

'Oh, it *is*, believe me,' I blub, my Poundland mascara smudging the collar of Céline's white Chanel blazer. 'These are happy tears. I can't tell you how relieved I am to see your familiar faces. It's all been too Mr Bean for words. I've aged about twenty years in the last few weeks.'

'Rubbish. You have lost weight, though,' says Lily, laying a

137

gentle hand on my arm.

'You were so hilarious as the maid,' chips in Céline.

I flinch. 'I never believed those people who said the stress some actors experience during performance is the equivalent of a small car crash – until tonight. Tonight, let me tell you, I felt like I was in a multiple pile-up on the M25. Anyway, it's over and you're here. Time to celebrate,' I say, slotting my arms through theirs. 'Let me buy us all a drink. I'm afraid there are no decent wine bars in this town, just the Lobster Pot. Their house white isn't bad though.'

'I know a place overlooking the sea that stays open all night, where we can drink champagne from crystal flutes, and eat smoked salmon by candlelight,' says Lily.

I look at her, puzzled.

'Ta-dah!' She beams as she produces a cool box from behind her back. 'Come on. We reserved a bench on the prom.'

Arm in arm, we saunter along the path to the shore, chatting and giggling non-stop. I give a quiet nod to the graffitied shelter, where I'd dined on fish and chips on that windy night eight weeks ago.

'Ahem! I'd like to propose a toast,' I announce, rising unsteadily to my feet, the bubbles in my glass fizzing. 'Be we in Branworth or Bermuda, may our friendship last for ever!'

'To friendship!'

'I know we don't see one another as much these days, but please don't ever think I've forgotten you. The last few months have changed me, and have made me truly appreciate having old friends like you in my life.'

'Less of the *old*, eh?' says Lily, wrapping her arm around me. 'But you're happy you made the move, aren't you?'

'Sure. It's not easy at times, scary even, but I'm learning that sometimes throwing yourself into unfamiliar situations can lead you somewhere unexpected, to new challenges, new people . . .'

'Like what, where, who?' asks Rachel.

'Well, I can rustle up a mean pasta sauce now, I can speak a bit of Italian, and I can make a palm tree out of balsa wood, should you ever need one for your next Hawaiian fancy dress party.'

'And any Ryan Goslings or Bradley Coopers we should know about?' probes Rachel, refilling our glasses, a cheeky glint in her eye.

'Nope. I wouldn't go out with an actor anyway.'

'Okay. Any Gino D'Acampos then?'

Colour rises to my cheeks.

'Knew it!' she squeals, throwing her hand up in the air and spilling her champagne.

'Don't get excited. It's nothing serious,' I say defensively. 'He teaches me Italian, that's all. Besides, I'm not the woman I used to be. I no longer *need* a man in my life. Now, enough of me. What about you, Lily and Randy, the LA Action Man?'

'Dating disaster.'

'Oh, why can't love be like in the movies?' says Céline longingly. 'You don't know just how lucky you are, Rachel – to have met and married the man of your dreams so young.'

'Hah! He's no romantic Darcy or Heathcliff,' she replies, 'but he's my best friend. I can't help wondering though how life would have panned out if I hadn't settled down so early on.'

'No point wondering *what if*,' says Lily. 'The way to happiness isn't necessarily about breaking all ties and travelling thousands of miles to Bali or India on some self-discovery pilgrimage, like in *Eat, Pray, Love*. The person sitting next to you at home may well be holding the key. I think what I'm trying to say, is that the grass isn't always greener.'

'Yeah. When we are young, we assume that there will be plenty of people out there in this big, wide world with whom we'll connect – and I mean *truly* connect,' I say, opening another bottle. 'But we ladies who – for want of a better phrase, *have been round the block a few times* – no, let me finish – we are walking proof that it doesn't happen very often – and in some cases, never.'

'True,' says Céline wistfully.

'We're so busy proving to the world how capable and independent we are, that we can overlook the very thing that could bring us lasting happiness.'

'But perhaps we all expect too much from life.'

'If guess if life were easy it would be boring and we wouldn't grow and develop.'

'Anyway, girls,' says Lily, lifting the mood. 'I wanted to wait until we were all together to share my news.'

We look at her wide-eyed. 'Go on. Don't keep us in suspense.'

'I've got a new job!'

'But you've got a job.'

'This is a volunteer job at the stables, supporting children with disabilities.'

'Wow. How did that come about?'

Lily shrugs. 'I used to ride as a child, and since Nick . . . well, I've been feeling I want to give something back, get involved in some kind of rewarding project.'

'You mean serving meals at thirty-two thousand isn't rewarding?' quips Rachel.

'I still love flying, but for a long time I've felt there's something missing. I've helped out at the stables a couple of times now and I love it. I guess it's helping me too.'

'I would like to make a toast,' says Céline, topping up everyone's glasses. 'To my wonderful friends for rescuing me. And to happy new beginnings for us all. Cheers!'

Chapter 9

Flying Solo

As the train gathers speed, I feel light-headed.

Closing my eyes, I unleash the thousands of lines, cues, stage directions, and quick scene changes of the last eight weeks, allowing them to flow out of my brain, through the window, and into the ether.

I am hurtling towards the Lake District, to indulge in long walks, yoga, and meditation in the company of . . . ME. After all the craziness, I need to press the pause button, to be on my own for a while; to recharge, to reflect, to plan, and find inspiration to finally finish writing my one-woman show, which currently comprises just one page of script.

This is another first for me; not so long ago the thought of going on a solitary mini break would have been my worst nightmare, making me feel exposed and self-conscious, but today I'm actually excited at the prospect.

'We are now approaching Oxenholme station. Oxenholme station, the next stop.'

Google Maps leads me along a main road, then left into a tree-lined, gravel drive. Sunlight flickers through the archway of heavy branches, the stillness broken only by falling droplets of rain from the earlier shower.

I turn the corner and gasp. The website hadn't prepared me for the spectacular grandeur of The Forest Hill Hotel & Spa, a converted Gothic mansion, surrounded by beautifully landscaped gardens, set against a dramatic backdrop of towering mountains. This is how the new Mrs de Winter in *Rebecca* must have felt when she first laid eyes on Manderley.

No Mrs Danvers to welcome me, but Max, the elderly proprietor, who greets me from across the reception desk with a smile.

After I've signed in, he unhooks a key from the rack, picks up my rucksack, and leads me up the wide, creaking staircase.

'You're in the Sycamore Suite,' he says, holding open the studded, panelled door and gesturing for me to enter.

I absorb my surroundings: very olde-worlde, dominated by a wonderfully opulent, four-poster bed and huge fireplace. There's a chaise longue in rich fabric and lots of scatter cushions in country house colours. There's a tiled washstand in one corner, complete with pitcher and bowl (none of your £24.99-shopping-channel tat, but the real deal), and dried lavender and a sampler hanging on the wall: *Catharine Alexander. Born in the Year of our Lord 1692.*

'Dinner's served between seven and nine-thirty,' says Max. 'And the spa is open from eight to eight. If you need anything just dial zero for reception. Enjoy your stay.'

He hesitates for a moment. Do I detect a pitying look fleeting across his face? I'm about to explain that I've come here alone through choice, in search of peace and quiet in which to write, but then why should I feel the need to explain my solo status?

'Thank you. It's perfect.'

He bows his head, smiles, and pulls the door to.

I kick off my trainers and socks, and like an excited child, I run around, wallowing in the luxury I took for granted back in my flying days.

I peek in the bathroom, which has one of those traditional,

roll-top, cast-iron baths with clawed feet. My radar homes in on the abundance of miniature bottles of bubble bath, shampoo, cleanser, toner, and moisturiser; and not the cheapo stuff either – the Molton Brown range, no less (my favourite) – all there for the swiping.

There are even His and Hers slippers with *FHH* stitched in green and gold thread. I wonder if you're allowed to keep those. I mean, it wouldn't be very hygienic to pass them on from one guest to another, would it? You could end up with verrucas or athlete's foot. Oh, and as for the fluffy, white, monogrammed, towelling bathrobes hanging on the back of the door . . . don't you dare even think about it, Emily Forsyth. That would be downright dishonest and not worth the risk of being rumbled.

I wander back into the bedroom, unhook the crooked, latticed window, and look out across the manicured lawn to the velvety hills beyond, dotted with grazing sheep, like balls of cotton wool. Not a rambler in sight, and the only sounds a rushing stream, a bleating chorus, and distant birdsong.

I rip open the complimentary chocs, uncork the half bottle of champagne and recline on the chaise longue, my eyes scanning the list of spa treatments. Now, which one will I choose?

* * *

Tired, sore feet? Yep.

Then why not try our fish pedicure? What?

Relax while they nibble dead and dry skin, leaving your feet feeling soft and invigorated. Eeuw!

I decide to play it safe and opt for the Thalasso Seaweed Wrap, followed by a paddle in the outdoor infinity pool, then dinner.

'Good evening, madam,' says the mâitre d'. 'Room number please.'

'Hi. I'm in room ten.'

'Ah yes, table for one,' he says, checking his list. 'This way please.'

I order a glass of red and study the menu. Oh, dauphinoise potatoes, mangetout, beef filet in a red wine jus, how I have missed you! I have been trapped in a world of frozen ready meals, soggy pre-prepared salads, and late-night pizzas for the last eight weeks, and I never want to go back there.

* * *

I awake next morning with the autumn sun on my face, the white muslin curtains swelling like sails in the breeze. I sit up in bed, rub my eyes awake, and let out a startled yelp at the scary vision in the wardrobe mirror opposite.

It's gone nine. So much for my early morning dip and Himalayan sauna.

I order continental breakfast from room service, take a shower, pull on my hiking gear, pack my rucksack, and head downstairs.

'Good morning,' says Max, handing me my freshly prepared packed lunch. 'Forecast is good. You're lucky. It rained every day last week.'

'Thanks, Max. I'll be back in time for dinner.'

He reaches under the desk and produces a pair of binoculars.

'As it's such a clear day, I thought you might like to borrow these.'

'Thank you.'

Placing the binoculars around my neck, map in hand, I exit the back lawn via the imposing iron gate, over an ancient stone-built bridge which leads me across a gurgling stream. A pheasant darts out of the hedgerow – frantically flapping its wings – then soars upwards, coming to land on a tangle of boulders, high above me.

The springy grass soon gives way to rough and rocky terrain. As the path begins to rise up steeply, I start to feel as if I'm wearing a corset, the laces being pulled tighter with every step I take, nasty blisters from my rarely worn climbing boots stinging my heels.

I clamber over a craggy ridge and collapse on a cushion of

lilac heather, the warm sun on my face. I open my eyes and study the billowy cloud formations. The word *nuvole* falls from my lips. *Nuvole*. How beautiful is the Italian word for clouds: light, floating, fluttery, just like in the Wordsworth poem.

My thoughts then turn to Francesco and my heart speeds up again. I look at my watch. He'll be in the market now, chatting with the stallholders, choosing the ingredients for tonight's menu.

I've missed my Italian lessons, the banter, the silliness. Can we pick up from where we left off, or will eight weeks apart have changed us? I can feel myself falling for this man, but romance only complicates things, and I'm determined not to allow myself to be derailed like before.

I haul myself up, scramble and claw my way to the top, draw the binoculars to my face, and scan Scafell mountain range, their summits poking through the band of hovering mist, like islands in the sky.

I have gasped in awe at the Rockies, the Himalayas, and the Grand Canyon, but through a tiny porthole at thirty-two thousand feet, they seemed unreal: remote, unattainable, aloof, inanimate. These mountains leap out at you, inviting you to reach out and touch their rough, rugged edges, to explore their rock faces and scree gullies, to dip your feet in their icy, tumbling waters, shelter in their shadowy crevasses, be bewitched by their unusual, brooding shapes, daunted by their noble magnificence. They are very much alive, their colours and moods constantly changing with the elements.

Forget the sun rising over Hong Kong harbour, the Manhattan skyline from the Empire State, or the thunder of the mighty Niagara Falls; there is nowhere on earth that I would rather be than here, atop Crinkle Crags, overlooking Bowfell and the Langdale Pikes, like felt cut-outs against a painted sky. I am drunk with fresh air and wonderment, possessed by a mad desire to run in the grass without any shoes, à la Julie Andrews.

I reflect on the last two months: the wobbly scenery, the terrible wigs, and the mixed-up lines, so stressful and torturous at the time.

But thanks to that chaotic mermaid, mature bride, farcical maid, and my chain-smoking, theatrical landlady, I now have the material and characters I've been searching for to write my one-woman comedy.

* * *

Back at the hotel, I light the honeysuckle-scented candles, find some Einaudi on Spotify and languish in the deep bath, intoxicated by the sweet, jasmine-fragranced vapour rising from the steaming water.

This is exactly how my fifteen-year-old self imagined an actress's life to be: floating in a flower-filled bath after a hard day's filming, reclining on a chaise longue, sipping champagne, eating fine food, sleeping in a four-poster bed, taking a dip in the private pool, being pampered with manicures, pedicures, facials, and expensive creams.

The now forty-two-year-old me is under no such illusion, but is allowing herself to relive that teenage dream for just a few more hours.

I hobble into the stone-walled dining room, bravely smiling through my pain at the other residents who bid me, 'Good evening.'

The moment I sit down on the carved chair, I slip off my heels and wiggle my throbbing toes.

As the waiter pours me a glass of wine, I peer at the faded tapestry suspended from a black, wrought-iron, fleur-de-lis rail next to my table. He tells me an army of local women wove this by hand some four hundred years ago, and that it represents the people and the community of the village. On closer inspection I am able to decipher the hotel (formerly the manor house), the church, the higgledy-piggledy farmers' cottages, surrounded by a tumult of peaks – Crinkle Crags, Bowfell, and Pike o' Blisco – the very same ones I've scrambled and clawed my way up, and slipped and slithered down.

They may be responsible for my aching limbs, calloused heels, and black toenail, yet they have stirred something in my soul. I wonder if this is the same 'something' that motivated those local women long ago, that inspired Wordsworth to write poetry, and that has given me the appetite of a hungry hippo.

Dinner over, I wander into the subtly lit garden, my feet cooled by the damp grass. I pass the tiered fountain, sparkling water spouting from a chubby cherub's mouth, on into the peaceful sanctuary of the verdant, aromatic herb garden, filled with rosemary, sage, thyme, chives, bay, and parsley. The heavily laden apple and plum trees, watched over by the moss-coated statue of the goddess Pomona, cast mystical shadows on the lawn.

I follow the illuminated pathway to a covered, ivy-clad alcove, where I settle in with a blanket on a corner sofa and open my notebook.

All at once my concentration is broken when, without warning, a low-flying jet from the nearby RAF station shoots across the black, star-spangled sky. The title I've been searching for pings into my brain . . .

Winging It
A Comedy in Two Acts

* * *

Thirty-six hours later, I'm walking through the iron gates for the final time and down the driveway towards the main road.

I stop, turn, and give one last, long, respectful look at the Langdale Pikes: strong, magisterial, graceful, and wise.

The last few days have instilled in me an inner peace and strength, which I will doubtless need to tap into as I re-enter the real world in just a few hours' time.

I take my seat in the quiet coach, the doors beep shut, and we're off, London-bound. The mauve and green hills flicker through my reflection and are then snatched away too soon.

I lean back into the headrest, close my eyes, and slip into a dreamy, cinematic state . . .

I'm once more at the summit of Crinkle Crags, looking out over Great Langdale, cut to Red Tarn lake, where I *finally* learned to swim (yay!), pan over to Fifth Avenue, downtown Manhattan . . .

CARRIE: *Em, honey, what* are *you wearing?*
SAMANTHA: *You'll never get a man looking like that.*
MIRANDA: *What happened to you?*
CHARLOTTE: *We're taking you shopping, hon.*

I awake with a jolt, painfully aware of several sets of scornful eyes upon me, the *Sex and the City* theme tune blaring from the overhead rack. I leap out of my seat, grab my bag, and pull out my phone.

'Hello,' I whisper.

'Lionel here. Got a casting for you, darling. It's . . .'

'Don't tell me; it's tomorrow.'

'Yes, how did you know? Anyway, someone . . .'

'Let me see, someone has dropped out at the last minute?'

'Their loss *could* be your gain.'

'Oh, Lionel, I . . .'

'No, let me finish. It's for a major tour of *Stepping Out*!'

'Isn't that about tap dancing?'

'Yes, but . . .'

'But I can't tap dance.'

'Doesn't matter, darling. You're up for the role of Andy, the tall, drippy one with no co-ordination. You're perfect.'

'Thanks.'

'Can't seem to find the relevant bit of script, but you'll be fine.

She doesn't say much.'

Past experience is teaching me not to go wild with excitement at Lionel's this-could-be-the-one casting calls. But then Portia's words ring in my ears. I've nothing to lose, besides which, it's all very well dreaming of producing and performing my own play, but even a one-woman show requires a venue, lighting, sound, publicity, and front of house staff, and my waitress's wage plus tips only just about covers my rent and living expenses. So, putting on my cheery, positive voice, I say, 'Great! Where's the casting?'

Chapter 10

Flying Blind

Drawing a deep breath I enter the doors of the drill hall. Think positive, girl! As Lionel always says, this could be the one, the audition that will lead to the lucky break you've been waiting for.

I toss my head and stride purposefully ahead, following the clickety-clack sound of tap shoes on wood.

A woman of around fifty, with mad hair and hula-hoop earrings, ticks off my name and takes my picture.

As I emerge through the double doors into the rehearsal room, I find myself in a scene straight from *A Chorus Line*: swarms of intense, highly trained hoofers in holey, faded dance gear arch their backs and touch their toes, some launching into little routines, spinning like tops, arms outstretched, oblivious to everyone around them. You can almost taste the adrenaline, the passion, the hope, the rivalry. I catch sight of myself in the full-length mirror opposite, all startled and skinny-legged, like a prize turkey.

I look around in search of other obvious non-dancers who might be up for the same role, but no one seems to fit that description.

Neville, the spray-tanned chief choreographer glides into the room, like a ship in full sail.

'Right, everybody, can I have a bit of hush, please? Thank you. I'm going to split you into two groups. Group A will work with me and group B with Trixy here.' (She of the big hair and earrings.)

'We're going to take you through a short and simple routine, which you'll perform to Peter – the director – and the rest of the choreography team. Those selected for the next stage will then be asked to read from the script. Any questions? Good. So . . .'

'Excuse me,' I say, half raising my hand.

Everyone turns to look at me.

'Yes?'

'I think I may be in the wrong place. I'm up for the role of Andy?'

'No, you're in the right place, darling. So, I'm going to divide you into two groups . . .'

I'm seconded to Team Neville with about twenty others, many of whom know one another.

'Darling! Mwah, mwah. How *are* you? What have you been doing since *Les Mis*?'

'Touring in *Joseph* – *again*.'

'I couldn't face another six months of *Hairspray*, so I've been resting, having some *me* time.'

'Mmm, I know what you mean. I was getting to the stage in *Phantom* where I was sleepwalking the routines.'

It's at this point I feel the panic and confusion start to bubble inside me.

'Now pay attention!' commands Neville, clapping his hands and striking a dramatic pose. 'Watch carefully, please. Okay, Julian, from the top,' he says, nodding in the direction of the pianist.

'Shuffle, hop, step, tap, sliiide, sliiide, kick, turn, cramp roll, shuffle, hop . . .'

Everyone starts to quietly mirror his steps in intense concentration.

'Right now, I'll do it once more, but this time I want you all to shadow me, so form a line behind me . . .'

'Excuse me,' I blurt out, my voice echoing around the hall.

'Yesss?' hisses Neville impatiently.

'Does Andy do the same dance steps as everyone else?'

'Does Andy . . .? Well, of course she does.' His voice is now caught somewhere between amused and irritated.

'Thank you, Julian. And five, six, seven, eight . . . shuffle, hop, step, tap, sliiide, sliiide . . .'

All too quickly it becomes a blur, as my brain staunchly refuses to cooperate with my body. Shuffle, hop, step, tap, kick, step, no, slide, shuffle, no, turn . . . aargh!

'Everyone got it?'

I clear my throat and tentatively put my hand up again, but then the door bursts open and the other group clatter in noisily, practising their little kicks and turns. I detest their serene confidence, their smugness.

I raise my hand once more, but yet again I am upstaged: this time by the arrival of the panel. As they take their seats behind the trestle table, the only sounds to be heard are the shuffling of CVs and photographs, accompanied by the glug-glug of mineral water being poured. Eventually they look up at us grim-faced, as much as if to say, *Well, go on then, show us what you're made of!*

'Okey-dokey, everyone ready?' calls Neville enthusiastically, flicking his silk scarf over his shoulder and flinging his arms wide.

'We'll have Group A first, please. Now remember, try to look as if you're enjoying it, and don't forget to give it some *razzmatazz*!'

I reluctantly drag myself to my feet, then shuffle along the back row until I am safely tucked behind a tall, willowy creature, who doubtless knows what she's doing.

'And when you're ready, Julian, from the top, thank you!'

'And five, six, seven, eight . . .'

It only takes a couple of bars of 'Steppin' Out with My Baby', before I'm a step behind, and why, oh why do I keep on turning the opposite way to everyone else? Gotta stop looking in the mirror . . . oops . . . now I've collided with the girl to my left. I duck, narrowly missing an extended arm belonging to the *Phantom* dancer in full spin before me. She darts me an icy glare. I now have a stitch in my side and have absolutely no idea what my feet are doing.

Julian ends the piece with a flourish, and we make way for Group B, who perform the routine with assured ease.

We stand about nervously as the panel scribble notes, then huddle together, whispering and pointing.

I fix my awkward gaze on a frantic bluebottle, buzzing about the windowpane, desperately seeking an escape route. What I'd give to be atop Crinkle Crags now.

'First of all, I'd like to thank everyone for coming,' booms the director. 'It's a difficult decision and I wish we could take you all . . .'

Come off it, Peter, let's be honest, don't you mean all but the red-faced, toe-tied, middle-aged clodhopper in the back row? I am among those called for elimination. Well, there's a surprise.

'Thank you very much for coming . . .' Blah, blah, blah . . .

Oh *God*, get me out of here NOW.

I don't hang around for the group-hugging, kissing, and sympathetic exchange of words, opting instead to trip out of the door to the changing room as fast as my shiny, new tap shoes will carry me.

Never have the busy streets felt so safe and welcoming. I walk around a bit, savouring my anonymity.

I'm about to nip into Costa when I notice the Lamb & Flag pub across the street.

I dive through its doors and order a G&T – a double – knocking it back in one, then slamming down the glass on the bar, like they do in gritty TV dramas.

I tell myself to stay calm. Fuelled by Dutch courage, I dial Lionel's number.

'Didn't I tell you, darling?' he says breezily. 'The actress who plays Andy also covers the role of Mavis, the dance teacher?'

'No, Lionel. You left out that tiny bit of information.'

'Sorry, darling. Anyway, how did it go?'

If I had another agent fighting for my business then I'd fire him, but I don't, so we are bound together – unless he fires me first, of course.

On the tube to Richmond I take out the Wish List I wrote after the shopping channel fiasco. I unfold it carefully and make a small amendment:

> Find ~~an agent.~~ a <u>better</u> agent.
> Do interesting work that fulfils me.
> Write and perform my own play.
> Learn to live in the moment.
> Find inner peace.

Finding a new agent is not as easy as it sounds. They have to see you perform, and without an agent it's nigh on impossible to get a job. There's only one thing for it: I will have to take matters into my own hands and follow Lily's advice by getting my one-woman show on the road. Quite how, where, or when, I haven't a clue, but it's no good waiting for something to happen, whingeing about Lionel or the fact that there's a lack of roles for older actresses. Time to take control.

> *The fault is not in our stars, but in ourselves.*
> ~ William Shakespeare

* * *

I collect my bike from the station and puff and pant my way up the hill.

As the green, white, and red awning begins to appear, the anger,

154

stress, and embarrassment of earlier is forgotten.

I peer through the glass and tap on the window. Luigi shuffles over from behind the bar, unlocks the door, and flings it open, sending the brass bell jingling.

'*Benvenuta, cara!*' he says, hugging me tight. 'We have missed our *piccola inglese.*'

'I've missed you all too,' I reply, removing my helmet and kissing his cheeks.

'*Ciao!*' says Carla, appearing at the top of the stairs, blowing me kisses, hair in rollers.

'*Ciao!*'

The aroma of fresh coffee, the sounds of Andrea Bocelli singing quietly in the background, the red gingham tablecloths, the piano in the corner, the candelabra, the Italian classic movie posters: *Il Postino*, *Cinema Paradiso*, and *La Dolce Vita*, all so reassuringly familiar. I run my hand along the back of one of the rustic chairs, happy to be home.

I hang up my jacket and helmet, change my shoes, put on some lippy, check my hair, and drawing a deep breath, I enter the kitchen, heart hammering.

Francesco has his back to me, head bent over the sink.

'Francesco. *Ciao.* I'm back!'

He swings round to face me, holding a giant sea bass.

'*E*-milee!'

My insides do a loop-the-loop as he kisses my cheeks, the smell of Dolce & Gabbana mixed with fish wafting up my nose.

I fall back into the role of server with ease. I know my way around here, am sure of my lines, and feel valued, nurtured, and safe.

Over the next few weeks, Francesco and I meet every day at Tamino's. The Italian lessons have been put on hold again while I write and rehearse lines for my play.

Poor Francesco. It must be driving him crazy, listening to me repeating the same dialogue over and over, like a broken record, while he prompts me whenever my mind goes blank.

'But I like to listen to you,' he always retorts earnestly, in that severely seductive accent of his, making it even more difficult for me to focus. 'And this help my English too.'

I often wonder if this is all a waste of time, as so far I haven't found a suitable venue that doesn't charge extortionate insurance and staffing costs. Even if I do find somewhere, how many agents and casting directors will turn up? I sent forty invitations to *Three Sisters* and not one replied, let alone came.

'I have an idea,' Francesco pipes up one afternoon as we are observing the deer feeding on the chestnuts in Richmond Park.

'Hmm?' I say distractedly, head nestling further into his shoulder.

'*Cena con spettacolo!*'

'Dinner with …?'

'Dinner show,' he says, turning me to face him, eyes alight.

'I don't understand.'

He tells me about this wonderful place in Venice which offers a dining and entertainment experience.

'Do you think Luigi will agree?'

'Why no? Maybe is good for the restaurant.'

'You, Francesco, are a genius!' I say, high-fiving him. We lock fingers then he pulls me towards him and kisses me gently.

'Maybe one day I take you to this restaurant, *sì*?'

'I'd like that,' I say, lost in his gaze, my heart pounding so hard I'm sure he can feel it.

* * *

'Luigi,' I venture that evening when I arrive for my shift.

'*Sì, cara?*'

'You once said if I needed anything to just ask.'

'*Sì.*'

'Well, there is something. It's just a crazy idea and you don't

156

have to agree, but I thought it was worth asking . . .'

'*Al punto, per favore!* To the point, please!' he says, chalk in hand as he writes the specials of the day on the blackboard.

I put the idea of Dinner Theatre to him, he checks the bookings diary, and that night – after the last customers have left – we toast Il Mulino's first Dinner Theatre Experience to welcome in the New Year on 5 January. Heelp!

* * *

I eventually climb into bed at 2 a.m., head buzzing with lists of things to do in the next couple of months.

I've come up with a cunning plan of how to lure agents and casting directors to my play: the invitation will include a welcome drink, set menu, and a bottle of wine. (Drinks courtesy of the ever supportive Luigi, who says the event may well attract new clients.)

8 tables x 2 covers per table @ £50.00 = £800.00. Yikes.

There's an obvious solution to this financial conundrum: find a daytime job for a few weeks . . .

* * *

I scrutinise the giant custard blob staring back at me in the full-length mirror and give a little start. I am wearing green tights with matching pixie boots, a yellow, hooped tunic with latticework design, complemented by a green tuft strapped to my head.

The changing room curtains swish open.

'Perfect fit,' says the wardrobe supervisor at Peach Promotions, looking me up and down. 'Could have been made for you.'

'Gee, thanks,' I say, the half-smile on my face disintegrating into a look of disgust.

Desperation has led me to join a promotions agency, offering around £300 per week after NI and tax. Three weeks and boom, dinner money sorted. What if nobody shows? 'Nothing ventured, nothing gained,' as the old saying goes. How many more times must I remind myself of this, I wonder.

While other women my age are dashing for trains in business suits, lip gloss, and high heels on their way to important meetings, I have rolled up at Waterloo station this morning dressed as a pineapple to promote a new brand of fruit juice.

I take up position on the concourse, waiting for battle to commence. I peer up at the clock: 7.05. I lower my gaze and wave to the orange and the strawberry, loitering by Lush. There's an apple reading a newspaper by WHSmith, and I realise things could have been much, much worse, as I spy the one in the banana costume pacing up and down outside Accessorize.

God, I hope no one I know passes by.

The station is starting to fill up now. I pick up my tray of Caribbean Crush from the tropical-coloured stand and brace myself.

'Good morning! I'm Pattie Pineapple. Would you like to taste a glass of Caribbean Crush to set you up for the day? It has all the vitamins you need . . .'

As the rush hour gains momentum, the gentle flow of sedate travellers turns into an ugly stampede. As fast as I can replenish my tray, the samples are snatched by a sea of greedy, clamouring commuters, sprinting full pelt for ready-to-depart trains.

I soon abandon my carefully learned spiel, realising I might just as well be saying,

Would you like to taste a glass of extra strong laxative? Guaranteed to make you go ten times a day.

The bulbous design of the costume makes me rather unsteady, so when I'm struck by a briefcase at high speed, I topple over, my green-clad legs flailing in the air, Caribbean Crush all over the concourse. I squeeze my eyes tightly shut and prepare to be trampled to death. What a way to go, dressed as a piece of fruit. I'd always had something a little more glamorous in mind.

'Here, hold onto me,' comes a deep, cultured voice at my side. My eyes focus on a pair of shiny, black, lace-up, city-slicker shoes, attached to charcoal tweed legs. The stranger slides his strong hands under my armpits, and I sag against him, knees buckling. Slowly, steadily, I am raised from the ground, like a sunken ship.

'Are you okay?' he says, coming round to face me, firmly gripping my shoulders.

'Yes, I'm fine, thank you,' I mumble, nails digging into my palms in acute embarrassment.

'Take care.' He smiles, handing me my sticky tray. I blush the colour of Caribbean Crush.

'Thank you, I will. This isn't my normal job . . . I don't usually go around . . .'

'Gotta dash,' he says, stealing a sideways glance at the departure board.

'. . . dressed like this. Bye.'

I bribe the lady who works at the information desk with Caribbean Crush, and she allows me to prop myself up there during busy periods to avoid any further mishaps. I've also cunningly hidden the wire to my earphones in my costume, so that I can listen to my lines while handing out samples.

With the temperature dropping as we move into winter, I'm grateful for the switch to playing Mummy Bear in a honey promotion for the final two weeks. The faux-fur costume keeps me cosy and warm on that freezing cold concourse, although the papier-mâché head has brought me out in spots.

* * *

I try with all my might to visualise a packed restaurant, a standing ovation, agents vying for my business, but with just one firm acceptance so far (from Portia, my old drama teacher), my old friend self-doubt has made an unwelcome return. Has all this effort been for nothing? Is it too late to cancel? What if Lionel finds out what I've been up to? I could end up with no agent at all.

I ration myself to just two email checks a day and try to focus on more rehearsal and Christmas.

Mum wasn't too happy when I told her that I can only stay for a few days.

To appease her, I found myself explaining that I'd been cast as the lead in a London play and have an intense rehearsal schedule – actually, I think the words *West End* popped out unintentionally. It then took several more phone calls to dissuade her from flying over for my opening night. I've definitely jinxed the evening now.

Luigi and I have worked out the seating arrangements and the set menu for the guests. Lily and Céline have volunteered to be front of house. (Rachel will be in the Maldives with husband Dave celebrating their wedding anniversary.) Luke has offered to play interlude music, accompanied by Carla, and lighting is courtesy of Francesco, who has given me an early Christmas present of fifty hand-crafted candles from Sorrento. Lighting rigs are too expensive to hire, and I want to keep it simple and intimate, like in Shakespeare's day.

I promise myself that if only Portia and a handful of others turn up, we'll all still have a great night and I won't let it ruin the start of a new year.

Don't get me wrong. I like Christmas, but being bombarded with cheesy holiday hits in the run-up to the big day sometimes makes me want to knock over the nearest Christmas tree and head for the emergency exit, screaming.

So how come, when these same songs are sung in Italian, I feel all cosy and Christmassy inside?

Il Mulino's secret is in the simplicity: the natural cone wreath hanging on the door; the candles, the boxes of panettone, and woven willow stars dangling from the ceiling; the traditional, hand-made nativity scene made by Sergio's children; the warm atmosphere, made warmer by merry people enjoying good food and wine – no crass commercialism here, no office party drunks letting off poppers while singing along to Slade's 'Merry Xmas Everybody' and exchanging tacky gifts from Secret Santa, like *Grow Your Own Boyfriend* or *Penis Pasta*.

Francesco and Nonna Rosa have prepared a typical Christmas Eve meal for us to celebrate our last shift before the New Year. Traditionally Christmas Eve is a day when you eat light food (normally fish) to give your stomach a rest before the next day's lunch.

I don't see anything light about the huge platter of calamari, swordfish, tuna, salmon, and eel before me. I won't be trying the eel again though, particularly after Francesco tells me it was alive and kicking just one hour ago.

'I'd like to propose a toast to you all,' says Luigi, rising unsteadily to his feet. 'And to absent friends. *Salute!*'

'*Salute!*'

'*Buon Natale!*'

'How is Sergio doing now?' I ask.

Luigi shrugs. 'No bad. He is with his family in Sicily. I tell him not to worry about us, but to get better.'

Carla raises her glass.

'To Sergio.'

'Sergio!'

It's gone two by the time we've cleared up and high time I was on my way if I'm to make my early flight in five hours' time.

I bid everyone a *Buon Natale*, my stomach diving into free fall as I realise the next time we meet will be the night of the cabaret dinner.

'I walk with you,' says Francesco, holding the door open.

He tells me he too is flying in a few hours' time to spend Christmas with *la famiglia* in Sorrento. Family? Who is his family? I'm reminded yet again of how little I know about him, despite our growing closeness.

'I have something for you,' he says, producing a beautifully wrapped gift.

'Francesco, that's so kind, but you already gave me a gift . . . I feel awful. With the play and everything I didn't buy . . .'

'*Silenzio,*' he says, putting a finger to his lips, one eyebrow raised sexily. He removes my cycle helmet, his espresso-brown eyes roaming my face. Parting my fringe, he drops a gentle kiss on my forehead, my eyes and lips. I close my eyes, head swimming, heart pounding.

'*Buon Natale, amore,*' he says, plonking my cycle helmet back on my head.

'Merry Christmas,' I whisper, giddy and tingling all over.

Unable to contain my excitement, I stop on Richmond Bridge and rip open his gift: *Sorrento Travel Guide*. There's a message inside:

Un invito . . . F x

Chapter 11

Winging It

'Cooee, poppet! Over here!'

I trawl the sea of expectant faces and drivers' meet-and-greet boards. There, in the midst of them all, are Mum and Dad – Mum waving excitedly, Dad towering over her, subdued as always. They look older, more frail, and I swear Mum has shrunk.

They had often talked of retiring early to the sun, and when Dad suffered a heart attack due to the stresses and strains of running a road haulage business, they were spurred into action before it was too late.

Nowadays Dad spends most of his time on the golf course, while Mum fills her days with yoga, Spanish language, and cookery classes.

'Oh, I have good news for you, darling,' chirrups Mum, turning to me as we pootle along the coastal road towards Dénia. 'According to Lydia, Giles has found himself a lady friend at last, so should be on his best behaviour at the Christmas party. She's called Crystal – or is it Charity, Brian?'

Dad shrugs his shoulders. 'Anyway, it's one of those footballers'-wives type names. We've not met her yet. I can't imagine what she'll be like.'

'I can't *wait*.' I smile, relief washing over me. I'd already decided that were Giles to pinch my bottom or make his usual quips about mile-high club membership this year, he would soon discover the sweet, self-conscious Emily he once knew has changed, and is not to be messed with.

'He's harmless. Don't be so melodramatic,' Ben used to say.

Hah. You wouldn't find Tom Hardy allowing another man to disrespect his woman – nor Francesco Rossi, I'm sure.

'And while we're on the subject of relationships,' continues Mum cagily, 'any word from Ben?'

'No, Mum.' I let out a heavy sigh, eyes boring into the back of Dad's seat.

'Such a shame. I really liked Ben. We both did, didn't we, Brian?'

I meet Dad's gaze in the rear-view mirror. He shakes his head wearily, runs his hand through his non-existent hair, and winks at me.

'I don't know what's wrong with men these days,' she ploughs on. 'But, darling, you know, you've got to make the best of yourself. When you were flying you never went out without make-up and you wore such pretty, feminine things. Now you're always in jeans and your hair makes you look like a man. I used to love it when you swept it up in a chignon: very Grace Kelly. Now, well now, you look like – Joan of Arc's mother.'

'I've changed, Mum. Designer labels, high heels, and manicures aren't me any more. I don't need those things to make me feel good.'

'I know, poppet, but without a proper job, you need to set about finding a man to look after you. Your father and I won't be around forever, and you're not getting any younger,' she says in an anguished tone.

'I don't need a man to look after me,' I say through gritted teeth, staring out of the window. What is it about being single at Christmas? Everything seems heightened. Here am I sitting in the back of my mum and dad's car behaving like a sulky teenager, reminded that most people my age are defrosting the family-sized turkey, baking mince pies, icing the fruit cake, decorating the tree, and wrapping the kids' presents.

Oh dear, things are not getting off to a very good start.

* * *

'I've put you in charge of canapés, poppet,' says Mum, hastily removing her apron, then thrusting two oval silver platters at me as she trots over to the door. 'And, Brian, I'm relying on you to keep people's drinks topped up, and oh, put some party music on – no brass bands or country and western though – some Julio Iglesias would be perfect.'

Before long the champagne corks are popping, crackers are being snapped, and guests are grooving in paper hats to Elvis's version of 'Here Comes Santa Claus'.

Back in cabin crew mode, I glide in between the guests.

'Vol-au-vent, Lydia?' I say, tapping Mum's posh yoga teacher on the shoulder.

'Emily! So lovely you made it home this year. Your mother told me about Ben. Men, eh? Always on the lookout for a younger model. But we middle-aged girls must never give up hope, must we?' She winks, her overly tanned face stretching into a sympathetic smile. 'Aah, you must be Chantelle,' she says, making a beeline for the bleached blonde sporting a cropped top and skirt the size of a Kleenex tissue.

We middle-aged girls? Excuse me! Lydia has to be sixty-five if she's a day.

My nostrils quiver as the unmistakable whiff of Brut drifts disconcertingly by, evoking memories of Christmases past.

'Well, hello!' says Giles in his creepy, innuendo-laden tone, waving his beer glass unsteadily with one hand, while trying unsuccessfully to pinch my bottom with the other. 'Great to see

165

you, old girl! Been on the telly yet? One of these days, eh? Better get your autograph now before you're rich and famous, what?' He guffaws, spraying my face with San Miguel. 'Well, go on, what do you think of my gorgeous lady? Isn't she something?'

'Yes, she seems . . .'

He leans towards me, voice lowering to a confiding whisper. 'And you won't mind me telling you that the sex is . . .'

'Breaded sprout anyone?' I say, beating a hasty retreat with the veggie platter.

'Thanks,' says Chantelle, attempting to scoop up a sprout between her bejewelled acrylic talons.

'Here, let me help you.' I smile, passing her one in a napkin. 'I'm Emily, by the way.'

'Oh, yeah, Giles told me about you,' she says, ejecting bits of almond through her Botoxed lips. 'You're trying to be an actress, right?'

'I . . .'

'Emily's got a leading role in a West End show, haven't you, poppet?' says Mum in a loud voice, butting in. 'That's why she has to fly off so soon.'

'Really? How exciting,' says Lydia. 'Congratulations. We should organise a London theatre break, shouldn't we, Brenda?' Lydia turns to look at Mum.

'Oh, it's a very short run,' I say, swallowing hard.

'We'd better get booked then. Do you hear that, girls? We're organising a weekend in London in the new year to see Emily in her *West End* show. I'll collect names later.'

'Excuse me, I just need to pop upstairs,' I say, breaking into a cold sweat.

I splash my face with cold water, sit on the laundry basket, shut my eyes, and take a few deep breaths. My mind wanders across the Mediterranean Sea to Sorrento, to Francesco, sitting around the Christmas table.

There's a knock at the door. 'Just coming!' I say and head

back down.

'Chantelle was just telling me Giles bought her *two* Christmas presents, the lucky girl,' shouts Lydia tipsily as I descend the stairs. 'But she hasn't told me yet what they are.'

'Well . . . you're lookin' at 'em,' says Chantelle, proudly sticking out her DDs. 'I'd wanted a boob job for ages but couldn't afford it, and Giles said he'd be happy to pay for the op.' (I bet he was.) 'He's a real diamond.'

'How very . . . *sweet*,' guffaws Lydia, pulling at her string of pearls, which snaps and sends the beads scattering all over the floor. 'Oops! I *adore* Julio Iglesias, don't you?'

* * *

'Come on, you two,' I say, collecting the last of the glasses. 'It's gone midnight and you both look exhausted. Why don't you go to bed and I'll finish clearing up?'

My parents exchange a knowing glance.

'Sit down, love,' says Dad tentatively. 'We need to have a little chat.'

'What is it?' I say, panic rising. 'You're not ill again, are you?'

'No, no, love. Nothing like that. It's just . . .' He shuffles awkwardly in his chair.

'Your father and I are worried about your future,' interjects Mum.

'Why?'

'Why? Because you may be over forty, but you're still our little girl, our one and only, and we want you to be happy.'

'But I *am* happy.'

'You can't live like this at your age. I mean, I know you've got this West End theatre job to go back to, but what happens after that? It's all right when you're young, living from hand to mouth, but not now . . . especially now that . . .'

'What? Now that I'm on the shelf, you mean?' I say in a

half-jokey way.

I'm sorely tempted to tell her about Francesco, to fill the sudden cheerless silence, to offer her a morsel of hope that her middle-aged daughter is not going to end up an old maid with whiskers and a cat. But I stop myself in time because I know from experience that I'll be bombarded with questions like, 'Could *he* be THE ONE?'

She'll get her hopes up, only to have them dashed – again.

'Why you gave up flying and your lovely little flat, I'll never know.'

'Because life's short, because I wanted new experiences and don't want to look back when I'm old and think I wish I'd tried that, because . . . because . . .'

'Look, if you got a steady job you could do amateur dramatics in your spare time,' she continues. 'Then you'd have the best of both worlds, wouldn't you?'

'Oh, Mum,' I groan.

'You're capable of so much more. With your degree you could have worked for the Foreign Office or the United Nations even. Couldn't she, Brian?'

'Come on, Brenda,' says Dad, getting up and gently guiding her to the door. 'That's enough. Let's go to bed. You've said your piece. It's Christmas. Don't spoil it.'

'We just want you to be happy, love,' says Dad, lightly kissing my forehead.

'I know.' I nod.

I get why they're saying these things – because they love me and are trying to help – but I don't need rescuing. I'm leading the life I want, and if they can't accept that, then there's nothing I can do to change it.

I pour myself the last of the port, snuggle up on the sofa in the soft glow of the Christmas tree lights, and put on my favourite Christmas movie, *It's A Wonderful Life* with James Stewart. Its powerful messages about love, family, and friends, about putting your heart and soul into what you believe in despite not getting instant results, hold even deeper meaning for me now.

* * *

5 January, Richmond

This is it. No backing out now.

I park my bike in the usual spot. It takes several attempts to secure it as I keep dropping the padlock key. I remind myself that if I can survive weekly rep with only a few hours' rehearsal, then this should be a breeze. But who am I kidding? If it all goes wrong, I can't blame the material, because I wrote it, nor can I blame the actors, because the actor is me.

Will I be able to show my face at Il Mulino again after tonight? There are people, loyal, valued customers, who are paying good money for this. And what about my friends and Luke, giving up their precious time, just so I can indulge myself in some self-promotion?

I feel sick. Tension tightens its grip further as I come face to face with the sandwich board outside the door:

DINNER THEATRE
Tonight at 7.30!
Winging It
A comedy

I'm naturally thrilled the evening's now a sell-out, but to say it's added to my anxiety is an understatement.

I tap on the window and Luigi appears, dressed in a navy-blue suit. He never wears a suit.

'*Buonasera!*' he says, kissing me on each cheek, his aftershave burning my nostrils.

'Luigi! How handsome you look! *Che bello!*'

'Tonight is a very important night,' he replies, waggling his fist.

Luke nods from the piano in the corner, practising his repertoire.

I change into my costume (Rachel's airline uniform) and study my reflection. Suddenly I'm back on board, pushing my trolley down the aisle.

'Chicken or beef, madam? Chicken or beef, sir?'

I enter the kitchen where Francesco and the agency sous-chef are busy preparing the starters, while listening to the football on the radio.

'*Ciao, bella!*' says Francesco, turning down the volume and kissing me on both cheeks. 'How are you feeling?'

I hold up a trembling hand. '*Nervosa.*'

He shrugs his shoulders. 'Don't worry. Enjoy! *Tutto bene!*' Leaning over he whispers, 'You look beautiful.'

'*Grazie, signor,*' I reply, dropping a curtsy and a wink.

I glance at the kitchen clock. My tummy flips over. Just forty-five minutes until curtain up.

'Emily!' calls Luigi from the dining room.

'Girls! Am I pleased to see you!' I say, rushing over to the gang, and we all huddle together.

'Look at the three of us,' says Lily. 'Back in uniform, just like the old days. Tea, coffee?'

'You f'coffee, sir?' we screech simultaneously.

I can feel the knot in the pit of my stomach start to loosen already.

'Ta-dah!' announces Lily, proudly producing a bag containing our props: three seatbelts, oxygen masks, lifejackets, and safety cards, on loan from the crew training department.

'*Buonasera,*' says Carla, appearing at the top of the stairs, dressed in the beautiful red gown she wore for the restaurant opening.

'Carla! Meet Lily and Céline.'

'*Piacere.* Nice to meet you.'

'Lovely to meet you too.'

'Carla!' calls Luke, running his fingers over the piano keys. 'Ready for your vocal warm-up?'

'I love your Italian family already,' whispers Lily.

'But when do we get to meet the fabulous Francesco?' blurts Céline with a twinkly smile.

'Shh. Later,' I say, blushing in spite of myself. 'The guests will be arriving soon. Follow me.' I lead them upstairs for a quick meditation and a group hug.

At seven-thirty on the dot, Luke opens the evening by playing 'Come Fly with Me', Luigi dims the lights and rings the bell, which is Carla's cue.

'Good evening, ladies and gentlemen. *Buonasera, signore e signori.* Welcome on board DaVinci Airlines. In charge of the cabin tonight are . . . Emily, Lily and Céline.' We descend the stairs, each of us taking a small bow to enthusiastic applause.

Carla then gives Luke the nod and he begins playing 'New York, New York' as we launch into our carefully choreographed emergency demo in time to the music . . .

Hysterical laughter, rapturous whoops and cheers ricochet off the walls. We glance at one another, battling to stay in character. Out of the corner of my eye, I spy Francesco in the half-light, leaning against the wall, foot tapping, a tea towel slung over his shoulder. A charge of electricity runs through me.

'Now, please fasten your seatbelts, switch off all electronic devices and enjoy the show!'

* * *

I don't remember much about the last ninety minutes, except for feeling relieved and sad at the same time that it's over. Judging by the audience's response, it couldn't have gone better, and of course the food is never anything less than five-star.

For the post-show party, just in case anyone's still hungry,

Francesco has prepared platters of bruschetta, baked *arancini*, Mediterranean houmous, focaccia, roasted red and yellow peppers, and slices of pizza.

'You were wonderful,' whispers a familiar voice in my ear.

'Portia! Thank you *so* much for coming.'

'You deserve some decent work after this.'

'You're very kind. I missed a line though . . .'

'Don't ever draw attention to that,' she says firmly. 'No one in the audience would have known. When I played Gertrude at the RSC, I beat myself up about missing a whole chunk of dialogue, but no one noticed – including the press. Is Lionel still your agent?'

'Uh-huh.'

'Well, I saw a couple of good agents in the audience tonight, so fingers crossed. Anyway, darling, I mustn't miss the last tube home,' she says, kissing my cheek. 'Thank you for the invite. It was fantastic. Goodnight.'

'Goodnight, Portia.'

'*Auguri!* Congratulations!' says Francesco. 'More wine?'

As he takes my glass, his hand brushes mine and my heart races.

'Emily?'

'Yes?'

I turn to face a tall woman in a cashmere camel coat and silk scarf, silver hair swept up in a chignon.

'Rosalind Holmes,' she says, shaking my hand. 'Holmes and Halford Agency? Got to dash, but I'd like to have a chat with you sometime. Call me,' she says, pressing her business card into my hand.

I waited a day before calling Rosalind. Never having been asked to call an agent before, I didn't know the etiquette. I know you should wait three days before contacting a date, but surely the same rule doesn't apply here?

* * *

'Miss Holmes will see you now,' says the immaculate receptionist, hanging up the phone.

Straightening my skirt, I head towards the glass office, feeling like I'm about to enter the boardroom, to be grilled by Sir Alan.

Rosalind Holmes swivels round in her leather chair to face me.

'Ah, Emily,' she says with a courteous smile, rising from behind her steel desk to shake my hand. 'Thanks for coming,' she continues, pouring me a glass of water and gesturing for me to sit down.

'Thank you for inviting me,' I say, my voice a little shaky.

'Loved the show. Very original. Funny. Tell me, was it semi-autobiographical?'

'I'm afraid I can't lie. Many of those stories are indeed true.'

'I travel all over the world with my work and I tell you, I shall be kinder to cabin crew in future,' she says with a broad smile and a twinkle in her eye.

'It was a great job really.'

'So why did you leave?'

I swallow hard. 'It's . . . it's a long story, but let's just say something happened that gave me the wake-up call I needed.'

'It takes courage and determination to do what you did.'

'Or madness,' I quip.

Rosalind lowers her glasses onto her nose and opens her laptop. 'Have you thought about what your boundaries are?'

'Boundaries?' I look at her nonplussed. 'Do you mean . . . am I happy to appear . . . nude, that kind of thing?'

She smiles. 'I wasn't thinking of that specifically, but have you considered what type of roles you're comfortable with, what your availability is, are you willing to tour, to understudy, to work abroad? What are your long-term goals, Emily?'

Truth is, I'd do anything (except appear nude), but does that smack of desperation?

'I'm open to gaining experience wherever I can and embracing whatever opportunities come my way.'

'Good. I ask only that you are honest with me – and with yourself. Don't accept work you're not comfortable with for fear of not being asked again. If you'd rather stick with straight theatre and not audition for TV or film, that's fine. Just tell me, so we both know where we stand.'

TV? Film? Am I dreaming? Play it cool, Emily.

Rosalind then sashays over to the printer and returns with a document. 'Here's a copy of our terms and conditions. Now go home, give it some careful thought . . .'

Play it cool . . .

'. . . and let me know by the end of the week.'

'I'd love to accept your offer, Rosalind. Today. Thank you.'

Those first few days after the show and the agency meeting, I wake up every morning, feeling rested, relieved that I have no lines to learn, and no commitments, apart from my shifts at the restaurant.

I resume my Italian lessons, go to yoga class, and take long bike rides in Richmond Park with Francesco. Freewheeling down the hill, the wind in my hair, the sun, the rain on my face, I feel happy and free, though I'm still trying so hard not to fall for him as once Sergio returns, will he disappear out of my life? And will my next acting role take me far from him?

I'm checking my phone and email constantly, just in case Rosalind is trying to get in touch. Half of me is relieved she hasn't been in contact yet so I may carry on living in this romantic bubble, but the other half is disappointed. *What is it you want, Emily?* screams my subconscious.

And then she calls.

'Casting for you. Number One Tour to cover the female lead in a period piece. Am emailing you as we speak.'

And then three days later, she calls again.

'They liked you. You start a week Monday. Sending you the contract right now. Any questions, give Becky – my assistant – a call.'

Chapter 12

Careful What You Wish For

I am beginning to worry. There's a dark side to my character emerging that I didn't know was there.

While I'm naturally over the moon and grateful for this job, as the days turn into weeks I'm becoming a teensy-weensy bit frustrated. I know the part now, and while I may not have starred in my own TV series or graced the cover of celebrity mags, dare I say it, I think I could play the role just as well. Does that sound conceited?

Wishing someone to be struck down with laryngitis or a mild tummy bug is one thing, but willing someone's foot to get trapped in a revolving set is something else entirely. Evil. I'm horrified that I'm capable of such a thought.

I breeze through the stage door, clutching the latest copy of *Hello!* and a bag of Jelly Babies.

'Evening, Arthur. Dressing room ten, please.'

'Reckon you'll no' be havin' much time for readin' the night, doll,' he wheezes, glancing at my magazine as he hands me the key.

'Mmm?' I say, signing in, then checking my pigeonhole, mind elsewhere.

'It's no' for me to say,' he says, hoisting a shaggy eyebrow.

I slowly start to climb the spiral staircase, calling in at the green room on the way for a brew.

'Company manager's been looking for you,' grunts one of the lighting guys from behind his *Autocar* magazine.

'Right. Thanks,' I say breezily, spilling milk everywhere, my stomach dropping ten floors. Surely not? I mean, I saw Sophie barely two hours ago. I watched her performance from the darkness of the stage-right wings and she was on fine form, giving her 'I-love-you-but-we-must-part' speech.

It was at that point that I'd decided to make a break for it. Technically, I'm not supposed to leave the building until the curtain comes down, but I've religiously watched and mouthed every performance from the wings of Brighton's Theatre Royal, to this, our final fortnight at The Dukes in Edinburgh. With just five minutes of the matinée left, what could possibly happen to her?

Mistake no. 1: leaving theatre early
Mistake no. 2: gorging on all-you-can-eat buffet
Mistake no. 3: succumbing to large glass of house red
Mistake no. 4: ordering garlic bread
Mistake no. 5: forgetting to switch on mobile phone
Mistake no. 6: arriving five minutes late for 'the half-hour call'

'. . . so, the silly cow's been whisked off to A&E to have it x-rayed. You know what this means?' says Simon, our company manager, running his hand nervously through his mop of unruly hair.

An eerie sensation ripples through my body. Maybe I really do have telekinetic powers. I hadn't intended anything serious to happen – just a minor ailment, something to lay her low for a week, a cold perhaps, allowing Rosalind sufficient time to arrange invitations and tickets for casting directors and producers.

I swallow hard and force my lips into a weak smile. There is an expectant silence. This is the stuff of Hollywood musicals: the leading actress is taken ill, and the understudy has to take over at short notice.

I can do it. I've been practising for months, says the heroine, with an assured toss of her pretty head. *Bravo! More! A star is born!* This is the moment I have waited for, *longed* for all these eight-show weeks, so why do I now have this overwhelming desire to flee the theatre and catch the first National Express coach out of town? Well, apart from my all-consuming guilt, the auditorium will be packed to the rafters with legions of excited fans waiting to see Sophie Butterfield and her co-star, Rick Romano, give their highly acclaimed, headline-grabbing performances as star-crossed lovers, Constance and Enrique.

The fact that their on-stage passion has spilled over into reality has fuelled the public's imagination. The House-Full sign is now a permanent fixture on the pavement, while armies of eager punters camp outside in all weathers, hoping for returns.

Exquisite pairing!
The chemistry between Romano and Butterfield
is electric. Beg, steal or borrow a ticket!
~ The Billingham Gazette

This romantic duo sets the stage alight.
You'd be mad to miss it!
~ The Yorkshire Evening Post

'You up for it?' Simon asks, knowing full well it doesn't matter whether I'm 'up for it' or not. Why else have I been travelling up and down the country, getting paid £500 per week plus touring allowance? So I may sit in my dressing room, stuffing my face with Hobnobs and tea while reading trashy magazines, or to be allowed to finally finish reading *Doctor Zhivago*, which I started during lockdown?

Nah – if it's all the same to you, Simon, I'd rather give it a miss.

'Of cour-hourse!' I reply, with a loud laugh, verging on hysteria.

'Knock 'em dead, girl!' he says with more enthusiasm than he feels, I suspect.

I feel my bottom lip trembling. Oh, my God. This is it. I'm trapped. There's no way out. Stay calm. Deep breaths. STAY CALM. I AM IN CONTROL. I AM A PROFESSIONAL ACTRESS. I CAN DO THIS. I AM IN CONTROL.

'Miss Forsyth to dressing room two *immediately*,' cuts in the wardrobe mistress's calm but commanding voice over the Tannoy. I float downstairs in a daze.

'Arms up!' instructs Doris with a sympathetic smile, as she unravels an eighteen-inch corset. Before you can say 'Mr Darcy', I am stripped of my jumper and jeans and unceremoniously wrapped up like a pound of sausages. She yanks the laces tight. I gasp for air, secretly cursing the waitress for having persuaded me to have the banoffee pie with whipped cream to finish.

'This is your five-minute call,' crackles the stage manager's voice through the speaker, barely audible over the excited laughter and chatter of the unsuspecting audience. 'Five minutes please.'

The show relay is switched off abruptly, and the only sound is Rick gargling in the dressing room next door. I stare at the stranger with big hair and heaving bosom looking back at me. God, I'm scared. My startled gaze falls on a bottle of Bach's Rescue Remedy, sitting among Sophie's numerous cards, flowers, make-up brushes, and other leading lady paraphernalia. *Directions: Pour 4 drops onto the tongue.* Bugger that. This is an emergency. Unscrewing the top, I swig what's left, in a desperate attempt to stop my knees knocking together and my teeth from chattering.

Our doubts are traitors, our doubts are traitors . . .

I toy with my mobile. To phone, or not to phone? Why not? I'm in need of some moral support, and who better to call upon in my hour of need.

'Francesco? Hi! It's Emily.'

'*Cara! Che cosa?* What's going on?'

I feel calmer already. 'I just wanted you to know I'm on!'

'*Scusa?*'

'In five minutes I'm on! Sophie had an accident and I'm on!'

I hear the sound of a pot lid spinning on the tiled floor at the other end of the phone.

'Francesco?'

'*Madonna mia! Fantastico!* Eh, Luigi . . .'

'Ladies and gentlemen, this is your Act One beginners' call. Miss Forsyth and Mr Romano. Act One beginners, please.'

'Got to go. I'll call you later. *Ciao!*'

'Good luck, my darling!'

Oh my God, just hearing my name mentioned in the same breath as Rick Romano's sends a wave of electricity around my body.

Little does he know that some twenty-five years ago, as the object of my teenage passion, his life-sized poster adorned my wall, smiling out at me, encouraging me through my A levels, comforting me when my pet rabbit died, and when Blair Galloway dumped me for Miss Young Farmer 2002.

His hair is flecked with grey now, and he may be sporting a paunch in place of a six-pack, but there's still something effortlessly magnetic and wildly attractive about him. His come-to-bed eyes are bluer than the sky, his seductive smile makes your legs wobble, and that mellifluous voice would make the football results sound like *Fifty Shades of Grey*. The moment I have dreamed of for a quarter of a century has finally arrived, and I'm so overfed and petrified I could vomit, and my breath reeks of garlic. I swipe an extra strong mint from my newly acquired cleavage, and crunch it fiercely.

Other cast members pop their heads round the door.

'Good luck!'

'Break a leg!'

'You'll be *fine!*'

Will I?

With lines swirling around my head, and pizza, pasta, Waldorf salad, red wine, and Rescue Remedy sloshing around my stomach, I lumber towards the stage area, one hand clutching reams of heavy, burgundy velvet, the other the wall. I now know how Mary Queen of Scots must have felt as she made her way to the scaffold. I can almost hear the solitary drum beat accompanying my every step.

As I take up position at the stage-right wings, I let out an almighty burp, the lace of my corset straining to the max. Rick gives me an encouraging thumbs-up from the dimness of prompt corner, opposite. I have only ever rehearsed with the other under-study, and wonder if he actually even knows my name. Until this moment he's probably been thinking I'm one of his many adoring fans, following the show religiously from Woking to Aberdeen.

'We have clearance!' hisses the stage manager. Oh, my God, what's my first line? Breathe, breathe, you can do this. You are ready. *Our doubts are traitors, our doubts are traitors.* What is my first line? Help! I can't remember! It's too late to rush round to prompt corner. Why the hell didn't I bring my script down with me? The lights are going down. *Our doubts are traitors . . .* The stage manager's stepping out in front of the curtains . . .

The excited chitter-chatter gives way to a deathly hush.

'Ladies and gentlemen, may I have your attention please. Due to the indisposition of Miss Sophie Butterfield, the role of Constance at this evening's performance will be played by Miss Emily Forsyth.'

A gargantuan groan reverberates around the auditorium. I feel like the booby prize in a raffle. I can almost hear them tutting and spluttering on their mint imperials, saying things like, 'Never heard of 'er.'

'Has she been on the telly?'

'Bloody cheek! These tickets cost a fortune . . .'

The lights dim and an eerie silence descends. *Our doubts are traitors, our doubts are traitors . . .*

I leave the security of the wings and venture out onto the vast stage. The curtain rises. Someone coughs. Any minute now they are going to start jeering, baying for my blood. All at once I am drowning in a sea of white light. I feel like a prisoner of war caught climbing the perimeter fence, exposed by the stark beam of a searchlight. Sweat trickles down my spine. I step forward, push out my diaphragm, open my mouth to speak and – nothing comes out. *Get a grip!* a voice in my head tells me. My brain is scrambling for the words. *You do know it.*

I can't stand here like something from Madame Tussauds, so out of sheer desperation, am about to throw myself on the floor and burst into floods of tears, hoping Rick will take it as a sign to come on early, when the lines tumble out in the nick of time.

The next two hours are a blur. It's as if I'm on autopilot, drifting through a fog, the dialogue and moves appearing out of nowhere . . .

Then all at once I am standing centre stage, hand in hand with Rick as we take our final bow to a standing ovation. It's over. I've done it, and I didn't muck up my lines or belch or bump into the furniture and no one demanded a refund at the interval.

I close the dressing room door firmly and lean against it, heaving a mighty sigh of relief. Alone at last. I feel giddy and ravenous. I unpin the heavy Antoinette wig, kick off Sophie's two-sizes-too-small shoes, and rip open the bag of Jelly Babies. Those little red, black, and green faces smile back at me sweetly as I devour them greedily. There's a knock at the door. Thank God! That will be Doris coming to unlace me.

'Yesh!' I call, through a mass of congealed strawberry, black-currant, and lime jelly.

'Well done, baby!' drawls Rick, bursting into the room, frilly shirt unbuttoned to the waist, a bottle of bubbly and two glasses clutched in his strong, manly hands.

Whoa! I blink several times, jaw scraping the floor. I need a reality check here. Standing before me is the demigod, Rick Romano: a man adored by millions of women the world over, inviting *me* to drink champagne with him. And here am I, with what resembles a pair of tights on my head, mouth so crammed full of Jelly Babies I'm unable to string two words together.

'Tank yub,' I drool, flashing him a gummy smile.

* * *

'Sophie's broken her foot,' says Simon in a phone call two hours later. 'She'll be in plaster for the next few weeks, so you'll be playing Constance until the end of the run.'

'That's great,' I blurt out. 'I mean, not great that she's broken her foot but . . .'

'We've scheduled an extra rehearsal for you tomorrow afternoon at three on stage. Okay?'

'Yes,' I reply, mind buzzing. 'Yes, of course.'

He hangs up. My stomach heaves. Oh shit, shit, shit. I've got to go through it all again tomorrow night, then another one, two, three . . . twelve performances after that.

'But this is the big chance you wait for, *cara*,' says Francesco during our now routine late-night call. 'It's your dream.'

'I know, I know. I just wish I had more time to prepare.'

'There is never enough time. Live in this moment, *cara*, and appreciate. Golden dreams.'

'*Sogni d'oro*, Francesco.'

I sleep with my script under my pillow, just in case there's any truth in that old theatrical superstition that lines can be passed from pillow to brain.

* * *

Rick is committed to a radio interview this afternoon, so I have to imagine his presence in rehearsal, while the stage manager calls out the lines from the front row in between frantic phone calls. It's fine during my soliloquies, but becomes a little tricky during our big love scene, where I have to embrace and kiss thin air. Even a tennis ball on a stick would have helped.

As the week progresses, I begin to relax into the part more and start to enjoy it, actually listening and reacting to what's being said on stage, instead of thinking, *Oh shit, I was supposed to shut the door when I entered just now, wasn't I?* or *I know it's my line soon, but which line?* The motion sickness I suffered due to the revolving set during my early performances has also settled, and I'm able to get on and off it quite smoothly now.

Rosalind made an unscheduled flying visit with some of her Scottish contacts, but thankfully I didn't know until after the show.

I have been living my acting dream in one of my favourite cities these last few days, not thinking about the past or worrying about the future but focusing on the now. I wish I could hold onto this feeling and keep it safe in a bottle. Then next time I'm having a severe case of what's-to-become-of-me blues, I'd uncork it, close my eyes, and inhale deeply. With just one whiff, my flagging spirits would be instantly revived, and I'd be back on track.

* * *

It's the last Saturday of the run, a two-show day. I arrive back at the theatre that evening for our final performance to find three bouquets of flowers waiting for me – *three!*

I close the dressing room door, switch on the kettle and rip open the envelopes.

Hear you're a triumph, darling!
Thank you & break a leg tonight,
Sophie x

Emily to the rescue!
Thank you for your hard work,
The Producers

Good luck
And thank you ~ Sergio

I let out a sigh, drink my tea then head to the stage for my very last warm-up. I look out into the silent auditorium, studying the glittering chandelier, the detailed plasterwork, the gilt cherubs, the plush red velvet seats, and the Royal Box – which, according to Arthur, is haunted by the Poet of Stockbridge, who was deeply in love with one of the actresses from the theatre, but she was the muse of the Duke of Stockbridge. In a fit of jealousy, the poet threw himself from the Royal Box during a performance and died in front of her.

Before I knew this story, I swear I fleetingly saw the hazy figure of an otherworldly gentleman in a top hat during a matinée, but without my glasses, I can't be absolutely sure.

I wave to the ushers and wish them well before returning to the dressing room to put on my make-up and wig cap.

* * *

As we take our final bow to cheers and whistles, Rick takes hold of my hand and kisses it. I smile as I think how impressed my teen self would be.

I look out into the packed auditorium through blurred eyes. In that instant I am reminded why actors struggle, do mind-numbing day jobs, and sacrifice the material things of life; it is for this. Nothing else has ever given me the same buzz, joy, and satisfaction, or feeling of camaraderie. But while I've now had a taste of where I want to be, I'm not prepared to get there by ruthlessly treading on another actress's toes – or by willing her foot to get trapped in a revolving set, for that matter.

Lily says it's all down to meaningful coincidences – that the universe is constantly sending us signs and guidance, but we need to be open and ready in order for the magic to work. It's taken time for me to fully understand this, but I now realise it's simply down to embracing new opportunities, instead of running for the nearest exit or the first National Express coach out of town.

After farewell company drinks in Rick's dressing room, I stagger out of the stage door, laden with flowers, my vanity case, towel, and yoga mat.

'*Buonasera, signorina!*'

'Francesco! What are you . . ?'

'*Brava, brava!* I am so proud of you,' he cries, picking me up and spinning me round, sending my yoga mat into the path of an inebriated passer-by tucking into a cone of chips.

'Sorry, sorry,' says Francesco, checking the guy's okay.

'Awa' and bile yer heid!' snarls the man, chips still in hand as he sways down the street.

'Excuse me?'

'Bit difficult to translate,' I say, stifling a grin. 'You saw the show? Why didn't you tell me you were coming? Why aren't you at the restaurant?'

'I ask Zio Luigi for two days' holiday. He call the agency and . . ?'

Large spots of rain are beginning to pelt the pavement, so he invites me to take his arm.

'My hotel is in the Royal Mile. Did you eat already?'

'Only a sandwich at the interval.'

'Will you come and have dinner with me?'

'Yes, Francesco. Thank you. I'd like that.'

He hails a cab, which drops us outside The Witchery, a sixteenth-century merchant's house near the castle.

As we enter the reception area, I catch sight of myself, hair like a toilet brush from being trapped inside a wig cap all day, scrubbed face, and ripped jeans. Had I known I was coming here – and with a stylish Italian in tow – I wouldn't have rocked up looking like a homeless woman.

With its dark panelled walls, low, heraldic ceiling, lavish tapestries, and dim candlelight, the dining room makes me feel like I'm walking onto the set of *Wolf Hall*. I half expect Damian Lewis as King Henry to appear and start ordering everyone about.

Over a dinner of Scottish salmon and Italian wine, Francesco opens up to me for the first time, recounting a little about his childhood.

'I live in an apartment, overlooking the sea. I can see Capri from the balcony.' He lets out a wistful sigh. 'My father and I, we make … made many happy adventures together in his boat.'

Apparently, as a teenager, he was a huge fan of Rick Romano's TV cop show, and I confess he was my first major crush after Doctor Zhivago.

'Francesco, I need to ask you something . . .' I blurt out, emboldened by several glasses of Verdicchio.

'What is it, *cara*?' he asks, putting his wine down. I bite my lip, heart accelerating.

'What will happen when Sergio returns?'

'Aah,' he says, the corners of his eyes crinkling. 'Yesterday he told Luigi that he has decided to go back to Sicily to be near family and he will work in his cousin's restaurant.'

'I see. And you?'

'Luigi has asked me to stay at Il Mulino.'

My heart leaps. 'And?'

He shrugs. 'I tell him I think about it . . .'

'I see.'

'. . . and . . .' As he tops up my wine, I try not to drown in his stare.

'. . . I think about it and then I say, "Why not?" The restaurant in Sorrento where I was working closed, so I need a job, I like Richmond, I wish to improve my English, and I have found a beautiful English teacher. She's a bit crazy sometimes, but she make

186

me laugh, and I think maybe, just maybe I begin to fall in love.'

I stifle a yawn.

'*Allora*, I am boring you?' he says with mock indignation.

'What? No! Of course not. *Scusa*. Two-show day.' I swallow hard. 'You were saying?'

'I don't remember,' he teases, signalling for the bill, a cheeky glint in his eye.

After a brief chat with the waiter, he takes my hand and leads me upstairs.

His room is entered via a stone turret staircase. He turns the pewter key, the door creaks open, and as I step inside, I travel back in time, landing somewhere resembling Anne Boleyn's bedchamber; the walls are upholstered in rich red brocade, the canopied bed is opulently draped in velvet, and the gilded ceiling is adorned with thistles and bagpipe-playing angels. I run my fingers along the bookcase and a secret door clicks open, leading to a chapel-like bathroom.

'It's lovely,' I gasp, desperately trying to keep my raging emotions in check, as Francesco drops a gentle kiss on my nose. *Stay cool, Emily.*

His liquid-brown eyes meet mine and I feel something jump inside. He ruffles my hair then slides his arms around my waist and kisses me again.

I let out a small gasp as I feel the warmth of his body pressing against mine.

By the fading glow of candle and firelight, he undresses me slowly and gently, brushing his lips all over me.

Why, oh why did I wear my tattiest Primark underwear today of all days? And dear God, I haven't shaved my legs or armpits since . . . I can't remember.

He laces his long fingers through mine. Our breathing becomes faster.

'Do you have any idea how much I want you, Emily Forsythhh?' he whispers, scooping me up and laying me onto the four-poster, which squeaks loudly. I bite my cheeks, determined not to ruin another *dolce vita* moment, but then I notice his mouth twitching. I let out an involuntary snort and we both end up in a giggling heap on the floor.

* * *

Hardly daring to breathe, I study Francesco's sleeping face: the small scar above his top lip (the result of an altercation with the neighbour's hungry Alsatian dog when, aged five, he carried home steak for Nonna), his slightly bent nose (broken at football as a teenager), his thick hair – inky black and silver in the morning sun's rays.

'*Buongiorno*,' he croaks, pulling me towards him and nuzzling me with his stubbly chin.

The promise I made to him over last night's dinner of a pre-flight, whistle-stop tour of Edinburgh is broken, because it's raining, and he says we can't possibly go outside. And who am I to argue with that?

We therefore make a deal: he will show me Sorrento, and Edinburgh will have to wait – for now.

* * *

As the train whooshes on towards London, I find myself wondering what would have happened if I had met Francesco sooner . . .

SORRENTO, ITALY. A HOT SUMMER'S DAY IN A GARDEN
    OVERLOOKING THE SEA.
A WOMAN IS HANGING OUT WASHING, A CHILD PLAYS
    AT HER FEET.
ALFREDO, THE POSTMAN, PASSES BY ON HIS BICYCLE AND
    WAVES.

ALFREDO: *Buongiorno, Emily! Buongiorno, Aldo!*

EMILY: *Alfredo! Ciao!*

THE SOUND OF CRACKLING GRAVEL AS A 1950s VESPA
    GRINDS TO A HALT.

ALDO (excited): *Babbo! Daddy!*

THE MAN REMOVES HIS HELMET AND RACES TOWARDS
    THEM. HE LIFTS THE CHILD HIGH IN THE AIR, SPINS
    HIM AROUND THEN RUNS TO THE WOMAN, WRAPS HIS
    ARMS AROUND HER, AND KISSES HER.

EMILY: *Ciao, Francesco.*

FRANCESCO: *Ciao, cara. What's for dinner?*

EMILY: *I made your favourite – pasta al forno.*

FRANCESCO: *Mmm. Ti amo, Emily.*

EMILY: *Ti amo, Francesco.*

Stoooop!! What's happening to me? Have I learned nothing from
past mistakes? I knew I shouldn't have let *romanza* back into my
life. If I'm not careful, I'll end up that fragile, pathetic woman
again, sobbing on the sofa into a family-sized tin of chocolates.

My life no longer revolves around a man; my happiness does
not depend on it. So yes, though I think I may be falling for
Francesco Rossi from Sorrento, I am not the same woman I used
to be, willing to give up everything for her man. I AM NOT.

* * *

As if reading my mind, Rosalind calls me the next day.

'Got a casting for you, Em,' she says in her customary blunt
tone. 'Nice little telly. Nineteen-forties period drama. One episode.'

'Wow, that's great. When?'

'Tomorrow morning.'

'Where?'

'Glasgow. I'm forwarding the breakdown to you now.'

'Glasgow? Hello?'

189

The line goes dead.

I spend the next two hours scouring the internet for cheap flights, but they've all been snaffled. The train won't get me there on time, and in any case, the only seats left are in first class, for the same price as a low-cost ticket to New York. It's dawning on me with sinking horror that there's only one solution: missing my shift at Il Mulino and taking the overnight coach from Victoria. Nooooo!

It's 07.30 and I'm staggering around the Glasgow streets half conscious, eyes like slits, mouth like sandpaper, looking for a coffee shop.

The only place open is a depressing greasy spoon, reminiscent of the losers' café on *The Apprentice*.

I order a coffee and study the script: just one page of dialogue, but four days' filming, as the character is in several crowd scenes, reacting to the action with a variety of looks, ranging from withering to firm.

I arrive at the TV studios in good time, so disappear to the ladies' to repair my face and hair, do some deep breathing exercises, and practise my lines and various looks in the mirror.

I return to the reception area, where there's now another candidate waiting nervously.

'Hi,' she says. 'You up for the middle-aged spinster role?'

'Yeah,' I reply, a little affronted. 'You?'

'The fiancée.'

'Ah.'

The door is flung open. 'Emily?'

'Yes, that's me,' I say, standing up, legs wobbly after my night on board the National Express, heart pounding, cheeks flushed.

'Thank you for coming,' says the casting director, pulling out a chair. 'This is Rob, our director.'

Rob stands up and shakes my hand, looking me over with a critical eye. Could I be the middle-aged spinster he's looking for?

'Take a minute to familiarise yourself with this bit of script,' says the casting director.

'Oh, I've prepared the scene you . . .'

'We've had a rewrite, so have a look at this,' she says, pushing a couple of pages across the table.

I fumble in my bag for my glasses.

'Take your time.'

My eyes scan the lines. A mobile rings.

Rob gets up and strides over to the window.

'Yep, yep. No. I don't care if he's not available. Tell him we start shooting next week. That's final.' Throwing his phone onto the table he sits down, turns to me, and says, 'Ready?'

'Ready.'

The red camera light winks at me.

'The key on screen is mental transmission,' Portia told us. 'Be subtle. Don't project. The microphone will hear you. Don't use your body too much. The camera will pick up the tiniest twitch, flicker of the eye. Don't blink. Don't pull faces. Use your brain. Less is more.'

'Good,' says Rob after I've finished. 'I'd like you to do it again, but this time put away the script and if you can't remember the lines, improvise.'

Improvise? Yikes. Come on, remember Branworth Rep? If you can improvise your way through an entire play, then what's two pages?

'Ready,' I say, looking unblinkingly into the eye of the camera.

* * *

One hour later, I'm back wandering the Glasgow streets, killing time until the two o'clock coach.

My phone buzzes, making me jump.

'Hey, *cara*. How did it go?'

'Fine, I think. I did my best. Will I get the part? Who knows? Just the usual "We'll be in touch." That's all.'

'I see you tomorrow night at the restaurant. Bring an overnight bag.'

'Why?'

'You will see. *Ciao.*'

We've just pulled out of a Welcome Break service station, and I'm tucking into my curly cheese sandwich, when my phone rings.

'It's Rosalind.'

'Hi, Rosalind. It went well I think, but whether . . .'

'You got the job.'

'I did?'

'Filming starts next Thursday. I'll send over the schedule and your e-ticket. Well done, darling.'

Whey hey! Even the smell of the chemical toilet and my unwashed, Big Mac-chomping neighbour can't dampen my excitement. My first proper telly, playing an actual character, with lines and a costume, and a backstory, as opposed to a rabbit-in-the-headlights shopping channel presenter.

* * *

'It's only a few lines, guys.'

But my Italian supporters are having none of it.

Luigi says he hasn't felt this excited since Bologna scored against Real Madrid, Nonna Rosa and Carla have prepared a special closing-time supper, and as for my late-night date with Francesco . . . let's just say my Primark pants have been ditched for lacy Intimissimi lingerie.

We toast my role in *Doon Place* with my gift of Laphroaig whisky, and I promise to prepare a feast of haggis, champit tatties, and bashed neeps for them on my return.

The taxi draws up to the Parkway Hotel on Richmond Hill, where Francesco has booked a deluxe room with spectacular views over the Thames. We sit huddled on the balcony, my head nestled into his chest, as we sip champagne and talk until the sun appears, casting an orangey glow over the meadows, the winding river, the moored boats, the trees.

'*Allora*, I had a feeling you would get this job, *cara* . . . But why you look so sad?' Francesco says, lifting my chin and tilting my head to meet his penetrating gaze.

'I wish I could freeze time, that's all,' I say, hastily turning away.

Here I go again. Feeling so pathetic makes me cross. So much for my newfound inner strength, eh? Get a grip, woman! Don't spoil things by getting all serious on him. I've been serenely self-sufficient for ages now, and one romantic fling throws everything into chaos, exposing my needy, insecure side. But then this isn't just a fling, is it? Talk about bad timing!

Gently turning my face towards his, he looks deep into my eyes and whispers, '*Ti amo, cara.*'

My heart races. I hang onto those three little words. He didn't have to say them. Does he really love me, or is he getting carried away by the romance of it all? My feelings for him go far beyond the physical; spiritual even. So why don't I say 'I love you back'?

He stands up, takes my hand, and pulls me towards him. Then, just like a scene from a Richard Curtis movie, he sweeps me up in his arms and carries me through to the bedroom.

Until Francesco no one had ever swept me up before. Ben had a bad back and my previous boyfriend had dodgy knees.

Chapter 13

Doon Place

'Right, that's you done,' says Ailsa from hair and make-up, snapping shut the can of hairspray and removing the towel from around my shoulders. 'Now pop along next door and see Bruce in wardrobe.'

My bloodshot peepers blink several times under the harsh glare of the high-watt bulbs. No girl should ever have to subject her face to foundation and blusher before sunup. Not that I'm complaining – quite the opposite. Call it positive thinking, cosmic ordering, or heaven-sent; four days' all-expenses paid filming at the historic Arbermorie Castle is the perfect distraction to keep my mind off Francesco and the future.

Bruce runs his stubby finger down the call sheet and ticks off my name.

'Now, er . . . Emily, I see Miss MacFarlane as your typical, nineteen-forties village spinster – disappointed by love, bitter, repressed, dowdy, frumpy . . .'

Yep, okay, Bruce, we get the picture. Loud and clear.

'She's definitely a tweeds and brogues sort of wee woman,' he continues, whipping the tape measure from his neck, and swiftly wrapping it around me. He bustles over to a rail of rather drab-looking garments and flicks through them, eventually pulling out a muddy-brown, herringbone-tweed suit.

'Try this on for size,' he says, pulling back the dressing room curtain.

I look at my reflection in the mirror. It's scary. I look like the sort of woman who lectures at the WI and knits toilet roll covers in her spare time. Bruce's arm bursts through, brandishing a suspender belt, a pair of seamed stockings, and clompy, vintage shoes.

'Sorry, dear, we've no size sevens – you'll have to try and squeeze into these, I'm afraid.'

I yank the curtain open.

'Give us a twirl,' he says, hands on hips as he gives me the once-over with his beady eyes. He plonks a battered felt hat firmly on my head. 'There we go! Frumpy spinster personified. The bus will meet you outside,' he says, resuming his ironing.

I am ON LOCATION! I have always wanted to say that. It sounds so glamorous and exciting, doesn't it?

I wipe the condensation from the minibus window with my moth-eaten glove, revealing a rather dreich car park, teeming with hordes of people, huddled round a mobile caff, sipping steaming liquid from polystyrene cups.

A figure in a bright-orange kagoul taps on the door and a hooded face peers round.

'Hi, I'm Jules, the third assistant,' she says breathlessly. 'We're running a bit behind schedule because of the rain, but we'll try not to keep you waiting too long. Help yourself to breakfast.'

'Round up the extras for the busybody/bicycle scene,' crackles her walkie-talkie, and she disappears.

My nervous nausea of earlier has now turned into pangs of hunger, so I make a beeline for the breakfast queue.

Mmm. My tastebuds tingle as the succulent bacon rashers sizzle in the pan. The chef thickly butters the soft, floury bap and slaps the bacon inside, adding a squirt of tomato ketchup, before pressing the top down with his palm. I reach up, like a kid in a sweet shop, and take it from him with both hands. I bite into it, and some of the melted butter, mixed with bacon fat, oozes down my chin. I am in paradise.

'Emily, come with me,' says Jules, suddenly reappearing at my side. 'I'd like you to meet Isobel, who plays Elspeth. You're doing your scene with her, yeah?'

'Fine,' I say, spitting crumbs everywhere. Jules strides off towards a huge trailer, and I teeter after her in my size five-and-a-halfs, cramming in the rest of my bacon roll as I strive to avoid the puddles.

We climb the steps and Jules knocks on the door.

'Come away in, dear,' comes a familiar voice from inside.

'Isobel, this is Emily, who's playing Miss MacFarlane,' says Jules.

'It's an honour,' I say, wiping my greasy fingers on my skirt and dropping a little curtsy. Aargh. Why in God's name did I just do that? She's not the Queen. But then Isobel is a legend in Scotland; she's been in *Doon Place* since it began, and is the only original member of the cast.

Her character has been through two husbands, has four children, seven grandchildren, and survived a war and a chip pan fire.

'You look frozen, dearie,' she says warmly. 'Let's have a wee cuppa and run our lines until they're ready for us.'

Jules's radio bursts into life again.

'I'll pop back when we've finished setting up,' she says.

Isobel may look like your typical, sweet, old granny. But take away the grey wig and padding, and behind that Mrs-Doubtfire exterior is a glamorous, go-getting sixty-something, who drives a Lamborghini, has a toy-boy husband, and is signed up to do the next series of *Strictly Come Dancing*.

'Just ignore the camera, dear, and if you fluff your lines, so what? You can do it again. If you survived weekly rep, then this'll be a doddle, so it will.'

A make-up girl bustles in to re-do us and tuts as her eyes are drawn to a blob of ketchup on my cream blouse.

'Okay, we're ready for you,' pants Jules, popping her head through the window of the trailer.

* * *

'Emily, my darling, can you hear me?' booms Rob through a megaphone at the bottom of the hill.

I give him the thumbs-up.

'Good. Now, on *action*! I want you to cycle like you're a woman on a mission – you're bursting to tell Elspeth that you've just seen the village floozy coming out of Tam MacLeod's house. Stop outside number nineteen, which is where the washing line is, okay? You then deliver your first line over the hedge. Clear?'

'Cool,' I casually cry, as if I'm an old hand at this, stomach churning like a cement mixer.

'Quiet, please! Cameras rolling . . . sound running . . . aaand . . . *action*!'

I swiftly pull my hat down so it's secure, firmly grip the handle-bars, take a deep breath, and I'm off.

'CUT!' roars Rob over the high-pitched squeal of brakes.

One of the crew runs over and hurriedly applies some WD-40. He pushes the bike back up the hill, while I totter behind, aware of several sets of eyes upon me, impatiently waiting to start the scene again. I'm tempted to shout out, *I'm not normally this slow at walking, but they didn't have any shoes to fit me*, but decide against it, as that would sound whingeing and pathetic. I tell myself just to get on with it, and mount the bike again.

'Quiet, please! Cameras rolling . . . sound running . . . aaand . . . CUT! Plane overhead!'

I abort take-off in the nick of time, saving myself from another embarrassing uphill stagger.

We roll again, and as I rattle downhill, I rehearse my first line quickly in my head:

Morning, Elspeth. I was on my way from the kirk, when I saw Jeannie MacLeod coming . . . aargh! . . . I was on my way from the kirk, when I saw Jeannie Frazer coming out of Tam MacLeod's house . . . Morning, Elspeth . . . I apply the brakes, but slither past number nineteen, eventually coming to a halt outside number twenty-seven.

'Cut!'

Someone pokes about the brakes with a spanner, as the technical crew prepare for another take. A make-up lady appears from nowhere and attacks me with a powder puff, tucks in some stray hair, and readjusts my hat.

'Right, can we crack on, folks? I'd like to get this done before the rain comes!' yells Rob, twitching with impatience as he glances up at the storm clouds gathering in the distance.

Huffing and puffing, I mount the bike again. Surely this time . . .

'Quiet, please! Cameras rolling . . . sound running . . . aaand ACTION!'

Morning, Elspeth. I was on my way from the kirk when I saw Jeannie Frazer coming out of Tam MacLeod's house. Morning, Elspeth. I was on my waaaaaay . . .

I'm applying the brakes, but nothing's happening. I fly past a bewildered Elspeth and her line of washing, and am now free-wheeling at dangerously high speed, heading for the huge light reflectors, lamps, crew, and extras at the end of the street. I swing my leg out and drag my foot along the ground, in an attempt to slow myself down, but end up parting company with the bike, falling flat on my face, tweed skirt over my head, stocking tops showing.

'CUTTT!'

I lift my grazed chin, just in time to see Rob smacking his forehead, throwing down his headphones, and storming off the set.

Concerned crew and make-up ladies swarm round.

'I'm fine, really I am,' I lie, forcing myself to my feet, mortified by all the fuss, stockings and pride in shreds. My knees and chin are stinging like mad, and I'm on the brink of tears – more from embarrassment than pain. I am whisked away, cleaned up, and brought a cup of hot, sweet tea.

'If you feel up to it, we'd like to try the scene again as the light's starting to fade,' says Jules with a sympathetic smile. 'And don't worry, we've tested the brakes and they're fine now.'

Poised for take-off, I shut my eyes for a moment, then take a deep breath. My chin is on fire, and my feet are throbbing, but goddammit, I will not be beaten by a wonky, old bone-shaker . . .

As Rob looks through the lens, a hush descends over the smoking chimneys and plastic cobbles of Doon Place.

'Yep, yep, not bad . . . check the gate . . . okay, everyone, thank you. It's a wrap!'

* * *

Back at The Glenfoyle B&B that evening, I lie in the bath, the warm water soothing my aching feet and grazed knees. My taut face cracks into a wide grin as I replay today's blooper in my mind. I wonder if one day it might be salvaged from the cutting room floor and reappear on *When TV Goes Horribly Wrong*. At least I was wearing the 1940s version of Bridget Jones's big pants and not anything too skimpy.

One of the highlights of the day was meeting Isobel. Women like her are an inspiration: comfortable in their own skin, living life to the max, still taking on new challenges, and doing exactly what they want, and not according to some ageist rule book.

There's a ceilidh at the local pub tonight, and Ailsa from hair and make-up has invited me along. I think she feels a bit sorry for me because of the bicycle incident, and it being my first day and all.

I haul myself out of the bath, hobble over to the bed, and look at tomorrow's filming schedule. My pick-up time is 06.30

for various crowd scenes. I wonder if I'll be required to do the withering or the firm gaze. I practise both in the wardrobe mirror.

I glance at the clock. All I really want to do now is run a bath, pull on my jammies, order a takeaway, and watch the latest episode of *MasterChef*.

* * *

Sucking in a deep breath and my stomach, I enter the swing doors of the Tam O'Shanter pub. I duck and dive my way past the maze of whirling revellers, in search of Ailsa et al.

'Yoo-hoo, Emily! We're over here!'

I weave my way over to the large table, where the crew, some of the actors, make-up and wardrobe girls are seated.

Before I've a chance to sit down, Ailsa drags us all up to the dance floor to join in with 'Drops of Brandy'. Admittedly I did a bit of Scottish country dancing at school, but being tall, had always to take the role of the man, so a fat lot of good that is to me now. Ailsa and the locals do their level best to steer us in the right direction, but we are hopeless, like dodgem cars, colliding with one another and causing multiple pile-ups. I've got a stitch in my side, but just when you think it's all over, that diddley-diddley music has a nasty habit of going round and round and round again and again – and again.

Finally it stops, and we stagger back to our table, gasping for air.

'Everyone enjoying themselves?' comes a gravelly Scottish burr behind me.

I swivel round on my bar stool.

'Oh, everyone, this is Duncan, my bro,' says Ailsa breezily.

'Please take your partners for "The Gay Gordons"!' announces the caller.

Duncan holds out his hand to me and says, 'May I have the pleasure?'

Though not as manic as the last reel, there's a twirly bit in 'The

Gay Gordons', and by the end, I'm starting to feel dizzy and sick.

'Are you okay? Would you like to sit down?'

'I'm fine,' I wheeze, running my sleeve across my sticky forehead.

Why don't I just tell him the truth? *Well, no, actually, I've got an excruciating pain in my chest, I'm seeing stars, and may well collapse in a heap at any moment.* But no, I opt instead to be relentlessly pushed and pulled and flung hither and thither until I am rendered a gibbering wreck. I have no control over my legs and am minus one shoe, and yet weirdly, the music makes you want to ceilidh all night.

'The Duke of Perth', 'Strip the Willow', 'The Dashing White Sergeant', 'Drops of Brandy' all merge into one, and suddenly it's midnight and we're all joining hands in a swirling, stamping circle. '"O ye'll tak the high road and I'll tak the low road . . . "'

Reunited with my shoe, I bid everyone goodnight. Out on the street, I can hear the blood in my eardrums. Barefoot, I head for The Glenfoyle via the beach, stopping for a moment to marvel at the full moon. I close my eyes, breathe in the cool, pure air, and listen to the gentle, rhythmic lapping of the waves. I dip my throbbing feet in the freezing water and gaze up at the stars.

I find myself thinking of Francesco again, remembering that magical night when he took my hand and drew Orion and the Great Bear in the star-filled sky.

'Emily!'

I spin round, startled. There's Duncan, breathless, his auburn hair glinting in the silvery light.

'You left this behind,' he says, holding out my bag.

'Oh my God, how stupid of me. Thank you,' I say, coming back down to earth with a bump.

'I was thinking . . .' he says. 'It's my night off tomorrow. There's a wonderful wee fish restaurant along the coast here . . .'

'That's kind of you to ask, but I've no idea what time our filming will finish . . .'

201

'Here's my number,' he says, whipping out a business card from his wallet. 'Call me tomorrow if you're back early and you fancy a wee change . . . Now, can I walk you home?'

'No, I'm fine, really, but thanks for the offer,' I say, taking the card from him, but all the while keeping a formal distance.

'Goodnight.'

* * *

As I descend the creaky, tartan-carpeted stairs five hours later in time to the piped accordion muzak, I am met by the pungent smell of early morning kippers and am transported back to the aircraft galley and those crack-of-dawn breakfasts from hell: call bells ringing, queues for the loo, babies crying, recycled air, snoring, sick bags, nappy bags, smelly socks, and dog breath.

When I'm not needed, I've found a spot with panoramic views out across the sea to a small, distant island. I lean over the balustrade, the crashing waves below spraying my face with salt water. I shut my eyes and inhale the sweet smell of seaweed, the sun's rays filling me with warmth and positive energy.

Jules touches me on the shoulder.

'Hi, Emily,' she says breathlessly. 'Found you!'

'Sorry, I . . .'

'As the light is better today, Rob would like to film your dialogue with Elspeth from a close-up perspective.'

'Right,' I say, pulling out my earbuds and straightening my skirt.

This wasn't on the schedule for today, but I'm learning that in screen acting, things can change at a moment's notice, and you have to be prepared for the unknown and not panic.

Isobel is shooting another episode today, so the chap from continuity feeds me her lines off-camera, while I revert to the tennis-ball-on-a-stick acting principle.

* * *

In the car on the way back to The Glenfoyle early that evening, I remember to switch on my phone. It pings immediately.

Céline: *Diverted to Prestwick Airport nearby. Are you free to meet?* x ☺

Arrangements made, I jump in the shower, belting out 'The Bonnie Banks of Loch Lomond', which has been relentlessly rolling around my brain since the ceilidh.

All at once the music stops as I'm struck by a flash of inspiration.

I burst through the shower curtain and dash over to the wastepaper bin. I rifle through the tissues and chocolate wrappers. Found it! I collect the torn pieces and set about reassembling Duncan's shredded business card.

Okay, so it's a mad idea. I don't know the guy, if he's good enough for her, or if he'll like her, or she him. I don't know if she'll agree, or if he's still free tonight, but knowing how much Céline wants to meet someone, what's the harm in trying to play Cupid?

As I'm towel drying my hair, I hear the quietly thrumming motor of a taxi below. I look at the bedside clock. Pulling on my tights, I hop over to the window. It's Céline. Uh-oh. She is destined to be subjected to a blow-by-blow account of my landlady's daily movements if I don't scarper – and I do not refer to the latter's busy schedule.

I leap downstairs but she's already in full flow . . .

'I get this pain at night. The doctor says it's trapped wind, but I'm no' so sure. I should go back to see him, but they're always sae busy. Still, I don't complain. Och, Emily, there you are.'

'Céline!' I say, hugging her tight.

'What a nightmare!' she says, rolling her huge eyes. 'Everyone complaining. I said to one passenger, "Would you prefer to fly with just one engine instead of two?" That bloody well shut him up.'

'How I miss the darlings . . . not,' I say, looking at my watch.

'Is it normal for your stomach to swell up when you fly?' pipes up Mrs McKechnie. 'I only ask because . . .'

'Lord, look at the time!' I interject. 'Come on, Céline, we're going to be late,' I say, pushing her out of the door. 'See you at breakfast, Mrs M.'

Linking arms, Céline and I walk along the shore road towards The Burns Hotel for a drink and a catch-up.

'I have an idea, and if you think it's daft, then you don't have to agree,' I say, pushing open the door of the hotel reception and ushering her into the lounge.

I order a bottle of Sauvignon and divulge my secret plan.

'Let's do it!' giggles Céline, eyes sparkling as she clinks glasses.

Taking a swig of Sauvignon, I dial his number. 'Duncan? It's Emily. Remember me? The clodhopper from the ceilidh?'

'Aye, of course I remember you. Are you up for dinner tonight? I made a reservation just in case.'

'My friend's flight has been diverted, and she's got an unscheduled night-stop, so she's here with me . . .'

'Well, I'll just have to take you both out,' he says.

'Oh no, I couldn't possibly expect you . . .' I say, giving Céline the thumbs-up.

'Or better still, I'll give my pal Drew a call and we'll make it a foursome.'

'Okay, if you're sure . . .'

* * *

Ladies, I have good news! The age of chivalry is NOT dead. I can report first-hand that this ancient practice is still being carried out on the Firth of Clyde.

Pulling out of Chair ✓
Buying of Drinks ✓
Listening Skills ✓

Helping on with Coat/Pashmina ✓

Drew's Land Rover whisks us away to Dunure, a small fishing village along the coast.

As we turn off the main road, we are tossed around on the back seat like pinballs, until Drew eventually parks up on a remote, steep, grassy bank.

'It's a short walk from here,' he says, pointing to a row of twinkling lights, high up on the cliff's edge. They each open a door for us (✓), and we are led along a twisty, narrow pathway. Had I known a pre-dinner hike was on the menu, I would never have worn my new, kitten-heel boots with pointy toes. I stumble and stagger up the hill, battling to prevent my gypsy skirt from billowing up over my head.

Céline, on the other hand, is dressed perfectly for the occasion, in a classically tailored trouser suit with flat pumps. She strides elegantly ahead, as if on the catwalk, flanked by our two hosts, her well-cut bob swishing back and forth.

Duncan turns and waits for me to catch up. 'Are you okay? Do you want to take my arm?' he asks, like I'm some old granny trying to cross the road.

'No, I'm fine, you go on ahead,' I say brightly, my scarf flying across my mouth and nose.

I look up, and coming into view, at last, is a stone-built, white-washed cottage, with tiny, leaded windows. A wrought-iron sign bearing the name 'Maggie's Fish Restaurant' in weatherworn lettering swings back and forth, squeaking in the blustery wind.

The heavy, wooden door creaks open and it's like we've stepped back in time: there's a fireplace big enough to sit in; a young lass, perched on a beer barrel, plays a reel on the fiddle; lobster pots hang from the beams; candles glow from wax-covered bottles; and the smell of fresh fish, mixed with smouldering, damp wood, hovers in the air.

Duncan and Drew pull our chairs out for us to sit down (✓)

and order a bottle of wine.

'So, ladies, how did you two meet?' asks Drew, while we wait for menus.

'On our cabin crew training course,' I say, nervously twiddling my napkin and glancing at Céline.

'Did you ever experience any emergency situations?' he asks eagerly.

'Nope. Sorry to disappoint you. But lots of hilarious ones, didn't we, Céline?'

'Well . . .?' says Duncan, filling our glasses, his voice enthusiastic.

'Don't get us started, please, we could be here all night,' I say.

'Go on,' they implore, sounding genuinely interested. Oh well, they did ask . . .

We are in our element now, and our initial awkwardness gives way to uninhibited, frivolous banter.

Before we know it, Maggie's coming over with the dessert menu. I drag Céline off to the ladies' for a nose-powdering expedition.

'Well?' I say to her excitedly, as I close the door.

'You have a little piece of broccoli in between your teeth, *chérie*.'

'Never mind about that,' I say, glancing in the mirror, horrified at my Edward-Scissorhands hair. 'So, what about Duncan?'

'Duncan? No, I really like his friend, Drew.'

'Oh, okay . . .'

Uh-oh. My attempt at playing matchmaker is not going the way I planned. I feel bad for Duncan now, but I guess there's just no predicting chemistry.

'Come on,' I say, baring my teeth, checking in the mirror for any more bits of vegetation. 'Our knickerbocker glories will be melting.'

As we return to the dining room, they both stand up and pull out our seats! Have these two gentlemen just stepped out of a Jane Austen novel?

'*Mistress Emily, Mistress Céline, we are indeed delighted to have your company once more.*'

Snapping out of my daydream, I clear my throat. 'Okay, guys, now it's your turn to speak,' I say, sinking my long spoon into gooey chocolate and whipped cream. 'How did you two become friends?'

'At school,' Duncan replies, pouring the coffees. 'More than thirty years ago now – I can hardly believe it. We used to go fishing and camping together in the holidays. We were inseparable.'

'Aye,' says Drew. 'Then when I was in my twenties, I went out to South America to work for the Forestry Commission. Since coming back, I've been running the laird's estate out at Brig o'Muckhart. Whenever I'm in need of a dram and a blether, I call in on my old pal here,' he says, draping his arm fondly over Duncan's shoulder.

Céline's starry gaze falls to her watch. '*Mon Dieu!*' she groans. 'It is almost ten. The last train leaves at ten forty-four.'

Duncan signals for the bill, and he and Drew fish out their wallets.

'Shall we go Dutch?' I ask, reaching under the table for my bag.

'Och, away with you, it's our pleasure,' says Drew, putting his bank card on the table.

'Absolutely! What kind of a man invites a lady to dinner, and then expects her to pay?' snorts Duncan.

Most of the men I've dated, I think.

Generosity: check ✓

* * *

I am woken abruptly by the buzzing of my mobile on the bedside table.

One eye focuses on the luminous numbers of the digital clock: 02:10.

'Hello,' I croak.

'Emily, it's Céline.'

I sit bolt upright. 'Oh, my God, Céline, what's happened?' I babble, my mind racing. I should have ordered her a cab instead of allowing her to disappear with a man we only met once. I can picture her at the other end of the line, battered and bruised, waiting at A&E for me to pick her up.

'I can't sleep,' she says, with breathless excitement. 'I had a wonderful evening, and when I come back from Chicago, I'm going to Breeg . . . Breeg . . . to visit Drew on the estate!'

'You call me in the middle of the night to tell me this?' I tease, beaming at her down the phone.

Like a pair of giggly teenagers, we dissect every bit of the evening, and by the time we say goodnight, the grandfather clock is clanging three, and I've demolished six shortbread fingers and a Bacardi Breezer from the mini bar. Wish I hadn't ordered kippers for breakfast.

Vanity working on a weak head produces every sort of mischief.

~ Jane Austen, *Emma*

* * *

Last day of filming today. More hanging around. More crowd scenes. More disapproving busybody acting.

While waiting to be called, I clamber onto the seawall, my gaze drawn to the sun bouncing off the dazzling, cobalt-blue ocean. A plane drones overhead, leaving a feathery vapour trail. The Proclaimers belt out 'Letter from America' through my headphones. Pulling out my notebook, I put pen to paper . . .

Dear Duncan,

Thank you for the delicious dinner – and for putting up with my very bad Scottish dancing. I hope you make a full recovery!

If you're ever down my way, there's an open invitation for you at the wee Italian restaurant where I work from time to time.

Best wishes,
Emily x

My thoughts then turn to Céline, who must now be five hours into her flight – lunch service over, pushing the duty-free trolley through the cabin, flogging Hermès scarves and giant Toblerone.

A sparkle of excitement flashes through me as I imagine her and Drew together, in matching tweed, hand in hand, roaming the heather-filled hills of the estate, stopping to admire a proud stag running along a craggy ravine, Drew putting out his hand to touch her face, parting her fringe, and kissing her gently on the forehead.

She so deserves to be happy. But then what if Drew turns out to be a no-good Celtic cad? Whatever happens now is not my responsibility. I may have given destiny a nudge, but I remind myself I can't fix people or control situations. After the Mike misunderstanding, Céline and I have made a pact never to fall out over stupid men again.

I deliver the note to the Tam O'Shanter pub en route to the airport and leave Scotland for London, having found my friend a braw Scotsman for a boyfriend (bet he looks good in a kilt) and having mastered both the withering and the firm look.

Chapter 14

Lost in Chelsea

I study Francesco as he queues up for our coffees at Heathrow; when I'm far from him I want to be able to recall the way his thick, greying hair curls up at the ends as it brushes his collar, how he talks with his whole body: the shrug of his athletic shoulders, the vibrant gestures of his strong, long-fingered, olive-skinned hands.

It's barely three weeks since I returned from Scotland and now I'm on my way to Vienna for *three months* to play the role of Chelsea in *On Golden Pond*.

I'm thrilled, of course I am. After all, this is what I've sacrificed so much both emotionally and financially to do. So what's the problem? I hadn't bargained for finding someone I truly connect with and for having to leave him again so soon. How long can our relationship survive at this rate?

He turns around and I drag my gaze away from him, pretending to study my boarding card.

'*Allora*, I have something for you,' he says, putting down the tray and reaching into his bag. I blink at him several times, trying to keep my simmering emotions from boiling over. A package is slid across the table. My hands close around it and I give it a shake.

'Open!' he says, throwing me one of his delicious, roguish grins. How I wish I could capture that now familiar expression and put it safely away in my pocket, to sustain me over the next twelve long weeks.

I lift the lid of the small, red velvet box to reveal an antique silver locket.

'This belong to my mother . . .'

'Francesco, I can't . . .'

'Please. Look inside.'

Inside there's a tiny photo of us taken at The Witchery in Edinburgh.

He fastens it around my neck, turns to face me, cups my chin, and kisses me tenderly. '*Ti amo, amore mio.*'

Please don't let me cry.

'The final call for passengers travelling to Vienna with British Airways. Please make your way to gate three.'

His molten-chocolate eyes rest on mine.

'Francesco?'

'*Si?*'

'I love you too.'

He puts his arm around my waist, pulls me close, and gives me a long, lingering kiss.

'Would any remaining passengers travelling to Vienna . . .'

'*Vai!* Go!'

'Yes, yes . . . plane to catch . . . bye, I mean, *arrivederci,*' I say in a silly, cod-Italian voice and stride off towards departures.

'*Cara!*' he calls after me.

'Yes,' I say, turning around, heart quickening.

'Your glasses,' he says, hand outstretched, the corners of his mouth twitching.

* * *

211

My eyes flicker open, and I focus my stare on the chandelier suspended from the cracked, wedding-cake ceiling. I reach out, tracing my fingers along the crocheted mat, feeling for my watch. I peer at the hands: 08:55. I pull on a woolly sweater over my pyjamas, pad across the tiled floor, and open the flaky shutters.

I step through the beam of sunlight, out onto the balcony, and soak up the sounds of the bustling Rudolfstrasse below: the rumbling tram, car horns, the shouts from the market stall holders, the putt-putt of scooters, and the ringing of bicycle bells. I lean over the wrought-iron railing, and the trailing geraniums (valiantly still flowering) brush my bare feet.

The church clock, around the corner in Ringstrasse, chimes nine, reminding me that I've had my daily dose of I-am-one-with-the-universe, and to get my arse into gear if I'm to squeeze in my caffeine fix by rehearsal at ten-thirty.

* * *

I am now the proud owner of one of those sit-up-and-beg bikes, complete with wicker basket, which I picked up for just sixty euros among the second-hand clothes, ornaments, paintings, and general junk at the flea market.

Vienna is great for cyclists, there being plenty of cycle paths and places to park. As someone who regularly runs the gauntlet of the A316 from Richmond to London, this city is a dream.

I slot my bike into the rack outside my favourite coffee shop. According to my guidebook, this has been a meeting place for poets, writers, and artists for centuries. It's rather shabby, but full of bohemian character, with its marble-topped tables, creaky wooden chairs, faded drapes, and ornate, gilt mirror.

'Good morning, *fräulein*,' says the tuxedo-clad waiter, bowing politely. He scrapes a chair across the floor with one hand, while holding aloft a silver tray in the other. He then serves me my usual order of Viennese coffee and an apricot jam-filled bun.

I run my hands across the cool, mottled table and wonder who else has sat here, learning lines, sketching, penning novellas and music, and did they too dunk their pastries in their coffee, or did the art of dunking not evolve until modern times?

I pull the script from my bag and scan my lines for the section we're working on today. It's a scene between Ethel (my mother) and me. Chelsea is a dream of a part to play: complex, at odds with her father, and unlucky in love.

There are some great emotional moments – something to really get my teeth into. I think I can safely say my days of stumbling about the stage sporting a dodgy wig and an even dodgier accent, grappling for my next line, are now firmly in the dim and distant past.

Ethel is played by Margaret Crawford (aka Mags), the only other female member of the cast.

We hit it off right from the moment we met in the departure lounge that day at Heathrow . . .

'Snap!'

My head had bobbed up. Sitting across from me was an elegant woman of about seventy, silver-grey hair piled up on top of her head, an identical green script clutched in her hand.

'My daughter, I presume?' she'd ventured, leaning forward.

I hesitated momentarily, and then it dawned on me. 'Ethel, how nice to meet you.'

By the time our plane touched down, we'd crammed two lifetimes into those two short hours. A retired French teacher and keen amateur actress, she'd turned professional after years of caring for her husband.

Norman, my father, is played by theatre veteran Oliver Simkins. With his Concert Artistes' Club tie, highly polished shoes, and trilby (which is raised whenever a lady enters the room), he is the archetypal courtly English gent. We love to hear his stories of the good old days, touring the classics to exotic places. I swear those rich, sonorous tones could be heard over the Rolls-Royce engines of a 787.

The same cannot be said for top of the bill, Alan Hastings, who has been cast in the role of my fiancé, Bill Ray. Alan has spent the last twenty-five years playing psychiatrist Doctor Chris Lane in the crime drama *Mind Games*, which has catapulted him into stardom.

This is his first foray into stage acting, and I can see why the casting director chose him: he's suave, sophisticated (if a little arrogant), and has earned a huge following of die-hard fans who are willing to travel in their droves to see him, so is a huge box office draw. There's just one small problem: he mumbles. This type of method acting is all very well if you're Marlon Brando in *The Godfather*, where an understated look, a grunt or a whisper is all that's required to subtly communicate emotions to an audience of one: i.e. the camera lens, but not in a one-thousand-seat auditorium.

But no matter, for there are always queues of adoring autograph hunters at the stage door every night, pens, programmes, and phones at the ready.

Alan is chauffeured between the Hotel Sacher and the theatre every day (I can't begin to imagine how many euros *he* earns a week) and is always jawing on about lunching at The Ivy with Idris Elba or golfing with Hugh Grant.

I imagine this must all be very galling for Oliver, who's a revered stage actor, with a list of notable credits to his name, yet walks to the theatre every day, and is staying in a three-star guest house. When I once asked him about his feelings on the subject, he simply said, 'Acting is not a contest, Emily. I'm proud of the work I've done, and am not interested in keeping score. "When envy breeds unkind division: there comes the ruin, there begins confusion." *Henry the Sixth, Part One*.'

How I would love to have Oliver's ability to quote Shakespeare at the drop of a hat – and to have the grace to think more kindly of Alan.

But try as I might, there's absolutely no chemistry between us, which is unfortunate, as we're supposed to be madly in love.

What was it Portia said?

'Acting is about finding the truth in imaginary circumstances.'

Charlie, the mailman, is played by Jason Holmes. Charlie's known Chelsea (my character) since they were kids, and still has unrequited feelings for her. He's gay (Jason, that is, not Charlie), but those soul-searching eyes regard me with such adoration on stage, that an unspoken frisson has developed between us. (Uh-oh, I'm falling for the wrong guy.)

The role of Billy Ray Junior, Bill Ray's teenage son, is shared between two young teenagers, who attend the American International Theatre School here, and play the role in rotation.

The scenes between crotchety octogenarian Norman and thirteen-year-old Billy Ray Junior are a masterclass in fine acting. The arrival of the young man at Golden Pond pulls the world-weary Norman from the quicksand of his melancholy, their fishing trips and man-to-man talks reviving the old man's zest for life. The powerful bond played out in their scenes together makes my heart hurt.

* * *

After two weeks in a church hall, today we are to rehearse on stage for the first time.

'Ladies and gentlemen of the *On Golden Pond* Company, please make your way down to the auditorium to walk the set,' announces the deputy stage manager over the Tannoy.

We enter through the swing doors and stop dead in our tracks. I feel the hairs on the back of my neck bristle. The cables and ladders have disappeared, and the hollow, cavernous stage of a fortnight ago has now morphed into Ethel and Norman Thayer's rustic, lakefront house in Maine, New England.

The audio engineers are hunched over a huge mixing desk in

the middle of the stalls, the lighting guys are working overhead, and day turns to night in an instant, the lake shimmering in the moonlight beyond the screen door. The eerie sound of the loons echoes around the auditorium. Mags and Oliver slip quietly unprompted into character.

"'Shh. Norman, the loons. They're calling. Oh, why is it so dark?'"

"'Because the sun went down.'"

"'I wish I could see them. Yoo-hoo! Loooooooons! Loony looo-oooons!'"

"'I don't think you should do that in front of Chelsea's companion.'"

Gerhard Schildberger, our director, sits at the front of the stage, calling instructions to the crew. We settle silently into the plush, red velvet seats until they are ready for us.

* * *

Opening Night

'*Guten Abend*, Olaf,' I say to the stage doorman as I tick off my name and eagerly check my pigeonhole for post.

'Good evening, *fräulein*,' he says, summoning me back to the desk with the crook of his finger. He disappears momentarily to the small office at the back and re-emerges with a bouquet of peach lilies.

'Thank you,' I reply, barely able to contain my soaring joy.

As I make my way up the stairs, Oliver's vocal warm-up exercises can be heard reverberating around the corridor.

The theatre manager, in full penguin suit, gives me a fleeting nod as he rushes past, squawking into his walkie-talkie.

'Sorry!' cries the wardrobe mistress, narrowly avoiding me as she clatters down the stairs, the mailman's costume slung over her shoulder.

The deputy stage manager's voice echoes through the Tannoy: 'Ladies and gentlemen of the *On Golden Pond* Company, the house is now open. Please do not cross the stage.'

I open the door to dressing room number three, which Mags and I share. She's already there in her paisley silk dressing gown, applying her make-up.

'Wow! Are those flowers from your Italian *amore*?' she asks, a girlish glint in her eye. 'How romantic!'

'I'm not sure . . .' I say, secretly hoping, as I rip open the card.

Good luck, darling!
Love, Mum & Dad xx

'Ladies and gentlemen, this is your half-hour call,' cuts in the deputy stage manager's voice again. 'Thirty minutes, please.'

A little jitter creeps into my tummy.

As I flick my powder brush to and fro, my thoughts drift to Francesco. I wonder what he's doing at this very moment. Concocting one of his delicious sauces, no doubt, while singing along to Zucchero or Renato Zero . . .

'Break a leg, my darling,' whispers Mags, pressing her cheek against mine.

'God, have I missed the beginners' call?' I say, coming back down to planet earth.

'No. Don't panic. I like to get down there early to check my props – and I have a daft little ritual I need to perform in the wings before every opening night,' she says confidingly. 'It's too silly for words, so don't ask. See you down there. Let's knock 'em dead!'

This is it. Two scenes, and I'm on. All the rehearsal and anxiety of the last three weeks, wondering if it would all come together in time, has culminated in this moment, and I'm thinking about Francesco and his pasta sauces. I give myself a severe ticking off, and take one last look at my lines, in an attempt to block him out and discipline my thoughts.

'Miss Forsyth, this is your call.'

A ripple of excitement mixed with sheer terror courses through my veins.

Flinging open the door, I bump into Olaf, face hidden by an enormous bouquet of velvety red roses.

'For me?' I gasp.

'For you,' he says with a lopsided smile.

'Miss Forsyth, this is your call.'

From the moment I make my first entrance, my nerves vanish as the magic takes hold, and I get lost in Chelsea; one moment a grown woman in complete control of her life, the next, a little girl, insecure and desperate for parental approval.

I am one of the lucky eight per cent of actors in paid employment, and to prove it, Blu-tacked to the dressing room mirror (with light bulbs all around it!) is the invitation to my first proper opening night party . . .

The Management of The Rieger Theatre, Vienna
invite the cast & crew of On Golden Pond
to first-night drinks in the Haydn Bar

'*Fräulein*?' says the waiter, clicking his heels as he tops up my glass of Sekt for the second time.

I give myself an imaginary pinch; I am in Vienna. I AM AN ACTRESS, WHO IS SIPPING CHAMPAGNE AT AN AFTER-SHOW PARTY IN VIENNA.

'Congratulations!' says a deeply familiar, über-smooth voice.

I veer round and find myself eyeball to eyeball with – BEN.

'Oh my God, what are you doing here?' I say, covering my mouth with my hand, heart hitting the floor.

'Hey, I didn't expect you to exactly fling your arms around me, but . . .'

'Sorry, it's just you're the last person . . .' I whisper, my voice disintegrating.

Why did I just come over all fluttery and apologise? This is the callous bastard who, in five minutes flat, sabotaged my whole life plan of moving to the country, having two kids (we'd even chosen names), a red setter, and a vegetable garden.

'Minnie, you were fab-u-lous. Didn't know you had it in you. Short hair suits you, by the way,' he says, his hand running down my cheek. 'It makes you look much younger. You should have had it cut years ago.' Excuse me? Is this not the same man who warned me never to cut my hair or he'd leave me? His thumb strokes my bottom lip as he holds me with his wolfish stare for longer than is comfortable. That old familiar scent of Paco Rabanne swirls around my head, awakening the past uninvited.

'God, the loos here are a bit funny, babe,' simpers a long-legged, lissom creature, bouncing over in an eye-popping, figure-hugging frocklet.

'Ah, darling, this is Emily. Emily, Natasha,' says Ben, not looking me in the eye.

'*Natasha?*' I say, raising a quizzical eyebrow. 'Sorry, I thought . . .'

'Natasha,' he says firmly.

'Hi,' she says with a coltish toss of her glossy, strawberry-blonde mane.

'We loved the show, didn't we, Benny?' she continues, resting her head territorially on his shoulder.

BENNY?! Who's Benny?

'So,' I say after an awkward pause, 'what brings you to Vienna?'

'Tasha had a night-stop and I thought I'd come along for the ride.'

'What a coincidence,' I say wanly.

'Actually, it wasn't . . . a coincidence,' he says, turning to 'Tasha' with a half-smile.

'I did a two-day Houston with Lily last week. She told me you were performing here, and then when Tasha discovered she had a night-stop, I . . . *we* thought we'd surprise you.'

'We fancy getting married in Vienna, don't we, babe?' says

219

Natasha in her little-girl-lost voice. 'It's *so* romantic. I saw the most gorgeous ring in a jeweller's near the opera house, but Benny says he can get something *much* bigger in Hong Kong.'

I take a huge gulp of champagne. That says it all. They make a good pair, these two. It's all about the size of the diamond, not the sentiment behind it.

And what became of whatshername . . . the Barbie doll he left me for . . . Maddie? Did she end up on the reject pile too? Did she have their baby? I actually feel sorry for her now.

'Tasha used to be in show business – kind of, didn't you, kitten?' says Ben, swiftly shifting the subject.

'Really?' I say flatly.

'Yeah, a model – I was with Models One,' she purrs. 'I could have gone into acting as I know lots of directors an' stuff, but I like this job for now. Maybe when I'm older, like you, an' we've had a couple of kids, I might do it for a while.'

My jaw drops. *When I'm older, like you*? The bloody nerve! Something inside me snaps. That's it. How dare they waltz in here and invade my lovely opening night? Ben may have movie-star looks, but to the new me, they now only accentuate his air of self-obsession.

'Emily, my darling, the cars are outside to take us to the restaurant,' calls Mags from the other end of the bar.

'Well, it was nice meeting you,' I say, switching on my haughty-yet-friendly voice. 'Hope the wedding and everything is all that you wish for.'

With that, I about-turn, and with a theatrical swish of my scarlet red, fitted and flared coat, I head for the door.

Out on the street, I slip into one of the waiting taxis and exhale deeply. The old me would have been swallowed up by sorrow. The new me is relieved that it didn't work out between us. What a fool I was back then. All those wasted nights spent waiting for Ben to call from LA, pretending to myself that he'd been delayed or couldn't get a signal. Were he to tell me now he'd made the biggest mistake of his life, I wouldn't be tempted to take him back – not for all the diamond rings in Hong Kong.

I tut inwardly as I recall how secretly upset I was when Ben bought me an exercise bike for my birthday. He'd casually informed me that he was doing me a favour, as he'd noticed I was getting a bit flabby around the waist. I'd felt instantly ashamed and unattractive. Now I've actually grown fond of my flabby bits, crow's feet, and the wee freckles that have started to appear on the backs of my hands. Francesco says they are beautiful because they are part of me and tell the story of my life. To misquote Whitney: 'Learning to love your cellulite. It is the greatest love of all.'

No more regret, bitterness, or resentment. In fact, I feel grateful; thanks to Ben's betrayal, I'm now following a path I would never have had the courage to take. I like my life now, with all its risk and uncertainty. It's given me an inner freedom. What if he hadn't dumped me? How would my future have panned out then? Would we have married, had children, been happy? Life is so full of what-ifs – just like when Gwyneth Paltrow misses that tube train in *Sliding Doors*.

'Come on, you old poop!' calls Mags, emerging through the stage door giggling, arm in arm with Oliver, his gait a little unsteady, trilby pulled down over his eyes.

She shoves him into the front seat, then plonks down next to me and says, 'Lord, Emily, who was that *divine* man in the bar?'

'Him? Oh, no one of any importance,' I say, flashing her a huge, self-satisfied grin as we are whisked off into the Vienna night.

* * *

My footsteps echo down the empty street under the pewter moon, my shadow flickering along the cracked walls of Rudolfstrasse. I raise the collar of my trench coat and am reminded of those old films noir, where spies silently disappear through enormous, heavy wood doors of once-grandiose buildings. The only things missing from the picture are the dark glasses and headscarf (and spies in thriller movies do not get drunk and waste five minutes fumbling for their keys).

I stagger through the shadowy entrance, up the long, winding staircase to the third floor, and tiptoe along the corridor to my studio, quietly closing the door behind me.

I kick off my shoes and the bed groans as I flop onto it. My mobile bleeps and the little screen lights up greeny-blue. One new message:

> **Francesco:** *Tonight, I think about you many times, cara. I hope the roses arrived. Ti amo. Sogni d'oro x* ☺

I curl up and slip into a smiley, alcohol-induced coma, clasping my phone tightly to me.

* * *

'What are you doing Sunday evening?' asks Mags one night in the dressing room.

'Hmm, let me see now . . . nothing,' I reply, plucking a *white* hair from my left eyebrow. 'Gotcha!'

'Good, because we, my darling, are going to the opera.'

'Opera? Blimey, isn't it awfully expensive?'

'I don't consider thirteen euros expensive, do you?'

'Thirteen euros! You're kidding me.'

'You don't have dodgy knees, do you?'

'What?'

'Varicose veins?'

'Nope.'

'Suffer from vertigo?'

'No. Why?'

'Good. Then you won't mind standing up on the balcony for three hours.'

'Three hours?'

'That's nothing. Olly and I saw *Tristan and Isolde* last Sunday. Four hours thirty. But it's worth it, believe me. Oh, and dress up. Everyone in Vienna dresses up for the opera – and bring a scarf to mark your place on the lean rail.'

'What, like reserving your sunbed with a beach towel?' I say, screwing up my nose.

'Now, Emily, darling, don't be a snob. And wear comfy shoes.'

* * *

I am having yet another pinch-me moment: I am standing before the majestic opera house, devouring a *Wienerwurst* (the Rolls-Royce of hotdogs), two tickets for *Tosca* in my pocket. Life doesn't get much better than this.

As I wipe the ketchup from around my mouth, a mature, well-dressed couple scurry past, hand in hand, laughing. Her scarf falls to the ground. He runs back, picks it up, places it around her neck, and kisses her lightly on the cheek. I sense the tenderness of this moment and feel a spike of envy.

Let me rephrase the above statement: life would be perfect if Francesco were here. I don't mean I miss him in a needy, hurting way, because I'm different to the woman I was before: the one who had to be in a relationship at any price in order to feel whole. No, the reason I think about him so much is because I miss his friendship, and the fact that he actually *enhances* my life.

Looking back, I realise that since I was sixteen, I've always had a boyfriend in tow. These relationships would usually end in dramatic circumstances, but then it would only be a matter of weeks until I found myself swallowed up by the next one. I now know it takes time to find a quality relationship with someone you are *truly* compatible with, and while we all have to compromise, moulding yourself into what your partner wants you to be is not the right way. No, I hardly dare admit it, but at last, here's a man who asks nothing of me – except perhaps to work harder at my Italian!

While I don't *need* Francesco as some sort of passport to happiness, I can't think of anyone better to share those special, pinch-me moments with. It's as simple as that.

* * *

From my corner vantage point, high up in the gallery, like a marksman, but armed with a pair of opera glasses, I scan the red, gold, and ivory horseshoe-shaped auditorium.

Two fifty-something, classy ladies – dripping with expensive jewellery – are chatting in the stalls aisle. From their body language, I imagine the English translation of their exchange to go something like this:

1st LADY: Mwah, mwah, daahling. How super to see you.
2nd LADY: Likewise. You look fabulous. Designer?
1st LADY: Naturally.
SWOONSOMELY HANDSOME YOUNG MAN APPROACHES
*   1st LADY.*
YOUNG MAN: There you are, sweetheart. (KISSES HER) We'd
*   better take our seats. Please excuse us.*
2nd LADY: Of course. (THROUGH GRITTED TEETH) Bitch.
PAN TO ORCHESTRA PIT . . .
BASSOONIST: I told him, how would you like it, to be stuck under
*   the stage every night behind the tuba?*
VIOLINIST: Honestly, mate, it's no better where I'm sitting. You
*   get the full force of the sopranos from the front.*
SWING TO A BOX . . .
GRUMPY MAN: Don't start. I didn't bloody well want to come in
*   the first place. You know how I hate the opera.*
PO-FACED WOMAN: Oh really? That's funny. Because a little

Mags taps my arm lightly with the programme, folded back at the
synopsis page. I pop on my glasses, but only get as far as *Rome.
1800. Inside the church of Saint Andrea della Valle* . . . before we
are plunged into darkness. The chit-chat fades as the conductor
appears in the spotlight, bowing to thunderous applause. He turns
to face his orchestra, nods and raises his arms. The string section
hold their bows at the ready, poised, waiting for the baton to be
lowered, like a starting pistol at the beginning of a race.

All at once the opening bars of the overture are released into
the air, and the heavy, red velvet curtains swish open.

Because we are so far away from the action, and because my
Italian is not yet up to comprehending the convoluted plots of
opera (people in opera never do day-to-day things, like ask for
directions or buy stamps, do they?), I haven't a clue what's going
on most of the time. I suspect the lady with the voluptuous figure
and high voice must be Tosca. She and Mario, her artist boyfriend,
seem to have a bit of an up and down relationship, if the constant
appeasing (him) and pushing away (her) is anything to go by.

Her diva-like strutting and petulant tossing of her black, pre-
Raphaelite hair, and the way she keeps jabbing her finger at his
painting of a beautiful blonde woman, tells me she's the jealous
type (it's only a painting, love), but then again, maybe Mario has
a wandering eye, in which case, I'm totally on her side.

When the action takes place upstage and our view is completely
obscured, I close my eyes and allow the music to swim through
me; otherwise my poor sightlines are more than compensated by
the very nice rear view of the conductor, who though not tall, is
rather cute in that young Al Pacino-way, with his black floppy
hair, which flicks back and forth as his whole body communicates
the subtle moods of the music to his players.

By the time the first interval arrives, I am transfixed, totally lost in the story (my version of the story at any rate), oblivious to the discomfort of leaning against a railing for over an hour. The safety curtain descends and the lights come up.

'I have a little treat for us,' whispers Mags, nudging me. 'Ta-dah!' She produces two quarter-bottles of Sekt and two plastic champagne flutes from her bag and proceeds to pop them open and pour while I keep a watch out for the hawk-eyed ushers.

Armed with drinks and a dose of schoolgirl daring, we descend the winding stairs and join the rich and the beautiful in the Schwind Foyer. Here, it is the Viennese custom for the audience to promenade among the paintings and busts of famous composers while unashamedly eyeing one another up and down, checking out who's wearing what and who's with whom.

This all sounds horribly pretentious, but believe me, if you're there, in the midst of it, you can't help but be mesmerised by the sheer elegance, the opulence, the self-assuredness, the *Devil-Wears-Prada*-ishness of it all: glamorous, expensive-smelling ladies in designer dresses with perfect tresses and heels as high as skyscrapers; distinguished, well-bred gentlemen with slicked-back hair, tailored jackets draped squarely across their shoulders, clutching Gucci man bags.

Do any of them suspect that there are a couple of impostors in their midst, I wonder? I half expect the Posh Police to burst through the doors, prise my plastic glass of supermarket champagne out of my hand, drag me by the collar of my flea-market dress, and throw me out onto the street, where I belong.

'So, you were here last Sunday?' I say to Mags, tearing my gaze away from a striking Amazonian woman with telescopic legs, wearing a slinky LBD, leopard-print turban, and matching shoes.

She falls quiet for a moment. 'Olly adores the opera, like me, and I can't tell you how lovely it is to be able to share things with someone again.' Lowering her eyes, she continues, 'You must think I'm awful.'

'Why?'

'Because I'm married, and am enjoying the company of another man, while my poor husband is in a care home with nothing more to look forward to than his next meal.'

'Mags, your friendship with Oliver is nothing to be ashamed of,' I say, squeezing her hand and looking her square in the eye.

'I should be at home, taking care of him,' she says, her voice breaking as she looks away, pulling an embroidered hankie from her sleeve.

'You've done the best you can, but you're entitled to a life too,' I say soothingly. 'And from what you've told me, it sounds like he needs professional care now, which you're not qualified to give.'

'All the same . . .' The three bells ring, summoning us back to our seats. 'Come on,' she says, her taut expression relaxing. 'I bet you five euros Tosca snuffs it in the end.'

* * *

I am woken early next morning by the persistent ringing of my mobile.

'Hello,' I grunt, holding it to my crumpled face.

'Morning, poppet!' trills Mum. 'Couldn't wait to tell you – your father and I have just booked a winter imperial cities tour to Prague, Budapest – *and* Vienna!'

'Really?' I say, propping myself up and rubbing my sleep-filled eyes. 'Brill! So you can see the play after all.'

'Ah,' she falters. 'I'm afraid we only have one night in Vienna. We leave for Prague by coach early the next day, and we're supposed to go to a Vienna Boys' Choir concert that evening – I've always wanted to see them, and it's all included – but if there's a performance of your play on Saturday afternoon, we could probably squeeze it all in, couldn't we?'

'Huh! So, the Vienna Boys' Choir takes precedence over me and my play, eh? How very dare they?' I reply, feigning offence. My former self would have been genuinely miffed by this, but the new me just thinks, that's okay. No problem. I don't want a fight. What's the point? I've been down this road too many times before. It accomplishes nothing and only leaves me feeling wretched. Mum doesn't mean to be blunt. She's just Mrs Say-It-Like-It-Is, whereas Dad is more Mr Keep-the-Peace, and Mum can't put a foot wrong where he's concerned.

Still, you can't change people – particularly those hurtling towards their eighth decade. Age, or maybe my new, more frugal life is forcing me to reassess situations and my reaction to them. I think, *hope* I am becoming more tolerant, less of a control freak.

'What do you say, poppet?'

'Hmm?'

'Is there a matinée on Saturday?'

'Yes. Fine,' I say brightly. 'I'll arrange two tickets, and maybe we can have an early supper afterwards. I'd like you to meet . . .'

'Darling, don't tell me you've met a new man? Not an actor, is he?'

'. . . Mags and Oliver. They play my mum and dad.'

'Oh. I see,' she says her voice dropping. Quickly drawing a deep breath, she yammers, 'Have a guess who rang me the other day? Dorothy Devine! Greg's *still* unmarried, you know.'

I pull the patchwork quilt over my head and count to ten, fighting my old instinct to snap back. She ploughs on.

'Dorothy says he's doing very well at the bank, got a lovely semi-detached house *and* a brand-new company car. He hasn't dated a girl since . . . well really, Dorothy and I could knock your two silly heads together . . .'

'Oh, Mum. I'm sorry, I know you don't want to hear this,' I say, crossing my fingers as I interrupt her mid-flow, 'but I've decided to steer well clear of men for a while.'

'I see,' she says, a surge of unspoken despair mixed with agitation crackling down the phone line.

Since Ben left and I set out on this crazy journey, a part of me has felt selfish and guilty for the anguish I cause my ageing parents. Like Chelsea, I long to prove something to them, and now here's my big chance.

I may not have turned out to be the high-flying United Nations interpreter, Supermum, or Kirstie-Allsopp homemaker they wanted me to be, but surely success is not necessarily a financial thing? I'm doing what makes me happy *and* getting paid for it. As a parent, surely you can't wish more for your child?

With my stage dad, Norman about to turn eighty and showing early signs of memory loss, the play is a reminder of my real parents' mortality and the significance of each passing day.

* * *

'They'll be here now, Mags. In their seats,' I say, glancing at my watch and continuing to pace up and down. 'Row C. I'm scared if I look down and catch their eye, I might forget my lines. In fact, a part of me wishes they weren't coming . . .'

'You're going to wear out what's left of this tatty carpet,' says Mags in an unusually firm tone. 'If you carry on like this, you *will* mess it up. Forget they're there. The auditorium is the fourth wall, remember? If you're thinking about your parents sitting a few feet away from you, then you're not playing it for real. Chelsea will become a caricature – a phoney. I've watched you grow into her these last few weeks, and I will not allow you to lose sight of her.' She shrugs. 'If your parents don't like the life you've chosen, then that's up to them. My son wasn't happy about me coming here, leaving his father behind in the care home. I visit my guilt every day, not only off stage, but on stage too. We get one shot at this, Emily,' she says, clasping my shoulders. 'As the old saying goes, "Life is not a dress rehearsal."'

I channel all my pent-up emotion into that afternoon's perfor-mance, and am aware of a subtle shift, in that Chelsea and I connect on an even deeper level than before. Through her I am forced to confront those negative feelings of inadequacy and guilt that I still haven't got my life together. The scene where Ethel tells me to grow up, forget the past, and move on has an added frisson of realism today, the like of which I haven't experienced before. Chelsea is teaching me about myself. All that stuff at drama school – about Stanislavski and 'being a role' – suddenly makes even more sense.

* * *

'Visitors at stage door for Fräulein Forsyth,' Olaf's voice announces over the intercom. I bound down the stairs, leaping off the last three steps into Dad's arms, just as I did when I was a child.

'What can I say, love?' he says, squeezing me tight. 'We couldn't believe that was our wee girl up there, could we, Brenda?'

I turn to face Mum. Is that approval I see in her eyes – pride even?

'I don't know what to say . . . I . . .' she says, quickly dabbing her eyes.

'Now, that's a first,' says Dad.

'That's enough, Brian!' she says, blowing her nose then checking her appearance in the full-length mirror.

Mags and Oliver join us for a traditional supper of *Wienerschnitzel*, complemented by a local wine, from the proprietor's own vineyard in Grinzing, on the outskirts of Vienna.

This being a special occasion, I break the actors' pre-show zero-alcohol rule.

'Amazing, isn't it?' says Mum later, as their taxi pulls up outside the stage door. 'Oliver and Mags – still treading the boards at their age. And they have no intention of retiring.'

'Precisely,' I say. 'To find what you love to do and be paid for doing it – well, you can't get luckier than that, can you?'

'It's all very well doing what you love, but it doesn't always pay the bills,' says Mum pointedly.

I take a deep breath. 'Let's put it this way – if someone had told you when you were young, *we know how much you love nursing, but sorry, we can't possibly allow you to do it.* How would that have made you feel?'

'That's . . . that's different,' says Mum.

'How different?'

'Well, for starters, I was in my twenties. You're . . .'

'. . . middle-aged, I know. But I don't have any responsibilities, so why not? Why shouldn't I have a shot at this before it's too late?'

'I just want you to be like other women your age . . .'

'Well, I *don't*, so shh!' I say in a mock stern tone, trying to lighten the mood. 'Away you go, or you'll be late for the concert.'

'Bye, smiler,' says Dad, kissing my forehead then pinching my cheek. 'I'm so proud of my wee lassie.' Lowering his voice he continues, 'And though she may not say as much, your mother is too.'

'Really?' I ask, that longing for approval never far away. 'You're not just saying this to make me feel good?'

'You should have heard her during the interval, telling anyone who'd listen that that was her daughter up there. Couldn't bloody well shut her up.'

* * *

'Do not turn around,' a stern, heavily accented Eastern European warns me. 'And listen carefully to your instructions. You will be met by Smollensky under the clock at Passau station. The code word is "loon".'

'Oliver, you *Schwein*! You almost had me going then,' I say, spinning on my heels and batting him playfully with my bag.

'The Salzburg train leaves from platform six, I believe,' he says, removing his shades and consulting Gerhard's list of directions. 'We change at somewhere called . . . Attnang-Puchheim for Bad Aussee.'

'Isn't this exciting?' says Mags, appearing at my side with three delicious-smelling coffees. 'So sweet of Gerhard to invite us.'

Austria has more saints than you can shake a ski pole at, and thanks to one of them, whose name I can't now remember, Monday is a public holiday, so Gerhard has invited us to his country house in Styria.

We climb aboard (and I mean *climb*. Tight jeans are a definite no-no when getting on and off Austrian trains). The whistle blows and we are on our way.

As we gather speed, the cityscape soon gives way to country hamlets, snow-laden pine trees, onion-domed churches, Babybel cows and frozen lakes. We thunder through inky-black, craggy tunnels and on, up into the mountains.

It's early evening and dark by the time the train pulls into Bad Aussee station. The squeal of brakes, the slamming of doors, footsteps crunching on tightly packed snow, the dimly lit, deserted station, the guard in peaked cap and greatcoat, all evoke a mood of winter romance. I am transported back to Zhivagoville once more.

After a long absence, Yuri and I are to be reunited at last . . . *Lara, my love! HE CALLS, HIS VOICE FULL OF LONGING. Yuri! I TUMBLE INTO HIS ARMS, MY WARM TEARS MELTING THE ICICLES IN HIS MOUSTACHE AS THE HAUNTING NOTES OF 'LARA'S THEME' ARE PLUCKED OUT ON THE BALALAIKA . . .*

'Fritz! *Nein! Komm her!*'

I am rudely awoken from my dreamy Russian fantasy by a crazed terrier in a tartan coat, which has launched itself at me from the darkness and is becoming a tad too friendly with my leg.

'Aaw, he's so cute,' I say, politely patting Fritz's head, while secretly wishing I could shake him off.

'He must like you,' says Gerhard, sliding down the hood of his enormous parka and grabbing the terrier firmly by the collar. 'Welcome to Bad Aussee!'

Fritz and bags safely loaded behind the luggage grille, we set off in Gerhard's Jeep Cherokee for Pension Dachstein, named after the Dachstein Glacier, which towers over the little village, like an ever-watchful bodyguard.

Gerhard's home is charmingly rustic: logs piled up outside, hand-painted, alpine furniture, huge, exposed beams, and a green-glazed tiled stove. The fire crackles and the air is filled with the smell of damp oak, mixed with cinnamon.

We squash around the beautifully laid table. Dried herbs hang from the ceiling and beeswax candles flicker on the windowsill.

Dinner is traditional and home-cooked. We discover during the evening that Gerhard's skills are not only confined to directing: as well as drama, he tells us he studied botany at university and is in the process of patenting his herbal spa products. He gives each of us samples of his latest creation: bath salts made from locally mined salt mixed with dried leaves and seeds from alpine flowers.

'If I turn up tomorrow looking like George Clooney, you'll know you're onto a winner,' says Oliver with a broad smile. But that's not all. This is the best bit: Gerhard is also one of Austria's leading Elvis impersonators. (I'd always thought there was something of the Fifties rock 'n' roll about him.) After a few Schnapps, we persuade him to fetch his guitar (disappointingly though, he refuses to don the white bell-bottomed jumpsuit and the black, high quiff wig).

Oliver and Mags know all the words and sing along with gusto. I pretend to know all the words while Fritz demonstrates that as well as a strong sex drive, he possesses a musical ear and a sense of rhythm as he howls and prances on his back legs. But when we start singing and dancing to 'Hound Dog', he gets overexcited again and is banished to his basket in the utility room.

* * *

The sun is coming up over the Dachstein by the time our party is over and, arm in arm, we steer one another across the road to our pension.

My room is pleasantly warm, the embroidered sheets pristine, the mattress firm but not hard, comfortable but not squishy, and the traditional loden wool blanket as warm as a sheep (not that I've ever cuddled a sheep). I close my eyes and wait for sleep to arrive . . .

Now, one of the annoying things about being the wrong side of forty is the digestion issue. I used to think Gaviscon was for windy grannies. Now it's as essential a part of my travel kit as deodorant. Only it was discovered in my hand luggage at Heathrow and confiscated by airport security.

Pulling on my slipper socks and Aran sweater, I stagger out onto the balcony, hand clutching my stomach. I inhale deeply, filling my lungs with freezing alpine air.

I close my eyes and imagine Francesco is beside me. I can almost smell his subtly sensuous aftershave, feel his breath in my ear, his stubble on my cheek. Without warning, a builder's burp is expelled into the sylvan silence, ricocheting across the glassy lake. I slap my hand over my mouth, looking around in shame. In that moment I am aware of muffled voices below. Eek. Did they hear?

Realising with a start that it's Oliver and Mags, I retreat into the shadows. I lie down in the half-light, like a starfish, and gaze up at the painted ceiling, the dying flames from the bedroom fire throwing a pale, intermittent light onto the cows and alpine flowers, making them look as if they're dancing . . . or is that the Schnapps?

Chapter 15

Phantom of the Opera

I arrive back in Vienna to find a letter. I instantly recognise the spidery handwriting. Francesco is a man of contradiction: someone who has his finger on the pulse of politics, literature, world music, films, fashion, and sport, yet still writes letters and refuses to be lured by social media or fast food. Texting is as far as he's prepared to venture into the push-of-a-button, click-of-a-mouse, ping-of-a-microwave, selfie world. I think of him as my Mediterranean Mr Darcy – minus the disagreeableness.

Ripping open the envelope, excitement ripples through me as I read the details of his planned trip. Checking my calendar, I realise Lily is pencilled in for some of the dates, so I call her from the theatre that evening to check if she now has her flight rota and can confirm.

'I don't think I'll make it now, hon. Liam is short of volunteers at the riding school and I've kind of promised I'll support him on hacks whenever I'm free,' she says.

'I see. Liam's name has been cropping up a lot recently on our WhatsApp group chat.'

'I told you – he's the new stables manager.'

'Hmm. And do I detect a smile in your voice?'

Ignoring this last comment, she continues, 'Those kids so look forward . . .'

'Yeah, yeah, yeah . . .'

Joking apart, there's no doubt in my mind that Lily's voluntary work at the riding school is a godsend; those horses and those disadvantaged children are helping her to heal. Catching a frisky pony in an open field or keeping a disabled child safe and happy requires the utmost concentration and doesn't allow your mind to stray elsewhere. Equine therapy, I believe it's called. All I'm suggesting is, where's the harm in her enjoying a little romance too?

'Don't change the subject,' continues Lily after a pause. 'What about Francesco's visit? It's high time you started putting him first. I understand why you're being cautious, but he's a good 'un, so you fix that up right away, d'you hear me? Francesco first.'

'But . . .'

'Ladies and gentlemen of the *On Golden Pond* Company, this is your Act One beginners' call. Act One beginners to the stage, please.'

'Lily, you still there?' The phone clicks. 'Lily?'

* * *

As I wait for Francesco to appear through the sliding doors of the arrivals hall, I realise even more how much I've missed him these last few weeks.

I'm practising mindfulness like mad, yet still anxious thoughts prod my brain, threatening to cloud our precious time together. Lily's right. Good men like him are hard to find, but how much longer can our relationship survive these long periods of separation?

'*Ciao, bella!*' And suddenly he's standing there before me, looking casually stylish in an army-green puffer jacket, jeans and brown leather cowboy boots, an expensive holdall bag swaying from his shoulder.

He wraps his arms tightly around me and kisses me for a long time, his familiar scent making me giddy.

'Hello again,' I whisper, dipping my head.

We interlace fingers and share a glance as we make our way down to the subway in contented silence.

The train clatters and jostles noisily along the track.

As we pull into Enkplatz, he nudges my foot with his and points to a poster advertising the play. Our eyes meet. He traces his thumb back and forth across my hand, kisses my forehead, and smiles.

* * *

My performance that evening is not my best, as I find it hard to concentrate. In between my lines, when I'm normally listening to what the other characters are saying, I'm thinking about Francesco and wondering if he found his way to the theatre, did he pick up his ticket, where should we eat afterwards, will he mind sharing a single bed in my tiny studio flat? I am playing with fire. It therefore comes as no surprise that I miss one of my cues; serves me jolly well right. Oliver, ever the consummate performer, comes to the rescue, jumping in with his next line.

As soon as the curtain comes down for the interval, shame-facedly I flee the stage to the dressing room, slam the door shut, and burst into tears.

Mags enters quietly, puts a mug of tea down in front of me, and stroking my hair says soothingly, 'Listen, sweetheart, it happens to us all, and tonight, well, tonight it was your turn. Not one member of that audience will have noticed you missed a line, believe me.'

'I wasn't concentrating. I was being totally unprofessional, and I've let everyone down,' I bleat through gasping sobs.

'Nonsense. Look, love, we all have our off nights,' she says, putting a motherly arm around me. 'We're not superhuman. And promise me one thing: if Francesco, or anyone for that matter, congratulates you on your performance, you smile sweetly and simply say thank you, do you hear me?' she says firmly. 'Don't you dare draw attention to the fact you missed a line, or Mama Mags will be very cross with you, do you understand? Now dry your eyes and drink your tea before it goes cold,' she says, snatching a tissue from the box on the table.

As the curtain goes up on Act Two, I can feel the adrenaline pumping round my body. Five pages of dialogue until my next entrance. Can I put my silly goof-up behind me, or will I freeze and ruin it for everyone? Is this what they call stage fright?

Our doubts are traitors, and make us lose . . . Our doubts are traitors, and make us lose . . . rings Portia's voice in my head.

Despite my initial tentativeness, it goes without a hitch, and I am the complex Chelsea once more, at odds with her father and finally reconciled. The pent-up tears of earlier come in very handy during my emotional scene with Ethel, and then finally with Norman.

'*Brava!*' enthuses Francesco, as I emerge from the stage door. 'It was *fantastico!*'

I give a modest smile and murmur, '*Grazie.*' The others file past, calling out their goodnights. Mags turns and darts me a knowing wink.

Francesco takes my hand as we make our way along the Graben (one of the many posh, pedestrianised shopping areas), past the fountain and illuminated statue of Saint Leopold, up the alleyway, and through the stained-glass doors of the restaurant the theatre manager recommended.

The waiter guides us through the snugly arranged tables to a discreet, low-lit booth. As soon as we sit down, he brings over two glasses of complimentary champagne, lights a candle, and hands out menus.

A pianist plays quietly in the corner.

In between sips of bubbly and goulash soup, I tell Francesco about Mags, Oliver, the play, the opera, the trip to the country. Francesco orders more wine, we eat, I talk some more, and because I'm a little bit squiffy, I divulge the Ben saga (not, you'll be relieved to hear, in a bitter, all-men-are-bastards rant, but rather in a some-things-happen-for-a-reason way). All the while he listens intently, his gaze unwavering.

'Hey, enough about me, Francesco,' I say, a voice in my head warning me my chattiness is verging on self-obsessed gabble. 'Tell me about the restaurant, Luigi, Nonna Rosa . . . I want to know everything.'

'Zio Luigi and Nonna Rosa are well. They send good wishes. Every Friday and Saturday we now have opera cabaret, just like at Sarastro in Drury Lane. Remember?'

How could I forget? That was the day I realised our flirting was growing into something more.

'Carla and Luke, they sing, and the restaurant is so busy you must make a reservation at least two weeks before. Zio Luigi is a ver-ry happy man.'

'With the compliments of the house,' says the waiter, delivering two liqueur coffees.

Francesco turns, raises his glass in thanks to the barman, then says, 'Look, *cara*, is your mother and father, over there.'

I lean forward, turn forty-five degrees, and sure enough, deep in conversation, oblivious to the world around them, are Oliver and Mags, the light from the candles illuminating their faces. He takes a neatly pressed hankie from the top pocket of his jacket and gently dabs her eyes. I bob my head back, pretending I haven't seen them.

'You don't say hello?' says Francesco.

'No . . . don't wave,' I say, grabbing his arm in the nick of time. 'I don't say hello because . . . well, it's complicated. But trust me, it's better they don't know we're here.'

'Aah,' he says with a sigh. '*Amore, cara*, is never simple – even when we are old.'

* * *

We turn up the cobbled street to my studio just as the cathedral clock is chiming midnight.

'Put your keys away, *cara*. I have a surprise for you.'

'What? I don't understand. We're here.'

Placing his arm around my shoulders, he propels me further along the street to a small pension. Two gargoyle lamps on either side of the wooden door illuminate the steps and the cast iron bell.

Francesco rings it once. The proprietor appears instantly in his dressing gown and slippers.

'*Guten Abend.*'

'*Guten Abend.* The name is Rossi,' says Francesco in a low whisper. 'Please excuse. We are very late.'

The landlord's eyes crinkle in a smile. 'No problem.'

Shuffling over to the reception desk, he fires up the computer which sits next to an old brass service bell. He checks us in, then unhooks a key from one of the highly polished cubbies.

After signing the visitors' book, we follow him quietly up the dimly lit staircase. To enter the room we have to stoop low and pick our way down a flight of narrow steps.

'Breakfast is served from eight until ten. *Gute Nacht.*'

'Goodnight.'

The room has a low, oak-beamed ceiling, exposed stonework, and the linen is embroidered Egyptian cotton. Francesco produces a bottle of Sekt from his bag, fetches two tumblers from the bathroom, sets them down on the oval table in the arched window, turns off the lamp, and opens the shutters.

'*Salute, cara,*' he says, clinking glasses.

We sit in the darkness, looking down onto the deserted, tree-lined street below, not saying a word.

There's something in the air tonight; something has changed or is about to change, I can feel it.

Francesco puts down his glass, pulls me onto his lap, his warm, dark, liquid eyes holding mine for a long moment.

'*Amore mio*,' he says, his voice low and serious. My heart accelerates. 'Tonight I understand very well why theatre is so important to you. I don't ever want to lose you, but this is selfish because you must be free to drop everything and go wherever the work will take you.'

I swallow hard, toying with my locket. 'Please can we not have this conversation right now? Let's enjoy the rest of the time we have here and not think about the future until we have to.'

Without warning a flash of silver rips across the sky, followed seconds later by a mighty crack of thunder. Heavy, sullen rain pelts against the window and onto the cobblestones below.

He pulls me closer to him with an intense yearning I've never felt before.

We lie side by side, holding each other tight, breathless in a tangle of limbs, staring at one another in the blackness, our faces eerily illuminated by beams of evanescent, blue lightning. No need for words. I fight the urge to sleep. Plenty of time for sleeping when he is gone from me.

* * *

Of all the places I have so far visited in Vienna, the little innocuous market just around the corner from Rudolfstrasse has to be one of my favourites. It's so . . . well, ALIVE. Sure, I appreciate the magnificence of the Opera House, the Spanish Riding School with its chandelier-lit paddock, the over-the-top, baroque, faded golden glory of Schönbrunn Palace, but they all have a LOOK-BUT-DON'T-TOUCH feel about them; whereas here, in this little market, I can see, feel, smell, listen to the Vienna of the here and now.

Francesco is in his element, disappearing into its maze of colourful stalls: pyramids of blood-red vine tomatoes; bunches of rosemary, oregano, and garlic bound up with raffia, swaying from metal hooks; roasted chestnuts, smoking in a coal-filled metal drum; speckled eggs, nestled together in straw-filled baskets; row upon row of freshly baked Kaiser rolls; rye, wholegrain, sourdough, and seeded artisan loaves that send your tastebuds into overdrive; trays of sausages; cuts of meat in pools of pink blood; and trotters with sprigs of parsley stuffed between their piggy toes. Aww. If I allow myself to think about those cute little porkers too much, I could turn vegetarian.

I seek refuge in the flower stall, where the air is perfumed with woodsy pine, cinnamon, eucalyptus, and orchids. With Christmas just a few weeks away, it's like entering an ice-white winter wonderland. Ladies in voluminous dirndls, fir-green jackets and heavy-duty gloves deftly create advent crowns from aromatic spruce, holly, metallic-frosted pinecones, red berries, cinnamon sticks, silver ribbons, garden twine, and candles.

I return to the food section where I left Francesco. Through the rows of hanging, cheesecloth-wrapped salamis and hams, pretzels, and dried chillies, I watch him as he zips from one stall to another, tasting olives, smelling herbs, feeling tomatoes and aubergines, checking they are ripe. He laughs and jokes with the amiable stall holders, cosied up against the cold in furry earflap hats and fingerless gloves, his hand vocabulary and humour bridging the language gap.

Ironic, isn't it? All those years hoping to meet 'the one'. Now he's finally here, so what's the problem? The problem is I'm not living in a Richard Curtis movie. This script is more complicated; the plotlines are unpredictable, harder to navigate, with no rehearsal or guarantee of a happy ending.

* * *

242

Sprinkling some of Gerhard's salts into the foamy bath, I slither down into the warm water, swishing my hand gently back and forth. I can almost feel the toxins draining out of my body.

'May I come in?' Francesco calls from the other side of the door.

'Erm . . . okay,' I say, sliding down further, the bubbles tickling my nose.

He stands in the glow of flickering candlelight, wrapped in a towel. I try not to stare. 'Champagne, *signorina*?'

'Thank you, *signor*,' I say, taking the glass from him.

He leans down and gently kisses my bare shoulder. I turn to face him, wrap my free arm around his neck, and boldly ask, 'Why don't you join me?'

'I wish I could, but we haven't time.'

'What? Where are we going?'

'It's a surprise.'

'Ooh. Is it somewhere posh?'

'Very.'

'I wish you'd told me. Is the dress I wore last night posh enough?'

'No more questions,' he says, chucking me a fluffy white towel. 'We have exactly one hour. Hurry.'

I scoosh some mousse on my spiky hair, apply a dash of red lippy, a spray of Prada, and fasten on my shopping channel diamante earrings.

'Ready?' calls Francesco.

'Almost,' I say, entering the bedroom.

'Close your eyes.'

'Why?'

He drops to his knees by the side of the bed. 'I said, close your eyes.'

I squeeze them tightly shut. 'What are you . . .?'

'Okay. You can look now.'

My eyes ping open to discover an enormous black and white striped box sitting on the bed.

'For me? What? When did you . . .?'

'I crept out this morning while you were sleeping. Open it.'

I undo the scarlet ribbon, lift the lid, and pull back the crisp white tissue paper to reveal a dark green velvet, below-the-knee, vintage dress with long, buttoned sleeves and fitted bodice. I lay it out on the bed, lips parted in disbelief.

Francesco unties my bathrobe, letting it slip to the floor. 'Try it on.'

I step inside the mound of rich velvety sumptuousness, wriggling into its contours. I feel Francesco's warm breath on my neck as he stands behind me, fastening the numerous buttons.

'It's beautiful – and will go perfectly with my new boots. Thank you, darling.'

Resting his head on my shoulder, he fixes his burning gaze on my reflection, then turns me around, kissing me, lightly at first, then again, more passionately.

Heat whooshes through me. I lead him to the bed and begin loosening his bow tie.

'No, no. We must wait, *cara*.'

'But . . .'

Checking his phone, he pulls me up, grabs my coat, and says, 'Hurry. We must not be late.'

'Late for what?'

He waves two tickets at me. 'The opera.'

'Which opera?'

'*Madame Butterfly*,' he deadpans. 'What else?'

I feel the heat creeping up my face as I recall the embarrassing day we first met at the restaurant, when he caught me unawares, belting out my very own version of the leading lady's dying lament.

* * *

We make it to the opera house with fifteen minutes to spare.

The orchestra is tuning up as we take our seats. I steal a

sideways glance at Francesco. He takes my hand in his just as the lights go down.

That Madame Butterfly will die is a given, but the circumstances leading up to this are doubtless complicated, and will require the utmost concentration, particularly as the dialogue is sung in Italian.

Despite not understanding the words, I find myself getting lost in the drama and the emotion of it all. The finale rises to a crescendo. Butterfly holds up her father's knife.

'Who cannot live with honour must die with honour.'

I feel Francesco's hand squeezing mine hard – really hard. Then I feel his shoulders start to shake.

I turn to look at him. He's staring straight ahead, the corners of his mouth twitching.

I try to stifle a giggle, letting out an unladylike piggy snort in the process. The woman to my left sighs theatrically. I can feel her glare searing through me.

Once the applause has died down, we make a hasty exit out onto the shimmering boulevard.

Hands on hips, I turn to Francesco, trying to look cross. 'Okay, *signor*, you've had your fun. Is that why you chose *Madame Butterfly*? To remind me?'

He's trying but failing to look innocent. 'Of course not, darling. I . . . I was lost in the moment too – until you started to lose control.' He shakes his head and tuts. 'And at the opera house too.'

'Me? Just you wait, Francesco Rossi!'

'Hah! You'll have to catch me first!' he cries, running and skipping backwards along the square.

What a loon.

A violinist, wearing an old army coat, plays a waltz before the Pestsäule statue, undeterred by the downpour and lack of audience. Francesco tosses a handful of euros into the young man's instrument case, gives a little bow, and offers his hand.

'What? Oh, no, Francesco, I can't dance. And anyway, it

wouldn't feel right, dancing here, in front of a memorial dedicated to plague victims.'

'Exactly! We must celebrate life, *cara – la dolce vita.*'

Taking my right hand, he places it in his, snakes his arm tightly around my waist, and pulls me close. I freeze.

'*Uno, due, tre, uno, due, tre . . .*' he whispers hypnotically, mouth grazing my ear as he gently rotates in time to the music.

'Francesco, please. Don't you think I've suffered enough embarrassment for one night?'

'*Uno, due, tre, uno, due, tre . . .*'

He pulls me closer, drawing me in with those come-to-bed eyes, his signature scent of Dolce & Gabbana tapping into my female senses.

Slowly, tentatively, my brain gives my arms and legs the green light to loosen up, and I yield to the ebb and flow of the music, the rise and fall of Francesco's body.

As we gather speed, I tilt my head back. Coloured lights flash across my eyes, buildings move, sounds are distorted, wind rushes in my ears. I am a child again: vulnerable, trusting, spinning, carefree, weightless, dizzy; like I'm back on the merry-go-round of my youth.

The music ends and he places a steadying arm around my shoulder. Steering me along the glistening street, he stops outside a cosy bar with heated terrace. 'Shall we?'

'I shouldn't really, but if you insist . . . Just one. To help me sleep.'

'Sleep? Tonight there will be no time for sleep,' he says, a wicked gleam in his eye.

My tummy does a backward flip.

'My flight tomorrow is not until the afternoon, so we have a little time together, *si?*'

'Sure,' I say in what I hope is a seductive tone, my head starting to swim with the giddy mix of Sekt and Strauss. He leans towards me, brushes my damp fringe aside, then raises my freezing hand to his mouth. I feel the warmth of his breath on my skin as he says in a low voice, 'Aah, *cara*, today is a beautiful day for me.'

I open my mouth to speak, but unusually for me, no words come, so I just grin, mixed-up emotions stirring inside me.

* * *

After a fitful few hours' sleep, I wake up the next morning, in dire need of caffeine.

I dreamed that Francesco and I were walking through the sun-baked back streets of Jeddah. He started to run really fast, and hard as I tried, I couldn't keep up. I called out for him to slow down, but he would turn his head and laugh mockingly. I kept catching glimpses of him, but then he'd disappear again. I woke up, pillow on the floor, heart pounding, sheet wound tightly around my legs.

The waiter takes a crisp, white tea towel from his long apron and flicks it across the table.

'Good morning. Your usual order?'

'Yes please. But for two.'

'Of course,' he says with a slight bow of the head and a click of the heels.

'Oh my God, Francesco, you are about to taste the crème de la crème of all pastries. They're called *Kipferln* and are shaped like a croissant, and they have the sweetest, most buttery smell, they're made from flour, sugar, butter, and almonds, sprinkled with just a light dusting of icing sugar, the baker here gave me the recipe and I'm going to make some for Luigi and everyone when I get back, they are simply the best things EVER, and once you've tasted one of these . . .'

'You are like we Italians,' says Francesco, propping his chin in his hand and grinning delightedly.

'In what way?' I reply breathlessly, meeting his intense gaze.

'Passionate.'

'Passionate?'

A thrill rushes through me as I relive last night; his tantalising, tender words, his toned, muscular body hovering over mine, our ardent lovemaking.

'*Sì*. Passionate – about food.'

'Aah,' I say, a hot flush coming on.

Fuelled by coffee and pastries, we head towards Belvedere Palace, which houses the world's largest Gustav Klimt collection. Now, I'm no art expert, but you can't be in Vienna and not notice the unmistakable metallic-gold-ink postcards, posters, key-rings, and tea towels for sale in every *Tabak*, every gift shop, on every street corner. This makes Klimt sound like tasteless kitsch, but to stand here, before the real thing is . . . well, I defy anyone not to be bowled over by the glittering, sensual beauty of his paintings.

'*Mamma mia!*' exclaims Francesco (told you) as we enter the gallery.

'For me, this is true, uncomplicated love,' says Francesco, rubbing his chin thoughtfully as he studies *The Kiss*. 'See the way the man protects the woman with his arm? And the woman, she feels safe with him. The love between them is equal. In many love affairs, there is imbalance, you understand?'

'Absolutely, Francesco, I know exactly what you mean.'

My gaze travels the length and breadth of him: his intense gaze devouring every detail of the painting, his strong hands emphasising every word.

'Here I see passion, of course, but this love is about friendship, respect, trust – the kind of love maybe you find once in your life – if you are very lucky.'

A wistful silence falls between us.

'Like . . . Antony and Cleopatra,' he continues.

'Like Posh and Becks,' I quip.

Francesco looks me at blankly.

Why must I always do that? Spoil magical moments by saying something flippant? And on our last morning together too.

* * *

Tears spill freely down my cheeks as Butterfly's 'One Fine Day' floats through my headphones.

I will never forget our last night together in Vienna – the opera, dancing in the square, Francesco's tender lovemaking, the secrets we shared. Only two hours have passed since we parted and I miss him so much it hurts.

I glance at my watch and tell myself to get a grip and concentrate on tonight's show. The prospect causes my tummy to flip over. It seems so long ago since Saturday's performance and my awful memory lapse. I must stay calm, not give in to stage fright, and give a stellar performance.

I turn off the music and pick up my script. I know I'll feel better as soon as I've got that dreaded scene over with.

* * *

The loons have flown and so must we. The run has sadly reached its end. Goodbye, Vienna. Goodbye, Chelsea. Hello, London. Hello, Insecurity. Are you going to accompany me on my journey once more? I'm trying to think positively and visualise drowning in a sea of scripts, but I'm well aware that, with very little on-camera experience, it's nigh on impossible to land a starring role in the West End.

The practical reality of everyday life is now looming large in my mind. There's no denying that I've been living a little too much in the moment of late, splashing out on pastries, coffees, expensive dinners and wine – oh, and a pair of must-have Ludwig Reiter winter boots.

* * *

Half asleep, I pull my bag off the carousel and head through the green channel towards the exit.

'Excuse me,' calls a customs officer.

I turn my head towards him and mime, 'ME?'

He nods and beckons me over. 'Mind if I check your bag?'

It's early, I've had about two hours' sleep, and there's a gorgeous man waiting for me on the other side of those doors, so of course I mind, but I doubt Mr Customs Officer would reply, 'No? That's okay, love. I'll try someone else. You have a nice day now.'

So with my best you're-barking-up-the-wrong-tree smile, I click open my suitcase and he begins to rummage inside.

'Olly and I will wait for you outside,' says Mags.

'Oh, don't worry about me,' I say airily. 'It's just a formality.'

'No, we'd rather . . .'

'Really. Your son will be waiting. Give me a call soon, yeah?'

'Don't forget our invitation to your Italian restaurant.'

'You just name the day.'

'I'm dying to meet Francesco.'

'He's so looking forward to meeting you too.'

'Ahem, when you're quite ready!'

I turn around to find the grim-faced customs officer waving at me.

'Oops. I'd better go.'

We hug and they disappear.

Snapping my bag shut, the officer says sternly, 'Come this way,' and I'm promptly ushered into a small interview room. As we enter, he slides the 'OCCUPIED' sign across sharply and firmly closes the door.

'Passport, please.'

I hand it over and he flicks through the pages in silence. Regarding me with a weighty stare he then asks, 'Apart from Vienna, where else have you been travelling to?'

'Where . . .? I . . . nowhere,' I stammer, face reddening, doubtless giving the impression that I've got bags of heroin strapped to my thighs. I wiggle the loose button of my coat nervously. One eyebrow raised, he studies me for several seconds, a smug, disbelieving look on his face. I swear he's deriving some sort of twisted pleasure in watching me squirm.

He then disappears, leaving me alone. I look around the stark white walls, my eyes coming to rest on the poster of a man behind bars. Underneath, in bold lettering are the following words . . ..

HM CUSTOMS AND EXCISE
DRUG SMUGGLING ZERO TOLERANCE

'NEVER leave your suitcase unlocked or unattended,' we were told in crew safety training.

I scream inwardly. Ohmygod, ohmygod, ohmygod. When I was waiting for Oliver and Mags at the airport this morning, I broke both those rules while I queued for coffee. Did someone tamper with my luggage?

The flickering strip lighting is starting to make my head spin. Small beads of sweat are forming on my neck. I glug a cup of water from the machine.

My phone buzzes. 'Rosalind Holmes Agent' flashes across the screen.

'Hello,' I whisper.

'Good morning, Emily,' she says brightly. 'You back from Vienna?' Without waiting for an answer, she ploughs on. 'Sorry to call so early, but I've got an audition for you. West End, my darling, with a possible Broadway . . .'

The door bursts open and the customs man reappears, accompanied by a female officer, wearing latex gloves – not someone you'd like to bump into on a dark night, let alone be body-searched by.

'Sorry, Ros. Bit of a bad time. May I call you later?'

I hang up abruptly. The chairs screech harshly as they are pulled out from under the table.

Several sealed plastic bags containing a white substance are shoved under my nose. Two sets of eyes glue themselves to my bewildered face.

'Can you explain what this substance is, and what it was doing in your suitcase?'

I look from one to the other in disbelief. 'I . . . what . . .? . . . Erm . . .'

Expelling a long breath, I shrug and innocently confess, 'It's bath salts.'

The customs officer pauses for thought, brow furrowing. 'Bath salts. So, you admit it then?'

'Yes.' I'm now fighting the urge to laugh out loud. 'What's wrong with that?'

'What's wrong with . . .?'

'Who supplied you with the substance?'

'Gerhard. Gerhard Schildberger. He's an Austrian director. And Elvis impersonator.'

'I see. And are you going to tell us where we can find this man?'

'Why do you need to know?'

'Why do we need . . .?'

'I can give you some if you'd like to try it. As you see, I've got loads. You'd both be very welcome to take . . . some.'

Without saying a word, they gather up the stash of salts and disappear, the male officer eventually returning alone and looking slightly flushed.

Averting his gaze, he places the plastic bags on the table and mumbles, 'You're free to go.'

'Right. Thanks,' I say, utterly perplexed as I quickly stuff my passport and belongings back into my suitcase before he changes his mind.

I make a hasty exit through the sliding doors to freedom, convinced that what just happened was some kind of set-up for one of those TV prank shows.

Francesco is pacing up and down by the barrier, looking overwrought and confused.

'Is there a problem? Your friends, they tell me you were stopped by customs . . .'

'No, no problem.' I smile, wearily holding up a mollifying hand, then pecking his cheek. 'Just a silly misunderstanding. It's a long story. I'll tell you in the car.'

Hmm. Not quite the cinematic, running-towards-each-other-in-slow-motion reunion I've been dreaming of.

Chapter 16

The Agony and the Ecstasy

I swing around the corner into St Martin's Lane, collar pulled up against the driving rain.

TONIGHT AT 7.30
Private Lives
by
Noël Coward

There's still a part of me that's convinced I've been dreaming, and whenever I arrive at the Congreve Theatre, the stage doorman will say, 'Not you again. Look, love, I've told you before, you can't come in. This is a *professional* theatre for *professional* actors.'

I mean, my name's not up in lights with the others, is it? No, but if you happen to have a magnifying glass handy, at the foot of the poster you can just about decipher . . .

Introducing Emily Forsyth as Louise

My character doesn't appear until Act Three, but it's a great little cameo role. My lines are all in French – my language degree may not have led to a job at the United Nations, but it has landed me the role of a French maid in a West End play. She's described as 'frowsy-looking' and her clumsiness and inability to speak English give her some of the best laughs in the show.

No cobbled-together costume here, stumbling on stage with half-learned lines, unsure of whose turn it is to speak; we've enjoyed the luxury of six weeks' rehearsal, carefully planned fittings at Angels Costumes, dialect coaching sessions, and previews.

I *may* also get to play the leading role of the glamorous Amanda, as I also understudy this part, but I shan't be disappointed if I don't; stepping into the shoes of a much-loved TV star and hearing the sighs and groans of disappointment as you're about to make your first entrance is an experience I'd rather not repeat.

'Evening, Doug,' I say, ticking my name off.

'Evening,' he grunts, slithering down from his stool and taking my key from the hook, eyes glued to *The One Show*. 'Those are for you.'

I scoop up the enormous tied sheaf of red and cream roses and wend my way up two floors to my dressing room. I still get a thrill when I see the shiny brass plaque on the door . . .

EMILY FORSYTH PRIVATE LIVES

Sadly, the glamour stops there: step inside, and you will be struck by the faded, peeling Regency wallpaper, the grubby, threadbare carpet, the yellowish-brown stain on the ceiling, the one-armed chair with foam spilling from a rip in the seat, the dusty light bulbs (most of which have blown) around the cracked mirror, the rusty, Victorian radiator that doesn't radiate, and the resident mouse, whom I've christened Colin. Yet, I am in paradise.

I rip open the envelope . . . *Good luck! Love Francesco & your Il Mulino Family.*

I smile to myself and begin rummaging around in the dusty cupboards for a vase. I'm busy arranging the flowers when there's a knock at the door.

'Come in!'

'Just to let you know,' says the company manager, 'I've moved your guests from the Upper Circle to one of the boxes close to the stage, and their interval champagne is on ice.'

'Oh my goodness,' I gush, accidentally giving him a bear hug. 'Thank you!'

'Right. Hope they enjoy the show,' he says, looking slightly discombobulated as he backs out the door.

Though I have a long while to wait until Act Three and my first entrance, I don't mind, as by that time the audience is well and truly warmed up, and judging by the reaction bursting through the show relay tonight, they seem to be truly listening, to be attuned to the actors and not laughing for the sake of it.

I wonder if my guests are enjoying themselves. Is that Luigi's cheery chortle I can hear crackling through the speaker? Will Francesco recognise me in my androgynous 1930s brown wig, beret, and Harry Potter-style spectacles? What do Luke and Carla make of the musical interludes?

I have a quick gargle and a Vocalzones lozenge before . . . 'Miss Forsyth, this is your call' filters through the show relay.

I catch sight of myself: face flushed under my beret, eyes the size of pizza pies.

Jelly-legged, I make my way downstairs to prompt corner, collect my string bag of bread and lettuce from the props table, and take up position in the wings, waiting to make my first entrance, heart battering my rib cage.

The assistant stage manager shoots me a thumbs-up and a glowing smile through the darkness.

Here I go . . . I inhale deeply and move towards the light . . .

* * *

'*Mamma mia!* Tonight, sitting in our own private box, I feel like the King of England,' says Luigi, puffing out his chest while proudly studying his reflection in my dressing room mirror.

'And we were so close to the stage,' says Carla, eyes shimmering with delight.

Luke sighs. 'I'm itching to have a go at playing that grand piano.'

'If you hurry up and finish your drinks, the stage manager said he'll give you all a backstage tour, and Luke, perhaps you'd like to play us something before he locks up.'

Carla holds up her phone. 'But first, a group photo please.'

Francesco draws me close. 'You were so funny, *cara*. I didn't recognise you.'

'Thank God for that.'

He then whispers in my ear, 'I cannot wait to be alone with you.'

'Ready? *Uno, due, tre!*'

* * *

Having waved Luigi, Carla and Luke off in a taxi, Francesco and I walk hand in hand along the deserted streets of London to our hotel, overlooking the Thames.

The bedroom door clicks open, he hangs up the 'DO NOT DISTURB' sign, then treats me to another of his swoonworthy romantic hero lifts.

'I have a proposition for you,' he says, laying me gently on the bed.

'Oh?' Desire gushes through me. 'And what might that be, Signor Rossi?'

'The show, it will close in four weeks, *sì*?'

I nod.

'Then you will come to Sorrento with me?'

'Hmm. I'll have to think about that . . . let's see now . . . I've thought about it . . . yes, yes, yes!'

I laugh as we kiss.

'I am owed some holiday and I want to show you my hometown and take you out on my father's boat to Capri, to the underwater Roman city of Baia, to my favourite restaurants, and introduce you to some of my family and friends.'

'Sounds perfect.'

He lies down beside me, alternately kissing my lips, my ears, my nose, my neck, my hair . . . 'Oh, Francesco, I am losing myself . . .' I groan, just as my phone vibrates.

'You don't answer?'

'No. Now, where were we?'

* * *

Full company call @1700 on stage please.

'Why you must go to the theatre early?' says Francesco the next morning over breakfast.

My stomach drops. 'I have no idea.' I wince at my lie.

I decided not to mention anything to him until it's confirmed. What would be the point? To be honest, I never felt it would actually happen. But the head of a Broadway production company was in the audience last night. I have a feeling this may well have something to do with it.

A few months ago I'd have been bubbling over with excitement at the prospect, but now it's sent my scattered thoughts into an anxious spin.

'I'll tell you tonight when I know more,' I say, forcing my lips into a smile.

* * *

'Ladies and gentlemen of *Private Lives* Company, please make your way to the stage. The producers have an important announcement to make. Full company to the stage please.'

This is it. Jumbled-up emotions whoosh through my veins.

Dressing room doors bang, footsteps pound the corridor, lively chatter echoes around the stairwell like a boomerang.

I join the cast and crew in the auditorium, heart galloping.

'That's everybody,' says the company manager, giving the thumbs-up and removing his headset.

A hush settles in the air.

'Hi, everyone. For those of you who don't know me, my name is Donna Wiseman of Wiseman Productions, New York City. Firstly, I want to congratulate you all on a terrific show. Five star reviews across the board, but more importantly, the warmth coming from the audience speaks for itself. Sold-out performances for the rest of the run, I understand, which is why . . .'

There's a collective sharp intake of breath.

'Which is why I'm delighted to tell you that we'd like to offer you guys a three-month transfer – to Broadway!'

'Broadway?'

'What?'

'Are you kidding?'

'No way!'

'Seriously?'

'When?'

Turning back to the group she says, 'We know you'll all have lots of questions, but I just wanted to give you the heads-up. Of course you must speak to your families and agents first, so please don't put anything on social media until everything is confirmed. Your company manager will send you an email tonight with all the details so far and we'll meet again tomorrow after the matinée before I fly back. Until then, focus on tonight and have a great show!'

* * *

Francesco is waiting for me at Richmond tube station.

We walk over the bridge to his studio above the restaurant,

our conversation unusually stilted.

He smiles and pours me a glass of Montepulciano. '*Allora*, how was your evening, *cara*?'

My stomach tightens. 'Fine, thank you. Yours?'

He shrugs and nods his head. 'The same.'

Our eyes lock into one another. I can feel tears teetering on my lashes. He reaches for my hand and squeezes it. 'What's the matter, darling?'

I blink and look upwards. 'New York. The show is going to New York.'

'But this is wonderful, your dream, *cara*.'

I swallow hard. 'But that was before I met you.'

'How long?'

'Three months – with a possible extension.'

'I see. When?'

'I don't know the exact date yet, but soon, I think.'

Francesco opens his mouth to speak but changes his mind.

He pulls me onto his lap and we hold each other tight, without saying anything.

We finish the wine and he takes me to bed.

'Do you remember in Vienna you said we shouldn't talk about the future until we have to?'

I nod, knowing exactly where this is leading.

'I think the time is now, *cara*.'

Don't leave me, Francesco Rossi, screams my inner voice.

'New York isn't that far, is it? Seven hours or so. That's nothing. We can do some fun stuff together. And I know lots of great Italian restaura . . ?'

He lifts my chin, silencing me with a kiss. Looking deep into my eyes he says, 'I love you so much, and it's because I love you that I will not hold you back. You have sacrificed so much for the theatre and having me in your life is a distraction . . ?'

'No.' I sniff. 'Ask me not to go and I'll be happy to stay here with you.'

He shakes his head, a sad smile crossing his lips. We make love; a desperate, fierce kind of lovemaking this time. Clinging to one another, we lie awake until the sun comes up.

* * *

How quickly my life has changed; one minute living in romantic bliss in a garret, now back to my single bed and a cat that hates me. Don't get me wrong; I am forever indebted to Beryl for giving me a roof over my head once more, but my heart is aching. How I miss him; the laughter, the excitement, the silliness, the aroma of fresh coffee brewing in the morning, but most of all I miss the intimacy – mental as well as physical.

Of course I still get a thrill of performing in the West End and am grateful that Mum, Dad, Beryl, and the girls got the five-star treatment too when they saw the show this week, just before our London run comes to an end.

But nothing is the same without Francesco. To be honest, I'm not even looking forward to going to Broadway. I realise of course how ungrateful and spoiled I sound. Most actors would give their eyeteeth to be in my shoes.

'So you turned him down?'

'No. It's not as simple as that, Lily,' I reply, running a tissue under my red-rimmed eyes. 'Neither of us wants this.'

'I don't understand.'

'I can't expect him to wait while I disappear again for three months – maybe even longer. How can our relationship possibly survive these long periods of separation?'

Lily takes my hand and sighs. 'As I see it, you have to decide what's most important in your life. When you left the airline you told us that your ultimate goal was to perform on the West End stage, and you've done it. Be honest. Do you want to go to New York?'

I hesitate for a second. 'No.'

'Then why are you going?'

'I can't back out now.'

'Have you spoken to your company manager?'

'No.'

'Then how do you know?'

'And my agent will be furious and probably dump me.'

Bang on cue, my phone vibrates. My mouth falls open. My stomach churns. Lily looks at me nonplussed. Rosalind Holmes Agent is flashing across the screen.

'Hi, Ros,' I squeak. 'How funny, I . . . I was just talking about you to my friend here . . .'

'I need to run something past you, darling. It's fairly urgent. Are you free to pop into the office today at around three?'

I swallow hard. 'Yes, but . . . if it's about Broadway, then . . .'

'Great. See you at three.'

I glance anxiously at Lily.

'What is it, hon?'

'It looks like I'm going to have to face the music sooner than planned. My agent has summoned me to her office. She's very intuitive. Maybe she suspects I'm having serious doubts.'

'Perhaps it's better all round to have the conversation sooner rather than later. If you're sure.'

* * *

Not much time has passed, yet so much has happened that it feels strange, nerve-wracking yet comforting to walk into Il Mulino this morning.

Luigi greets me like long-lost family.

'I expect you are looking for Francesco?'

'Yes. Is he in?'

He shakes his head. 'No, *cara*.'

I swallow hard. 'He doesn't answer my calls or texts.'

'He is in Sorrento.'

262

My heart drops. 'Oh.'

'Now we have found a permanent sous-chef, I tell him to take some time off – to clear his mind.'

'I see.'

Fighting back tears, I bite my bottom lip, turning away from Luigi's kind and intense gaze. He squeezes my hand.

'Go to him. Please.'

Grabbing his order pad, he starts scribbling. 'Here is his address. If you don't find him at home, you will find him at the Marina Grande. His boat is called *Canto del Mare*.'

Epilogue

Sorrento

The taxi slows to a halt by the water fountain in the piazza.

'*Grazie mille.*' I thrust a twenty-euro note into the driver's hand. '*Arrivederci.*'

'*Arrivederci.*'

I jump out and swing my rucksack onto my back.

Taking a deep breath, I hold it for a moment, taking in the dazzling world around me.

The sun casts a warm glow on the rust-coloured walls and flaky green shutters of the glorious old stone buildings.

I pull Luigi's note from my pocket and look up. This is it. I walk up the cracked, uneven steps and peer at the apartment number panel. 'ROSSI'. My trembling finger is poised on the buzzer.

I can see that my WhatsApp messages are unread, so I take it Francesco has no idea I'm here. My pulse quickens at the news I have yet to share with him.

Will he be overjoyed to see me or will these few weeks apart and being back in his homeland have changed his mind? With too much time to think, I'm now convinced his insistence that he's holding me back is an excuse for wishing to break up with me. Very soon I will know for sure . . .

I wait with bated breath for him to answer, rehearsing in my mind what to say:

'*Surpriiiise! Bet you didn't expect to find me on your doorstep, did you?*'

Nope. Too flippant.

'*I can't live without you, Francesco . . .*'

Too needy.

'*I have exciting and unexpected news . . .*'

God, no! He'll think I'm pregnant.

Hoping the perfect words will trip off the tongue unrehearsed, I press the buzzer again – harder and longer this time. No answer. I about-turn, checking my phone for directions to the marina.

The sun is rising higher in the sky. Wiping my sticky palms on my cotton dress, I make my way over to the fountain and splash cool water on my face, then head down the cobbled pathway to the harbour.

Squinting from under the brim of my straw hat, my eyes scan the rows of boats bobbing serenely on the glassy, turquoise sea.

I walk along the water's edge, imagining him beside me. Then, through the shimmering haze, I see a tall, dark-haired, tanned, and toned figure running towards me. Can it be? My heart soars.

'Francesco!' I wave, running and stumbling along the rocky shore as fast as my new floral-printed plimsolls can carry me. 'Francesco!'

As he approaches, my heart sinks as I realise it isn't him at all, but I carry on running, calling out his name in an attempt to cover up my embarrassing faux pas.

When I've run far enough away, I surreptitiously turn around and begin my search for *Canto del Mare*.

What will I do if I don't find Francesco here? I guess I'll have to head back to his apartment and wait on the doorstep. I'll only try calling him as a last resort. These things are better said face to face.

What's the worst that can happen? That I'll be on a flight back to London tomorrow morning. My stomach twists in a tight knot at the prospect.

Just then a boat noses around the curve of the glittering bay.

Shielding my eyes from the sun, I walk towards the jetty. The engine slows as I pick up the pace, gaze pinned to the figure at the helm, his white, unbuttoned shirt flapping in the breeze.

As I draw closer, the lettering on the side of the boat becomes clearer. My heartbeat accelerates.

I watch him as he jumps off and secures *Canto del Mare* with the ropes.

Kicking off my plimsolls, I run into the water. He has his back to me, his faded jeans rolled up to his knees. I tap him lightly on the shoulder. Straightening up, he turns around and does a double take, mouth open, eyes wide in disbelief.

'What . . . what happened? What are you doing here? Why aren't you in New York?'

I try not to drown in his stare. 'It's a long story, but . . .'

He raises an eyebrow. 'Please don't tell me you turned down this opportunity because of . . .'

'No. I didn't have to.'

'New York was cancelled?'

'No.'

'I don't understand.'

'Don't look so worried.'

'Tell me.'

I take a deep breath, my heart picking up speed. Here goes . . . 'It all happened so fast, Francesco. Two days before I had to sign my transfer contract, my agent called me to her office. The casting director had asked for me specially and the next day I had a meeting with her and the producer . . .'

Francesco wrinkles his nose. 'The casting director? The producer?'

'Yes. The casting director saw my showreel – the clip of me

playing the nosy neighbour in *Doon Place*. Remember? Anyway, she then came to see me in *Private Lives*. I had no idea until Ros, my agent, called and asked to see me. You could have knocked me down with a feather when she told me. Anyway, where was I?'

'Shh,' he whispers, gently putting his index finger to my lips to stop me speaking. '*Al punto, per favore!*'

'What? Sorry, I'm rambling, aren't I?'

He nods, running his hand through his hair in confusion.

Drawing a steadying breath, I compose myself and peer up at him, heart fluttering like a trapped bird.

'I've been offered a regular part in a new TV comedy series to play a . . .'

'What? Where?'

'It will be filmed at Ealing Studios.'

'Where is this?'

'About five miles from Richmond! I can even cycle there if the trains . . .'

He silences me with a kiss. Coming up for air, I blurt, 'Are you going to come back to Il Mulino? I keep having these dreams that you're going to stay in Sorrento – and who could blame you? It's beautiful.'

He pulls back slightly, looking directly into my eyes. 'But you are even more beautiful.' These words are swiftly followed by a self-mocking smile, flickering at the corners of his mouth.

He shrugs his shoulders and shakes his head. '*Dio mio.* What are you doing to me? I sound like an Italian gigolo.'

I stifle a giggle. 'I love you, Francesco Rrrossi.'

'Not as much as I love you, Emily Forsythhh.'

He draws me towards him, kissing me passionately, both of us now knee-deep in the sea. Then, scooping me up into his arms, he carries me ashore.

♥ ♥

THE END

Acknowledgements

Thank you to my editors, Amal Ibrahim and Rachael Nazarko at HQ HarperCollins, for their guidance, expertise and patience, and to Ernest Thompson and the Earl Graham Agency, New York, for granting me permission to quote from *On Golden Pond*.

Excerpt from *Three Sisters* by Anton Chekhov, translation by Peter Carson, is reproduced with permission from Penguin Books Ltd.

The extract from *Miranda* by Peter Blackmore is used by the express permission of the publishers, Creselles Publishing Company Limited, Colwall.

Author photograph: Sacre Images.

Finally, love and gratitude to my much-missed parents, for always believing in me, and to all my loving family and friends for their unwavering support and encouragement in everything I do.

♥

Dear Reader,

We hope you enjoyed reading this book. If you did, we'd be so appreciative if you left a review. It really helps us and the author to bring more books like this to you.

Here at HQ Digital we are dedicated to publishing fiction that will keep you turning the pages into the early hours. Don't want to miss a thing? To find out more about our books, promotions, discover exclusive content and enter competitions you can keep in touch in the following ways:

JOIN OUR COMMUNITY:
Sign up to our new email newsletter: http://smarturl.it/SignUpHQ
Read our new blog www.hqstories.co.uk

🐦 https://twitter.com/HQStories
f www.facebook.com/HQStories

BUDDING WRITER?
We're also looking for authors to join the HQ Digital family!
Find out more here:

https://www.hqstories.co.uk/want-to-write-for-us/

Thanks for reading, from the HQ Digital team